Kevin,

HOUNDS OF THE
HOLLYWOOD
BASKERVILLES

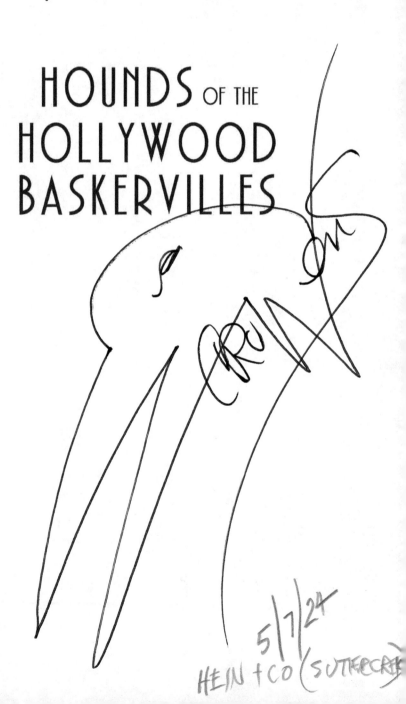

5/7/24

HEIN + CO (SUTTERCREEK)

HOUNDS OF THE
HOLLYWOOD
BASKERVILLES

ELIZABETH CROWENS

Author Photo Credit: Kim Gottlieb-Walker

First edition

ISBN: 978-1-68512-542-4

Cover art by Level Best Designs

This book was professionally typeset on Reedsy.
Find out more at reedsy.com

To Lola, my lucky star

Contents

Praise for Hounds of the Hollywood Baskervilles

"I heartily enjoyed Elizabeth Crowens latest book *Hounds of the Hollywood Baskervilles*. This comedy-mystery is set during the golden age of Hollywood. Crowens' detectives, Babs Norman and Guy Brandt, believe the case (involving dognapping and other nefarious doings) could put them on the map—especially with a star client like Basil Rathbone and suspects such as Myrna Loy, William Powell, Nigel Bruce, Dashiell Hammett, Lillian Hellman—and more. A nice look behind the scenes of the dream factory known as MGM and Hollywood in its glory days with a delicious whodunit with witty repartee to boot. This book is a real winner."

—Charles Tranberg,
author of *Murder Over Cocktails: The Thin Man Films*

"Move over, Holmes and Watson. Stand aside, Nick and Nora Charles. Make room for PI Babs Norman and her Guy Friday, Guy Brandt! Author Elizabeth Crowens deftly combines humor, excitement, and epic name-dropping in this entertaining adventure set in Hollywood's Golden Age."

—Carla Coupe,
editor of *Sherlock Holmes Mystery Magazine*,
member of the Adventuresses of Sherlock Holmes and The Baker Street Irregulars.

"Elizabeth Crowens' *Hounds of the Hollywood Baskervilles* is a thrilling and hilarious romp through the days of Old Hollywood. If you ever wanted to jump into the screen and spend time with Nick Charles and Sherlock

Holmes, this is the next best thing. I, for one, can't wait for more adventures with Babs and Guy! Delightful!"

—Phoef Sutton,
Emmy Award-winning producer of *Cheers*,
author of the *Crush* novels,
and co-host of the *Film Freaks Forever* podcast

"Travel back to old Hollywood to meet a fantastic cast of old Hollywood characters in this fast, fresh, and wildly entertaining new novel. As you read, you'll feel like you're watching a movie. Hell... you'll feel like you're IN the movie. So sit back, relax, and take the trip with Elizabeth Crowens."

—William Martin,
New York Times bestselling author of *December '41*

"A fine example of historical fiction that will find an enthusiastic audience among pet lovers and fans of classic Hollywood."

—*Kirkus Reviews*

"A pack of famous canines, movie star cameos, and oodles of banter brighten a dognapping mystery set during the Golden Age of Hollywood. You'll be howling by the time you finish *Hounds of the Hollywood Baskervilles*."

—Leigh Perry,
author of the Family Skeleton Mysteries

"Silver Screen idols, Golden Age styling, and hardboiled humor — *Hounds of the Hollywood Baskervilles* marks a fast-paced, fun-spirited start to this new series."

—Art Taylor,
Edgar Award-winning author of *The Adventure of the Castle Thief*

Chapter One: Flea Circus

Hollywood, 1940

B abs Norman bundled Miss Marple in a beach towel while her disgruntled partner held onto a box of kittens and flinched from fleabites. She looked around the vet's waiting room to see if she recognized anyone, but all she noticed were an unknown house frau with a French-cut Miniature Poodle, a uniformed nurse with a Cocker Spaniel, and a frumpy elder with a Shirley Temple hopeful hugging her Saint Bernard.

The front door flew open, revealing a tall, thin, but athletic gentleman with his chestnut hair slicked back. His striking profile rivaled classic sculptures, except for the sweat that dripped down his forehead. Under one arm were photostat flyers. Under the other, a folded-up copy of *Variety magazine*. Both featured photos of dogs.

Guy poked Babs in the ribs to get her attention. "Recognize him?"

She observed the newcomer, who explained his dilemma in haste to the assistant, but most of what Babs could see was from behind. "Who?"

"Rathbone…Basil Rathbone."

"The actor who plays Sherlock Holmes?"

"*Shush*. Don't advertise it to everyone on Sunset Boulevard."

In a whisper, he disclosed the highlights of the actor's resume. "That, and *Captain Blood, A Tale of Two Cities, Great Expectations*, and more, not to mention quite a bit of theater. If we keep it discreet, maybe we can find out why he's here."

1

Basil approached the lady with the cocker and asked if he could scratch him under his chin. "Such a handsome boy. My Leo looks a lot like him, except his coat is a deep red rather than brown."

He pointed to the bulletin board with listings for lost pets and adoptions and handed the front desk assistant his entire stack. "I'll have more printed. Please give them to all of your clients. If I can't find my poor Leo, I don't know what I'll do."

Babs saw this as an opportunity to get acquainted. She sprang from her seat, clutching the hissing fuzzball wrapped like a jellyroll. "Maybe I can help in your search."

Basil narrowed his eyes. "Do I know you?"

"Babs Norman." She attempted to extend her hand for a proper introduction, but struggled with the snarling feline. "Cast as an extra in *The Adventures of Robin Hood*."

"Ah...with Errol Flynn, in the days when the studios always had me play the villain."

She gleaned from the subtle shift on his face he didn't care for his co-star.

He eyed her with sudden skepticism. "Refresh my memory. What scene were you in? Almost all parts were male."

"When Sir Robin of Locksley revealed to Maid Marion that he saved the lives of desperate villagers. I played a peasant wife, but my back was toward the camera."

"What a shame," Basil said.

Babs blushed. "I *used* to be an actress, but not anymore."

"What do you consider yourself now?" Basil asked.

The vet's assistant came between them. "Miss, maybe he desires privacy." He ignored Babs and asked Basil. "Sir, have you filed a report with the pound?"

"I tried, but I have little faith they can help. Everyone laughed and said, 'Sherlock Holmes has lost his dog!'"

Babs cleared her throat to get everyone's attention. First, she addressed the rude assistant. "Excuse me, but you interrupted us before I could answer his question." Then she turned to Basil. "The reason I'm no longer an actress

2

is *now* I'm a private investigator. The gentleman next to me is my associate, Guy Brandt."

Basil dismissed the employee's well-meaning intervention. "Such an odd transition from acting. What compelled you to get into that business?"

She lowered her head. "It's a long story." He didn't need to know the truth about her father's murder. "I also have an acute talent for finding things, whether they are people...or pets."

"You have an actual private investigator's license?" Basil asked.

"In my purse." She tried to fish it out while wrestling with the cat, who broke free from her grasp. Between Guy and another staff member, they corralled the anxious tabby into a handheld cage.

"I'm so sorry." Babs looked around at the bedlam of barking dogs. "This stray doesn't want to nurse her kits, and I think she has—"

"Fleas." Basil scratched his arms. "Looks like we're both having kittens."

She also felt an oncoming rash. "Come again?"

"Ha! It's a peculiar old English expression. People believed a witch's curse caused painful pregnancies, but instead of a child, they thought the woman had kittens inside her, clawing to get out. Since I'm not expectant, it shows my uncomfortable position in more ways than one."

Babs flushed, aware this was an awkward introduction for a potential client. Meanwhile, staff members brought the kittens into the back for examination.

She plucked her ID and her business card out of her purse. "*B. Norman, Investigations.* In case you need proof."

He put down his copy of *Variety* to accept her card. Babs swiped his tabloid, attracted by a photo of another dog on its cover.

"Someone else's dog is missing." Babs read the article out loud. "Skippy, the wire-haired Fox Terrier known as Asta in the *Thin Man* movies, has vanished. Production is supposed to start on the next film featuring the lovable detectives Nick and Nora Charles. A one-thousand-dollar reward. No questions asked."

Guy whistled. "That's one hefty jackpot."

Basil looked at her business card one more time. "Well, if it's any

3

consolation, I'll match that for the return of my red cocker. My wife will think I'm insane. I was offering one hundred." He showed them his flyers. "For you, as professionals, I guess I'll make an exception, since now it looks like I have serious competition from producers with studio funds. Is that enough of an incentive?"

"Our agency is on Hollywood Boulevard, close to La Brea," she said with a confident smile.

"Let's say I stop over tomorrow on the way to the studio. Perhaps I should trust your expertise if you say you're so good with animals."

Babs nodded and forced herself to contain her excitement. "Sir, do you mind if I borrow your newspaper?"

"Keep it," Basil said. He handed her both his copy of *Variety* and several of his flyers.

After he left, she turned to her partner. "Who says we can't go after both Asta or Skippy and Leo?"

The vet returned with the verdict. "There's no doubt your adult cat has a case of fleas, which might have also infested your furniture. The kittens are another matter. They're too young to eat food on their own. The obvious issue you overlooked is the adult is not their mama, because she's a he. Not so obvious with his long and thick matted fur. That's why he wouldn't nurse the little ones."

Babs turned red. "I can't believe I was so caught up in the moment that I overlooked something that simple."

"A coincidence, I'm afraid. You must've put two and two together when you found this fellow near a box of abandoned kittens," the vet explained. "The newborns will need around-the-clock attention, and Old Tom will need a few flea baths before he's ready to go back to anyone's home."

Babs grimaced. She looked at Guy and then back toward the vet. "Can't play nursemaid while running a business."

"Don't worry." The vet reassured her. "Leave them here. My staff will handle it. We'll find good homes for all of them."

Chapter Two: Rude Awakening

Babs returned to her apartment in the heart of West Hollywood and encountered another surprise—an eviction notice on her front door. Someone had changed the locks, boxed her belongings, and stacked them in the hallway. With rent four months overdue, pleading with her landlady proved futile. Even when she explained it was pay the rent here or have the phone and electricity shut off at her office. The woman allowed Babs a five-minute phone privilege to call Guy to help load her stuff into his jalopy and take it to their office, which would have to serve as her temporary residence.

"I'll find good homes for everyone." Guy mocked what the vet had said about their stray kittens. "Looks like you got left out of that solution. Babs, maybe the two of us need to wise up. Didn't you tell me you used to always fall back on modeling gigs when the chips were down?"

"Call it quits? More often than not, my auditions have wound up as casting couch situations in disguise. What would you do?"

"Become a rich old dame's gigolo. Not that I want to, of course, and one who desires platonic companionship. Besides, it might be the perfect front."

"In order to hide your true inclinations?" Babs asked.

Guy made a quick glance from side to side to make sure no one had overheard and gave a subtle, affirmative nod.

* * *

An unwelcome ray of sunlight beamed through her broken Venetian blinds.

Babs jerked upright from her office couch and stared in horror at the windup alarm clock she'd failed to set the night before. "Oh gosh! Basil will be here any minute."

She grabbed a robe and prayed she wouldn't run into anyone in the hallway. Taking a quick peek, she made a mad dash into the public restroom to wash her face, do a quick sponge bath, rinse the horrible overnight taste out of her mouth, and fill up the coffeepot. Then she bolted back to her office, started the coffee, and stared at a stale, half-eaten chocolate éclair left over from yesterday.

She took quick sips of coffee from her lipstick-stained cup, in between dressing and putting on her makeup, and panicked as soon as she heard a knock on the door. "I'm not open yet! Come back in an hour."

"I would, but my driver has the motor running, and I have an urgent meeting at the studio. This is Basil." He opened the front door, which she left ajar, and hung up his hat and coat. "Your boss should give you a raise for arriving before normal work hours."

"Excuse me, but I am the boss. You assumed B. Norman was a man?"

Basil scratched behind his ear. "My sincere apologies. I guess it's hard to accept a female in the role of a private investigator, and you look too young to run your own business."

"Looks can be deceiving, as the old saying goes. I already married and divorced at seventeen, but I'm wiser now and use the magic of Max Factor's cosmetics to hide those battle scars."

"Please refresh my memory on your friend's name."

"Guy, he's both my secretary and my partner." She pointed to the name plaque on his desk. "How can I help you?"

Yesterday's rushed move out of her old apartment left her office reception area in disorder. Babs ushered him into her inner sanctum, which showed obvious signs she spent the night. He tried to make himself comfortable on her couch and moved her bathrobe aside. She worried about leftover fleas from the stray cat.

"I wish I could offer you tea," she said.

"Please, don't worry. I have a breakfast meeting within the hour."

She was about to smooth back her hair, but when her fingers got caught in a tangle, Babs realized she hadn't taken out all the bobby pins yet.

"Look, I'm beside myself about the disappearance of Leo, our poor Cocker Spaniel," Basil said. "He always reminds me of my best friend, Jack Wiltern. I witnessed the horrible tragedy when he stepped out into traffic on Los Feliz Boulevard. He and three of our dogs got hit by a car. It was terrifying to see four bodies lying in the middle of the road. Somehow, as I tended to Jack, Bunty, and Cullum, our two Westies got to the other side of the road, unharmed. Leo had broken his leg.

"Not only had my friend's death caused me to be overcome with grief, but every time I'm around Leo, I become nostalgic and remember all the good times I had with Jack." Basil looked at his watch. "Heavens, I'm going to be late."

"You mentioned it yesterday, but do you wish to hire me, Mr. Holmes?" Babs asked.

Basil sighed. "I wish you, or anyone else, wouldn't equate me with the roles I play. God forbid, I received vicious hate mail when I played Judas in the theater circuit."

She took a pencil and notepad from her desk. "I enjoyed your film, *The Hound of the Baskervilles*. No one else could've been better suited for the part. That aside, let me ask you a question. Where was your dog when you last saw him?"

Basil's gaze bounced off the ceiling as he searched his memory. "Come to think of it, I'm not sure, except I was probably on set and not at home when Leo must've disappeared. My wife Ouida and I always let our pets have the full run of the place. Until now, I considered Bel Air a safe neighborhood."

"Can anyone else recall who was there at the time?"

"Various members of the household staff. With them, it's been like a game of musical chairs, as if there's been some sort of citywide conspiracy with domestic help. We gave our regular house servants holiday time and had to resort to referrals and several agencies to fill the positions. My wife comes and goes as she pleases every afternoon, so there's no telling where she was when Leo vanished. Plus, there are always deliveries from the dry cleaners, the florist, and messengers from the studio. We just adopted a baby girl, so we have a diaper service, and we've had a terrible time with nannies. My wife fires them on a whim."

Babs wrote his wife's name on her notepad and drew a bold circle around it.

"*Hmmm*, so it sounds like you don't have a set routine."

"After the dogs eat their breakfast, we let them loose to play in the backyard. Since we have so many of them, it's much better than discovering they've done their business somewhere inside our house."

"None have tried to run off before?"

Basil shook his head.

"I know you're in a hurry, but you and I will need to sit down and make a list and try to narrow this down. My partner will be glad to follow up."

"This is rather blunt, Miss Norman, but is your interest in my case monetary or based upon the fact I'd be your celebrity client?"

Babs cleared her throat. "For me, this is personal. When I got married, *ugh*, to a horrible man, someone—thank heavens, who should be out of my life forever by now—he failed to tell me he hated animals in the house. This was one of those unfortunate instances of character misjudgment that was impossible to pick up beforehand and, mind you, before I became a private investigator and learned how to read people better.

"Anyway, I insisted we welcome my Cocker Spaniel into our new household, but he'd have nothing of it. Then, one day, he took her to the park. Maybe he unleashed her on purpose, lied, and allowed her to run off. Who knows, but he came home without her. What upset me the most was he didn't even have the sense to ask my mom to take back my favorite pet when he knew how much I considered her a part of my family. I feel your loss."

Basil took a wad of bills out of his wallet and plunked it down on her cluttered desk.

"Will this suffice as a suitable retainer?"

Babs wanted to slap herself in the face. "Uh, yes. More than enough."

He sized up the boxes and suitcases in her office and made a point to comment about the scattered cosmetics and overdue bills on her desk. "Bear with me if I've jumped to false conclusions, but I assume being a female private eye must be a hard life. If I were to think like the famous detective I portray, I'd deduce your landlord or landlady forced you out of your flat, and that's why you camped out on your couch. In no way would I believe an excuse about a case with a stiff deadline, and you just went through an all-nighter."

"An admirable deduction," she replied with disdain.

"If you agree to take my case, you'll need to be presentable around the company I keep. Our business arrangement will be conditional on straightening this place to appear like a proper professional office. You'll take a temporary residence in one of my guestrooms. I own a mansion in Bel Air with nine bedrooms. Our pantry always has plenty of tea, coffee, and a lot more sustenance than chocolate éclairs," he said, drawing her attention to the remains of her breakfast. "Agreed?"

Still foggy in the brain, she verified her suspicions by the wedding ring on his finger. "I couldn't impose upon you and... What about your wife?"

"Think nothing of it," he replied. "She loves to entertain guests, and our staff handles the household."

Babs wiped the sleep out of her eyes. "Are you sure? You're a handsome man and around every attractive leading lady in Hollywood. She's never accused you of having eyes for another?"

"Of course she has, but she should know me better. Besides, we just adopted a child. If that isn't commitment, I don't know what is."

Babs blushed. "Well..."

"While on the subject of hospitality, my wife Ouida and I will throw a party, posthaste. She's so used to it, she could do it in her sleep. For the life of me, I can't imagine why I'd have any enemies who might desire some sort of retribution or payback. All things considered, we'll send invitations to anyone who might be a potential suspect or have an insight into Leo's whereabouts."

"Sir, I have a request. Asta, the adorable dog from the *Thin Man* movies, is also missing. The studio offered a one-thousand-dollar reward for his safe return. My hunch is there might be a connection between the two disappearances. If you assist me and assume the guise of Sherlock Holmes, I think we'll have a better shot at finding both dogs—yours and theirs. Consider both my trusted partner and I as your two-for-the-price-of-one, Doctor Watson."

"We'll have to deal with Powell…"

"Do you have a problem if I take on a second case?"

"Not at all. Just professional rivalry and public opinion about who plays the superior detective on-screen. People will side in his favor because they think Holmes is outdated." He scratched his chin. "Perhaps I should talk this over first with Nigel Bruce, my on-screen collaborator. The public expects to see us together as a crime-fighting team."

"That's unnecessary, or at least not at the onset. Between Guy and I, we should have everything under control, but you will add credibility if others know you're assisting us."

"I'm only a thespian putting on a show. Sherlock Holmes is just an act."

"Yet, a believable performance, and one which might intimidate our culprit. Is that a promise?'

Basil gave a reluctant nod. Then he opened his wallet and added two more hundreds. "Make sure this keeps the electricity running and the phone working here in your office. Once we've made up your room, someone will call you with directions to my place. Meanwhile, I must be going."

After he left, Babs gulped down a sip of cold, bitter coffee and stuffed the cash in her brassiere. Yes, this was odd, she thought. Maybe a dumb, quick move into a luxurious retreat, but much more tempting than bathing in her office building's public restroom.

Chapter Three: Meet the Suspects

Just days after Babs left her temporary encampment and moved into one of the Rathbones' guest bedrooms, Basil and his wife planned a lavish soirée with a live band. The moment Guy arrived, Babs ushered him past security and spared no time introducing him to their host and new client.

"To be honest," he said and shook Basil's hand, "my real name is Gary... Gary Brandt, but there's a gentleman over at the bar freshening up his martini who has a similar name and is already more established in his acting career than I am.

"That aside, you've done up this place to the nines," Guy said. "Embarrassed to say, but I think my eyes went straight to your master chef's seafood extravaganza. Those mountains of King crab and lobster tails... You have enough shrimp cocktail to make Poseidon sea-foam green with envy. It must've required an architect to squeeze those festive floral arrangements among those mouthwatering food displays. Well, anyway, I'm at a loss for words, but glad I brought my appetite."

"If you think this is impressive," Basil said as he reviewed his guest list, "when Rodion, my son from my first marriage, got married, Ouida filled our pool with orchids. Neither he nor his wife appreciated our efforts. All the press photographers cared about was the who's-who roster of celebrity attendees. They took more pictures of Charlie Chaplin and Douglas Fairbanks, Jr. than the bride and groom."

"Ah, there's William Powell." Guy peered through the crowd. "The woman he brought with him seems to be quite—"

Babs wanted to know why he was at a sudden loss for words. She stood up on her tiptoes to catch a better glimpse. "Is she his wife?"

"Heavens, no," Basil replied. "I've never seen her before. He married another actress, Diana Lewis. His third marriage so far. His second wife, Carole Lombard, left him for Clark Gable."

"Didn't she die in a horrible plane crash?"

Basil nodded. "After their divorce, he wanted to get married to Jean Harlow."

"Another tragedy, too," Babs said.

"Diana is doing a film on location and won't be here today. Studio executives must've pushed him into this. Publicity, you know...it never looks appropriate for a handsome actor to show up alone, but I've never seen her before."

Basil spotted a familiar face and changed the subject. "See the man with the red carnation on his lapel...over by the pool? He's Asta's owner and original trainer, Henry East. The lady next to him is his wife, comedienne Gale Henry, who was big in silent pictures. At some point, I'll have to introduce you."

Babs wanted them to hire her to find Asta and make this official. Meanwhile, Basil excused himself to tend to the other guests.

Once the two detectives were alone, Babs reacted to Powell's guest's excessive use of fur. "How many exotic animals did she murder to make her outfit?"

"Do I sense a hint of jealousy?" Guy asked.

"What's your first impression of that fur-drenched fiend?"

He snickered. "She reminds me of a cross between Dietrich and Garbo with a hint of jackass, if you want my honest opinion."

"Guy, you missed your calling with comedy. Why don't you mingle and circulate? We must find out more about *la femme dangereuse.*"

* * *

Basil headed back toward Babs. "Look, Powell is alone, and your partner seems to be entertaining his strange companion." He waved and beckoned William Powell to join them. "Well, well, well, if it isn't *Our Man, Godfrey.*"

Powell raised Babs' hand to his lips and gave her a gentleman's kiss worthy of royalty.

He noticed her naked fingers. "How come a stunner like you isn't wearing a wedding ring? Some lucky gent doesn't know what he's missing."

"Somehow, I'm always surrounded by handsome men, but like my present company—they're all married."

Both men blushed.

"Flattery will get you everywhere with me, I'm afraid." Powell chuckled. "Should I assume the gentleman I spotted you with earlier wasn't your beau?"

"Guy?" Babs laughed. "You thought he was my husband? He's my business partner, like Fred Astaire to Ginger Rogers."

"Are you an actress?"

"A former one who's suffered too many pratfalls and pitfalls and without such sublime dance skills," she replied.

"Don't tell me you gave it all up. With a face like yours, the camera's lens would never crack."

Basil glossed over the news of the day about Hattie McDaniel's surprise win at the recent Academy Awards, food rationing in Britain, the Three Stooges' release of *You Nazty Spy!* which made fun of a Hitler-like character played by Moe Howard, and the real-life threat where Hitler agreed to bring Mussolini into the war overseas.

Babs stepped aside when Guy returned. "Have anything to report?" she asked.

"She goes by the name of Countess Velma von Rache. Don't know if the title is real, or if she's putting us on. She's German and a newcomer in town."

"Funny," Babs replied. "*Rache* is the German word for revenge and is mentioned in Arthur Conan Doyle's first Sherlock Holmes story, *A Study in Scarlet*. Anything else?"

"Her late husband was from Transylvania," Guy added.

Babs kept her voice low. "Is Bela Lugosi on Basil's guest list?"

"Dracula? Babs, for heaven's sake. Give me one solid reason you're so quick to despise her."

"Her furs clash," she said with disdain.

"You're too cruel. Nothing about her congenial personality?"

"Maybe she is in heat."

Guy bit his lip to keep from laughing out loud. "Despite any jealousies you might have, she is a major patroness of the arts in the Hollywood theater scene. Her goals include financing and producing films independent of the big studios, along with radio shows, and…drumroll please…she will be sponsoring a huge, prestigious *dog show* at the Beverly Hills Hotel."

Dogs? Babs' ears perked up. Before Guy could disclose anything else, Basil raised his hand to capture another party's attention. "Come, it's the rest of the *Thin Man* gang. This is the perfect opportunity to introduce you. Dashiell Hammett was here earlier but seems to have left."

Basil escorted the detectives over to a close-knit clique comprised of Henry East, his wife, Frank Weatherwax, who was another animal trainer, director W. S. Van Dyke II, who insisted everyone call him by his nickname, One-Take Woody or Woody for short, and producer Hunt Stromberg, wives included. Also present, Myrna Loy, who explained her husband was hobnobbing somewhere on the Rathbone compound unless he had fallen into the pool.

"Babs Norman has diverted her aspirations toward an acting career and has carved a little niche for herself as a private detective," Basil said. "I was so impressed that I hired her to retrieve my dog, Leo."

"You're interested in Asta's disappearance, as well?" Powell asked.

She looked Asta's owners and trainers in the eye. "Of course."

Myrna tested her. "You don't look like much of a detective to me. Why do you think you're so qualified?"

Babs stood erect and proud. "Ask Howard Strickling, the VP of Publicity at MGM. My partner and I returned all the stolen pairs of ruby slippers from the *Wizard of Oz* after they disappeared from the MGM Wardrobe Department."

Powell scratched his head. "How come I never heard anything?"

"Because it never made front-page news. Everyone involved did a spectacular job of keeping quiet," Guy replied.

Stromberg explained that so far, they had produced *The Thin Man*, *After the Thin Man*, and *Another Thin Man*. "Our next project is *Shadow of the Thin Man*. We hope to release it next year and expect it to be another box office success."

Basil interrupted. "Ladies and gentlemen, I suggest you keep an open mind and consider hiring them to find Asta. You won't be able to start your new film without him."

Guy handed all the members of their group business cards. Myrna examined hers, but backed away with such a scowl it was hard to dismiss.

Babs viewed everyone's skeptical faces with a stern eye. "Aren't you concerned about his welfare?"

"Of course, but..." Stromberg replied.

She started to ask Stromberg if he knew of anyone who would wish him ill, but he excused himself and said he needed to catch a guest before they left. Babs remained fearless and would not let this opportunity get away.

"Do you mind inviting me to your kennels, Mr. East? I'm curious what it takes to train dogs for motion pictures."

"Just call me East and refer to my wife as Gale. Between my first name being Henry, and her last name, Henry, it's much easier."

Babs had already retrieved her appointment book. "How about this Wednesday? Does 2:30 p.m. work for you?"

East tested his memory. "I suppose we can arrange that. If not, either Gale or I will call and reschedule."

Guy frowned and whispered in her ear. "That's just swell. I have an audition then."

"Break a leg. There's nothing saying I can't hoof it...or paw it...alone."

"Don't you need a ride? If you take a city bus, you won't enjoy the uphill hike with heels."

"I'll take a taxi. We can write it off as a business expense, but thanks for the reminder not to wear my favorite pumps."

Guy shrugged. "As you wish. Our fate now lies in your hands. Just make sure you give me the skinny on what happens. When you go solo, you have a tendency to keep the fact-finding to yourself."

Babs suggested that before or after his audition, he should inquire about domestic workers' employment agencies to investigate the Rathbones' temporary household staff.

She glanced over at Myrna and changed the subject. "Compared to her, I feel so underdressed."

"I'm surprised you've been more focused on her outfit rather than her cool reception," Guy said. "To me, she looked rather put off."

Babs would never satisfy her curiosity if she didn't find out more about Myrna's gown, so she put forth her best effort to make a new friend. "Nora, oops! I meant…"

"Please, call me Myrna. How can I be of help?"

Babs looked down at her feet and blushed. "I'm dying to know who designed your dress?"

Myrna threw back her head and laughed. "Heavens! You had me scared for a minute. I would've sworn you were about to interrogate me. Dolly Tree designed our *Thin Man* wardrobe for MGM. Talented, for sure, but I hired Adrian."

"Whose talents are also impressive," Babs mused. "He's the one who came up with the original design for the ruby slippers."

Myrna toned her voice down to a whisper. "Just between us, I didn't steal any items from MGM, but you don't think I'm guilty of making off with Asta?"

Babs gave her the side-eye. "I wouldn't be doing my job if I didn't, at least, try to rule you out."

"*Hrffmph*. I guess I'll just have to prove my innocence in any way possible to get on your good side," Loy replied.

"So will everyone else."

Babs escorted Myrna back to her friends. Her next move was to make sure everyone would agree for Guy and her to take on Asta's case. Who did she need to speak with? Who could sign off on a deal memo, and who could write the check?

* * *

On the verge of tears, Basil's wife, Ouida, interrupted them. "I'm afraid something dreadful has happened. I can't find our Bull Terrier, Judy."

"Have you searched the servants' quarters?" Basil asked. "She loves to give us the slip and hide in there. The washroom is another one of her favorites. Judy loves to play in piles of dirty laundry."

"That's the first place I looked," Ouida said, still shaky.

"You don't suppose someone here at the party tried to steal her?" Babs asked.

Mimicking Sherlock Holmes, regardless of whether on purpose, Basil paused to light his pipe. "The thought crossed my mind."

Babs' brain switched into detection mode. "Have you asked your hired help?"

His wife pleaded, "There are so many unfamiliar faces here today for the party since I gave our regulars time off. I wouldn't know where to start. Please, help me look for her."

Basil insisted someone needed to remain poolside and entertain their guests, but Ouida wanted to hear nothing of it. Powell volunteered.

"Ouida, why don't you ask if anyone wants a tour of our new house? It won't be obvious, but I'll be on the lookout for signs of Judy. How does that sound?"

"What a brilliant idea," Powell said. Others agreed.

A server swished by, and Basil placed his half-finished drink glass on his tray. "Then it's settled. Rally the troops, my bride, and I'll be glad to oblige."

* * *

While Basil gave his tour, Guy suggested he and Babs split up, and he would scout out other suspects. They both couldn't believe there might be a second dognapping. Babs searched the rented cabanas. She opened one, still occupied, with Nigel Bruce, Basil's on-screen Doctor Watson. Embarrassed she caught him changing, she hoped she wouldn't have to ask him for any future favors.

Next stop: the Rathbones' laundry room, where she discovered a tattered, unusable leash, which she stuffed inside her purse. After that, she slipped into the gardening shed, the garage, and the pool house.

She was just about to call it quits when she realized she'd forgotten to look under the Rathbones' hedges and examine every square inch of landscaping big enough for a medium-to-large-sized dog to hide. Then she had thoughts about how Leo could have wiggled through or dug a hole and escaped. Their property had no actual fences, walls, or gates. Only typical California shrubbery. Their errant Bull Terrier was close to the same size, or even smaller than Leo.

Against her better judgment, she bent over and heard a telltale rip in the seam of her pristine silk chiffon dress.

"Goodbye, dear friend," Babs said with a sigh. Between the rip getting larger and grass stains impossible to get out, with one last look, she hiked up her skirt before she got down on her hands and knees. The moment she saw Guy heading her way, she dipped her dirty hands in the swimming pool, shoved a handful of hors d'oeuvres into her mouth which tasted like chlorine, and caught up with him.

"Any more news on the countess?" she asked.

"I felt guilty spying on her when everyone else was on a dog hunt."

Before he said more, Basil, who finished his tour, came over holding three flutes of champagne. "So, what or who were you talking about?"

"Powell's so-called companion," said Guy.

Basil took a quick look over his shoulder, which turned into a subtle scowl. "Someone else is also a piece of work," he mumbled. "I wouldn't have invited him if my publicist hadn't insisted on his *social* importance."

"Who? Errol Flynn?" Babs asked.

"Look at him! Surrounded by six infatuated women. Don't think I'm jealous; it's disgusting. I bet you he'll take every single one of them to bed with him this evening."

In between sips of champagne, Babs kept a watch on Flynn.

"Any luck?" Basil asked.

"I looked for signs of both Leo and Judy," she said.

"Good show; anything noteworthy?"

"No signs of Judy anywhere, but I found this when I entered your house through the back door." Babs opened her purse and handed him the ripped leash. "Behold, Exhibit A. Could Leo have broken away? Maybe he's loose somewhere in the neighborhood."

"Or someone could've cut the leash and set him free," Guy added.

Basil shook his head. "We always used that leash for another dog, not the Bull Terrier or Leo, but it's useless. I swore I'd thrown it out."

"Anything show up on your tour?" Guy asked.

"We had a delightful time until I cracked open the door to Babs' room and came upon an offensive odor. My maid had to fetch smelling salts when one woman fainted."

Babs gasped. "It didn't smell bad the last time I was in there."

"When was that?" Basil asked.

"When I dressed for your party, but I haven't been back since. Maybe I knocked over a bottle of perfume."

"This was no bottle of Paris's finest. Perhaps toilet water, and I mean the other, vile kind you flush down the loo." Basil checked his watch. "The stench will remain long after our guests have left, but that sums up my awkward adventure for the afternoon."

* * *

At the close of the party, the Rathbones continued to panic; their Bull Terrier, still absent. They were quick to point fingers at Powell, East, his wife, Weatherwax… Even the band members and Nigel Bruce. No one, however, had the chance to interrogate Dashiell Hammett or the countess before they left. Basil and Ouida gathered their house servants who were on-call that afternoon for questioning. Guy and Babs, the only others remaining, joined them for an all-out search of the grounds before giving up and calling the pound.

Exhausted and without answers, Guy drove home. When Babs returned to her room, she forgot about Basil's earlier comments. Something smelled so terrible that her nose rebelled. Given away by the sound of sad whimpering, she found the Rathbones' Bull Terrier under her bed, probably terrified of the crowd and the music from the live band. Locked in and with nowhere to go, the dog had a minor accident.

Chapter Four: The Hounds of the Hollywood Hills

Basil insisted going to the pound was a waste of time. Babs refused to believe him. On the day after their party, she taxied over there to find out for herself. As he predicted, the city employees made her a laughingstock and asked why Sherlock Holmes would hire someone else to locate his missing Cocker Spaniel. Jokes ranged from, "Why? Wasn't Watson available to solve the crime?" to one smarty-pants worker who quoted from one of Conan Doyle's stories: "No man (or woman, in your case) burdens his mind with small matters unless he has some very good reason for doing so."

The only person who offered anything useful suggested she might make inquiries at the upcoming Beverly Hills Dog Show, convincing her this was an event she shouldn't miss. Other than that, Babs became fed up with the wisecracks which weren't solving her case.

Despite the Rathbones' housekeeping staff doing their best to deodorize Babs' room, whoever stayed there would have to make use of the shower across the hall. When Ouida caught Babs with her bathrobe half-open by accident, she was up in arms. She ordered one of her housemaids to transfer her to another room with its own bathroom.

Babs tried to do anything she could afterward to cozy up to Ouida. Her household staff was less than cordial. Basil was correct. There seemed to be unknown faces all the time. Under normal circumstances, they had three maids, a cook, and a Japanese houseboy. Ouida had given them time off and replaced them with temporaries. Gretchen filled in for their head housekeeper, who turned out to be a never-ending source of contention. If she didn't remind Babs of Mrs. Danvers from Alfred Hitchcock's film *Rebecca*, then she'd revive memories of the wicked witch from *The Wizard of Oz*.

Wednesday barreled around the corner. Babs stopped by her office before her appointment at the Easts' kennels.

"Please don't tell me you're taking public transit," Guy said, relieved she wore sensible flats but still concerned. "It's too bad you couldn't convince Basil's driver to take you there."

"Right now, I need to earn my merit badge with his wife, so I didn't have the heart to ask. And no, don't ask me to elaborate. We don't have the time, and I don't need a headache. One of these days, after we win this case and collect the full reward, I'll buy a car," she said.

"Does this place have a particular name?" Guy asked.

"Henry East owns a few acres up in the hills. I think it's just called the Hollywood Kennels. Why?"

"Nothing cleverer like the Hollywood Hound, or the Hollywood Dog Bowl...you know, like the Hollywood Bowl, the music venue, or the Hound of the Hollywoodland-villes?"

"Like *The Hound of the Baskervilles*?" Babs said, making last-minute touch-ups on her lipstick. She wished Guy the best of luck on his audition and assured him she'd call a cab.

* * *

East came out to greet her with an affectionate collie in tow. He gave a brief introduction and insisted the dog welcome Babs by shaking her hand.

"Otto, I need help," he shouted, opening a gate and shutting it behind.

A massive, snarling Rottweiler hurtled toward them, dragging his poor handler. Not the response East expected. He yanked Babs out of danger. She tumbled backward. He tightened his grip on the collie.

"Cig? I wasn't expecting you. Where's Otto Braun? Weren't you supposed to be training Bruno?"

"*Bruno mit Otto,*" he replied in guttural German.

"With Otto? He's Walter Jäger's responsibility. Get this vicious dog out of here. Tell Otto to come at once."

East apologized and helped Babs to her feet. "Cig?" Babs asked. "A chain smoker?"

"Short for Siegfried. Puffs on too many stogies around the animals."

"Wow, that was a close call," Babs said. "Has Cig been here a while?"

"He's a new hire, and I don't recall ever seeing this dog before. Maybe he forgot *who* is the boss. No new animal is supposed to get past me."

East helped Babs brush grass clippings from her skirt. "Seems like I've gotten a lot of calls from German, Austrian, and Eastern European animal handlers willing to shovel shit around here." He realized his gaffe and apologized for the use of his language around a lady.

Otto came and took the frightened collie back to his pen. As soon as the handler was out of earshot, Babs remarked, "If I were a casting director, I'd have no trouble putting any of your assistants in an anti-war propaganda film, or as dress extras in a Wagnerian opera if they had suitable voices."

East was already steps ahead. "Now, let's talk about Asta, whose real name is Skippy." He raised his voice so Babs could hear him above the din of barking. "He was a young pup when he made his first appearance in a Three Stooges film. Among his many projects, he's starred in *The Thin Man, After the Thin Man, The Awful Truth, Bringing Up Baby* with Katharine Hepburn and Cary Grant, and he played Mr. Atlas in *Topper Takes a Trip* with Frank Weatherwax as his trainer. Of course, there's a lot more."

"Weren't you nervous about having him around a leopard in *Bringing Up Baby?*"

"Of course. He could've wound up as the big cat's lunch, but he was a real sport, acted like a pro, and never antagonized the feline. I'm sure someone fed the leopard before every scene where they performed together. However, if you read Dashiell Hammett's original book, *The Thin Man,* rather than just watching the movie, Asta was a Schnauzer. When it came time for casting, there wasn't a single Schnauzer in Hollywood well-trained enough to fit the bill. Everyone fell in love with Asta, who's a wire-haired Fox Terrier."

Babs made a quick visual scan toward the hills. "You seem to own a lot of land. Is this a lucrative business?"

"Asta is the highest-paid animal star in the business, earning two hundred and fifty dollars per week. He's MGM's top dog."

"You don't say."

"Well, guess what? His trainers get only sixty per week. I started out as a motion picture prop master but wound up doing this full-time. Maybe it pays to go to the dogs."

"I bet William Powell or Myrna Loy offered to buy him."

"Countless times. Myrna loved to tease and flirt with me right in front of my wife and refused to take no for an answer, but Asta was never for sale. He is so much brighter than the average dog, and I'd venture to say, but don't repeat this: he's smarter than any of the actors he's worked with. He can hide his head, play hide-and-seek. Even play dead..."

East got misty-eyed. "I need to remain hopeful." He made a sharp right through his maze of animal pens. "One of our little animal stars will show you the stuff he's made of, and we'll give you a demonstration."

"Can't wait." Babs removed a piece of gravel from her shoe and tried to catch up.

* * *

East led her over to an open corral. He returned, escorting a French bulldog.

"Dogs have their own language," he explained. "They can interact with their eyes and their tongues and have also displayed a sense of humor. Figuring this out is like trying to understand another person who speaks a foreign language. Let's put this little pup to the test, and Babs, one more thing..."

"What's that?"

He pointed to his baggy pants. "Stuffing an ample supply of dog treats in your pockets will do wonders. Meet Ripley. We named him after the *Ripley's Believe it or Not!*

"Ripley, sit down. Good boy. Now, hold it...h-o-l-d it..."

The dog seemed to strain under the pressure.

"All right." East rewarded him with some kibble. "Remember to praise him for his good work."

East asked Ripley to crouch, crawl on his stomach, and climb a ladder.

"I loved the scene in *The Awful Truth*," Babs said, "where Asta retrieved a man's hat, hidden behind a mirror. Then, when he perched on top of it with the hat in his mouth, it toppled over."

"If it makes you feel better, a Foley sound effects team did the sound of shattering glass after the filming."

"I wondered about that."

"Babs, we make sure none of our valuable stunt animals get harmed."

"Besides Asta, are any of these dogs your favorite?"

"*Shush!* They might gang up and go after me if they thought I liked one over another."

"Would they attack?"

"Nah, but I might get licked to death, or buried like a bone in my backyard."

Babs needed to be less star-struck and more of a sleuth. "East, when did Asta disappear, and who was with him at the time?"

"We were in the middle of a rehearsal on the studio lot with a large cast and crew. It was impossible to keep track of everyone around him."

"Isn't his trainer responsible?"

"Well, uh...yes, but often actors and directors and even producers won't listen. They think they're above everyone else, and the rules don't apply. Seasoned professionals like Myrna Loy and William Powell can be the worst. They think they know everything about proper behavior on set."

"This is a serious issue, Mr. East. Aren't you concerned there'll be another dognapping?"

"Babs, I'm a bit confused. Are you interested in what it takes to train a dog, or are you interrogating me?"

"Who says I can't do both?" She gave him a crafty smile. "You shouldn't be concerned unless you're the guilty party, am I right?"

Even if it was in jest, she could tell by the look on his face he took offense, and it was time to change the subject. "You kidded me about dogs burying you in the backyard, but could you teach a dog to dig for bones of dead animals?"

"That's a search and rescue specialty, usually reserved for police dogs. Some of what we do here overlaps with that kind of training. Our major focus is on entertainment and what looks good for the camera. Consider contacting the K-9 unit of the Los Angeles Police Department for more insight."

He led Babs inside his onsite office and pointed to his collection of animal celebrity portraits on the walls. "In these frames are testimonials from proud clients—Al Christie, the president of the Christie Film Company, Mack Sennett Comedies. Even Marie Dressler said her animal actor acted like an old trooper."

"If I got a dog, what breed would you suggest?" she asked.

"Ask others who own the breed you've been considering. It's not much different from deciding what model of car to buy, except you're factoring in temperament and personality. Do you live in a tiny apartment or in a large house with a yard? Some dogs need constant play and exercise. You might prefer a more docile pet like a Maltese or a toy Pomeranian."

Babs frowned. *An intruder could kick one of those across the room.* She hesitated to admit she'd taken temporary residence at the Rathbones. The norm was a smallish space because that was all she could afford.

"All I can say is a Fox Terrier, like Asta, cooped up in an apartment, would drive you berserk. Same with a sheepdog who's used to having his run of the ranch."

"What about a guard dog, considering my line of work?"

East looked like he was about to offer suggestions when another assistant burst through the door and looked distressed.

"We have...situation. Into the hills—Bruno. Dog... Ran off."

East rubbed his forehead and muttered, "Coyotes," under his breath. "Where's Walter?"

The handler shrugged.

"Clark Gable wanted to buy him. *Beweg dein Hintern!*"

"German?" she asked.

"Bits and pieces I pick up from the movies, but with a lousy accent. Means, 'Move your ass.' Sorry, we'll have to cut this short. We'll have to form a search party."

East called a taxi and said one would arrive in five minutes. While she waited for the car, he reached into his pocket and pulled out a check.

"What's this?" she asked.

"A retainer…to find Asta. When you bring him home, safe and sound, you'll receive the balance."

The down payment was much more than she expected.

"The sum came from a group of us—our producer, Hunt Stromberg, our director, and Weatherwax, who will be the next trainer on *Shadow of the Thin Man*, the next *Thin Man* movie. We'll send a signed agreement to your office."

Chapter Five: Two Civilized Gentlemen

William Powell stood outside of the Brown Derby for a last-minute tête-à-tête with Rathbone. With a cigarette dangling in his mouth, he patted down his jacket pockets, unable to find his lighter. Basil, seeing his friend in distress, offered him a light. They removed their hats, and the maître 'd ushered them to Basil's favorite table.

"Can't figure out why they call it the Brown Derby," Powell said. "I know it's supposed to resemble a hat, but it reminds me more of the Griffith Park planetarium. The only stars we'll see over here are ones with studio contracts."

Basil pointed out a few of the celebrity caricatures on the walls. "The artist drew Jimmy Durante's nose so large, it takes up two separate picture frames. Isn't that your portrait to the right of his?"

Powell could care less and buried his nose in his menu. "It smells too good in here to suffer any longer, and I'm famished."

"You're aware of the peculiar acoustics in this place, I hope," Basil said. "The architects built this place on purpose, where it's easy to overhear everyone else's conversations."

Powell laughed it off. "But of course, I've dined here since you were still in your nappies."

"Born in 1892, am I correct?" Basil gave a hearty laugh. "The same year as I. On June 13th."

"A Gemini," said Powell.

"If you believe in astrology," Basil replied. "Are you superstitious?"

"Well, I'm a Leo, just like the lion at MGM, born on July 29th," Powell said.

Basil's mood turned somber. "About poor Leo..."

"Your dog?" Powell asked.

Basil nodded. "Two dogs connected to celebrities—one my personal pet, and the other featured in your next film, and it's turned our lives upside down. Be honest, William. Did you have a hand in this?"

"Why would I sabotage my project? I've done one film a year instead of three since Harlow's death. We were to be married, you know, but we kept it between ourselves. I didn't think I'd ever get over my grief until Diana came along. She renewed my sense of *joie de vivre*."

Basil asked for one of Powell's cigarettes and gave it a long drag. "Pay or play, perhaps? Worried you're no longer considered the sexiest man in Hollywood?"

Powell crunched his brows. "Pardon me? Am I losing my sex appeal to Clark Gable?"

"If that were the gist of my inquiry, I'd consider myself more viable competition. Don't you have it in your contract that you get paid whether your next film gets made? Wouldn't it be nice to extend your honeymoon for a few more months?"

Powell gave him a dirty look. "Now, Basil, if I weren't born yesterday, I'd suspect you were painting me into a corner."

Basil blushed. "Bad acting, I guess. You can't expect me to be on point all the time."

"How dare you jump to such conclusions! Perhaps I should pick up the check and call for a ride." Powell got up and alerted their waiter.

"My apologies." Basil told Powell to hold his horses and requested two more martinis.

"Changing the subject," said Basil, "tell me more about your royal highness."

Dumbfounded, Powell couldn't interpret his question.

Basil dropped a hint. "Your escort...at my party."

"The countess?"

"If that's what she really is," Basil replied. "Sounds dubious to me. Call me a poor host, but I never spoke with her at length outside of a hasty introduction."

"Can't tell you much, either. It's too bad my wife wasn't available to join me."

"A studio publicity stunt?"

"Of course. How can you guess? I don't even know where she lives."

"How did the two of you arrive?"

"She wanted my driver to pick her up at the Riviera Country Club. Said she was having drinks with a friend beforehand."

"I guess one could always rent or borrow fancy finery, but she appeared affluent," Basil said. "People do it all the time for the Oscars."

"If you dare to think I'm in with her on some cockamamie plan, you are dead wrong. To be frank, I think her attention was on Errol Flynn."

"I think Flynn caught every woman's eye at my party, including my wife's," Basil said.

Powell patted his lips with his cloth napkin and smoothed his pencil-thin mustache with his finger. "Have you been playing detective this whole time?"

"In a manner of sorts. I hired that persistent little lady and her partner in an official capacity, but for my dog only. You haven't been curious about Asta?"

"Basil, wouldn't it have been easier to just file a report with the pound instead of hiring private investigators?"

"My wife and I wanted to avoid publicity. If the staff at the city pound didn't take me seriously when I tried to make a report, could you imagine all the crank calls and false alarms I'd receive if fortune hunters thought *Sherlock Holmes* lost his dog? Not to mention the absurd newspaper headlines. I gave Babs Norman my blessing if she wanted to try, but she encountered similar ridicule. I can't rely upon underpaid public servants. Yesterday, she met with East at his kennels, in part to find out more about training dogs, and in part, to ferret out any suspicions."

"You think he might be guilty?"

"Who knows? He, along with Weatherwax, your producer, and the director, pooled together a retainer toward the reward for the safe return of Asta."

Powell sighed. "I wondered how anyone came up with the outrageous amount. Maybe the screenwriters chipped in, too. Wouldn't you want to assume coughing up that kind of dough would prove their innocence?"

"On the flip side, what if the considerable sum was a ploy to get the detectives to look in another direction?"

"Like a bribe?" Powell asked.

"Or a diversion they weren't aware of."

"That sounds more like a plot twist Dashiell Hammett would put in one of his future detective stories."

Basil retrieved a pen from his inner jacket pocket and scribbled a note on his napkin. *Don't forget. Question Hammett.* Realizing it was not a cheap paper cocktail napkin, but a fine cloth one, he made sure no one else was looking and stuffed it in his pocket.

He turned his attention back toward Powell. "It's not farfetched, if you consider the profits the studio expects to make after they release your next picture and the losses if production comes to a halt."

"Please don't tell me that little lady...Babs, that's her name...is going to pick my brain."

"She or her partner wouldn't be doing their jobs if they didn't."

"Well, there's no dog-do on my hands. Please don't tell me you've also questioned my co-star."

"Myrna seemed skittish when introduced to the detectives at my party. Is there something you're not telling me?"

Powell snickered as he helped himself to a miniature crab cake.

"What's so amusing?" Basil asked, taking a dive into his shrimp cocktail.

"We've both had our fair share of playing detectives on film," Powell said. "Even you tried to take away my role as Philo Vance."

"In the *Bishop Murder Case*? That was the studio's doing. Not mine, but it was refreshing to play the hero, for once, after an unbroken string of roles as the bad guy. Don't blame me for *The Dogville Murder Case*."

"Ha! At one point, the studio titled it *Who Killed Rover*. MGM had a field day with those canine parodies. That one was a spoof on *The Canary Murder Case*, where I played Philo Vance for Paramount." Powell leaned in closer and kept his tone low. "Man to man, do you trust that dame?"

"Babs Norman? Don't you dare underestimate her."

"Isn't a private investigator—"

"A man's job? Our little Miss Holmes has her own sidekick."

"Oh, that pansy?"

Basil rolled his eyes. "That's an inappropriate remark. He's a competent young man."

"Then you have more faith than I. Listen, I need this film, and I'm sure I can speak for Myrna as well. Besides, I adore Asta—poor fella. I feel as close to him as if he were my child."

"I have the same sentiment with my dogs, especially Leo. He's my constant, everyday reminder of my dear friend Jack."

"Patience, my friend. You'll get your dog back soon enough." Powell reached over and clasped Basil's hands. "Whatever you want. Whatever you need. Even if you need me to pose as Nick Charles or Philo Vance, or any other fictional detective, I'm at your disposal. You have my word. This is hurting my purse as much as it's tugging at your heartstrings."

Chapter Six: The Thin Man, Hard-Boiled and On the Rocks

Basil and the two detectives went down the list of party guests. One of the most elusive attendees was Dashiell Hammett, the author of the book *The Thin Man*, on which the films were based. The consensus was he hadn't been well and had left their party earlier than most.

Guy sweet-talked one secretary at MGM into giving him Hammett's temporary address, which turned out to be a lavish penthouse apartment at the Beverly Wilshire Hotel. He and Babs greeted Basil in the lobby to go up as a team.

"No Inverness cape?" Babs looked at their famous friend with disappointment.

"A more subtle choice, don't you agree? Minus the passé hat, cape, and walking stick, I'm sporting my paisley silk ascot and the smart double-breasted herringbone suit, the one I wore on the moors in *Hound*. Are you sure you saw my film?"

Babs buttoned her lip as they entered the elevator.

* * *

Hammett greeted them upon arrival, shrouded in cigarette smoke almost as thick as the San Francisco fog he wrote about. He insisted his visitors join him for a round of Scotch.

While he prepared everyone's drinks at his private bar, Babs shouted,

"Extra soda in mine, please." Then she whispered to her partner, "If I don't water this down, I'm a goner."

"If you're going to remain in this business," Guy said, "you'll have to be better at holding your liquor."

Fidgety, Babs looked around, as if expecting some sort of surprise.

"Are you still having a problem with fleas?" Guy asked.

"Heavens no." She straightened the hem of her skirt. "This place reminds me so much of the upscale place where Nick and Nora Charles stayed in *The Thin Man*. I keep imagining Asta will poke his head around the corner."

Hammett laughed. "Often, I've wondered if someone had that in mind and selected this room for me, on purpose."

Basil cracked a smile. "Perhaps its *raison d'être* was to get you in the mood to write your next *Thin Man* installment, or to quote Oscar Wilde, 'Where art imitates life.'"

"Maybe to get past my writer's block," Hammett said and took a sip of his drink. "Everyone's waving money in front of me for more detective stories, but I can't seem to churn them out anymore. Now, how can I help?"

Basil started the inquiry. "We might as well be upfront from the get-go. I hired Babs Norman and her partner, Guy Brandt, to find my missing red cocker, Leo."

"Are they detectives or dogcatchers?" Hammett made an all-out effort to keep a straight face.

"Private investigators and, so far, fine ones at that," Basil replied. "After you left my party, I introduced them to the director and producer on the *Thin Man* films, who chipped in to hire them to find their missing mascot."

"I'm afraid my role is rather insignificant," replied Hammett.

"Although I'm sure it's safe to say you're not involved with the disappearance of my dog, anyone affiliated with Asta, unless ruled out one hundred percent—"

Babs cut in. "Sir, we're looking for a solid motive why someone would steal Asta."

"You don't have to tell that to a former Pinkerton detective," said Hammett.

"We also can't dismiss you're the author of Sam Spade," Guy said.

"Whom I'm often compared to, although that's unfair. Like Nick Charles, I am also retired," Hammett replied.

"To be honest, we wouldn't be doing our jobs if we overlooked a possibility," said Babs.

Hammett appeared uncomfortable. When he had a violent coughing fit, he pulled out his handkerchief and spit out blood. When it wouldn't abate, he excused himself to go to the bathroom.

"I heard about his chronic health issues," Guy said. "I wonder if that's why his hair turned white since he's not old—only forty-six."

"Amazing, only two years younger than I," Basil said.

Hammett apologized for his brief absence. "Sorry, the Great War took its toll."

"Where did you serve?" Basil asked.

"Enlisted in the United States Army Ambulance Corps in 1918, but never made it out of our camp in Baltimore," he replied. "Came down with the damned Spanish flu, which developed into tuberculosis. About as much action I ever saw, and you?"

"Second Lieutenant in the 2/10 Battalion King's Liverpool Regiment with B Company in the trenches near Bois-Grenier," Basil replied. "My brother served, too, but didn't make it out alive."

Hammett coughed again but cleared his throat. "Sorry for your loss. War is god-awful, no matter how you look at it. Getting back to the purpose of your visit, you're wasting your time if you think I might've had something to do with Asta's disappearance."

"Mr. Hammett, isn't it true in your book that Asta was a Schnauzer?" Babs asked.

"You are correct, but people make adjustments all the time."

"Do you think someone, perhaps a breeder of champion Schnauzers, could've been upset with the switch?" Guy asked.

Hammett stroked his chin. "I'm not buying it. If you want to know, including Asta in my original story was because of a private joke I played on a screenwriter friend in New York, Sid Perelman, a great humorist who wrote several scripts for the Marx Brothers. One day, I arranged for a stripper to surprise him at his apartment and timed the practical joke so his wife Laura would discover them. Ironically, I wound up having an affair with Laura, and she owned a dog named Asta. When I wrote in a pet for Nick and Nora Charles, I stole the name of her dog."

"Could there have been anything else from your novel that might've upset a crazed fan—someone who insisted the films follow the books to the letter?" Basil asked.

"The screen adaptation of *The Thin Man* was pretty true to the original. That was the only book I wrote, and it never turned into a series in the literary sense. The screenwriters hired by MGM concocted the ideas for sequels. Not my doing at all, except as an advisor on the initial characters. They have the power and artistic license to rewrite a Schnauzer into future scripts, or they can always come up with the excuse the Charleses gave Asta to a relative and replaced him with a wise-cracking, foul-mouthed myna bird, if the director demanded it."

"Is there anything related to your background or view on politics, on the war, or about Hollywood, which might've prompted someone to take Asta?" asked Babs.

"Now you're coming across as a journalist. Are you sure you aren't a reporter in disguise?"

Guy answered for her. "Detective work, as you know, involves a lot of the same talents."

Hammett nodded and offered another round of drinks.

"There's been talk of postponing the next *Thin Man* film," Basil said. "Although Myrna Loy and William Powell are under contract, the studio might need to assign them to another project. As you can imagine, the investors are nervous."

Chapter Seven: Best and Worst in Show

They didn't get too far in trying to question Dashiell Hammett. Par for the course in his profession as a writer of detective novels, whether they were hard-boiled or whimsical like the adventures of Nick and Nora Charles, he was a man of many contradictions. Few understood him beyond the surface. Babs and Guy wanted to believe he was innocent in regard to the missing dogs, but it was too soon to be sure.

Gale East reminded the detectives about the exclusive dog show to be held at the Beverly Hills Hotel. Too many people in that crowd knew Gale and her husband, but she urged Babs and Guy to go, since it might provide a few leads. William Powell pulled a few strings to get their press credentials from MGM's publicity department, so they could pose as journalists for the studio. He also felt it best not to accompany them because his high profile could blow their cover. Basil felt the same.

On the day of the big event, Guy did his last-minute primping. "We had better solve this case," he said.

Babs straightened the seams of her stockings. "What if we don't?"

"If I keep blowing my share of our advance on looking dapper, I'll wind up in the poorhouse."

She gave him a quick inspection. "No one pays attention to men's clothes compared with women's."

"I beg to differ. Besides, they made this suit with tropical-weight wool. Much better as we're heading into warmer weather."

"Picky, picky." She loved teasing him, but with good reason.

"If I didn't pay such attention to fine details, I wouldn't be a good detective, would I?"

"I hope you pay equal attention to balancing your checkbook," she said with contempt as she pinned a festive silk gardenia in her hair. "About Basil's dog...did you ever come across anything useful when you called those domestic employment agencies?"

"I need to learn how to speak German or Russian or whatever," he replied. "Nothing conclusive. One woman, who sounded like she could've been the missing daughter of Tsar Nicholas II, said a pipe burst in her office and ruined all of her recent records. Seemed too convenient."

He packed his Rolleiflex camera in a carryall and double-checked his inventory of flashbulbs and film. "Even if I pretend to shoot it and not waste expensive film, it's the perfect accessory."

She handed him his badge. "Make sure you wear it where officials can see it. I don't want to hear a peep out of you if it pokes a hole in your lapel or hides your flashy tie."

* * *

After they checked in with hotel security and made a stop at the press table, officials handed them a copy of the program. When asked why MGM had a particular interest in the event, Babs said she and her partner were also scouts for fresh doggy talent.

Guy pored over their brochure. "'Countess Velma von Rache proudly sponsors this year's first Beverly Hills Dog Show. Profits from this event will go to the Thespian Development Fund and the ASPCA.' Babs, she might be eccentric, but she seems to be a legitimate philanthropist."

"According to this," Babs said, "the actual competition will be in the ballroom, but not for close to another hour. There's a special pre-show event—the Parade of the Stars. The animal handlers will strut their pooches around the pool."

A server passed by, and Guy grabbed two glasses of champagne. He handed one to Babs and took a sip from his. "What are you waiting for?"

Babs frowned. "You, my friend, will be working. Even if you have to fake it."

With no convenient place to dispose of it, Guy took one last gulp with a burp, and dumped the remaining contents of both glasses into the nearest potted plant. On the way to the pool, he insisted on having a quick look-see of the hotel's famous Polo Lounge.

"Now that's the life," he said, nodding in approval at its posh Deco decadence. "Just imagine all the stars who've dined here...the glamorous people, the booze flowing... Hey, I heard their bungalows were going for half a million clams."

Status-conscious, he pointed toward the relevant pictures on the wall. "Did you know they built this place near actual polo grounds?"

Babs didn't need a historian. She grabbed her chatterbox partner by his camera strap to ensure they stayed on schedule and ushered him toward the exit. Once they made it outside, she recognized a familiar face shading herself in one of the poolside tents reserved for judges and VIP guests.

Guy got a lump in his throat. "The countess. She'll recognize me from Basil's party."

"You didn't tell her you were a private detective?" Babs asked. "Or did you?"

"Of course not. I guess I should introduce you...as a reporter."

Despite the heat, Von Rache wore fur. The detectives kept her under surveillance as she engaged with a couple who had an elegant silver-and-white Borzoi wearing a diamond collar. Babs took charge and led Guy to a closer vantage point where they could listen in.

"*Oooh*, I just adore furry little things. I hear Mae West has two of these." The countess spoke perfect English, like someone who had a command of the language, but with an obvious accent.

She outraged Babs by grooming the Borzoi's silky hair with her elongated, blood-red fingernails. "Try picturing her affectionate with an American Hairless."

Guy grabbed her wrist and pulled her aside. "Shut up. Just because you're jealous, you don't have to—"

"Criticize her?" Babs pulled out her compact and reapplied the powder.

"Maybe she needs a little dressing down."

"*Grrrr...* Whenever anyone wears an expensive outfit you can't afford..." Guy was ready to tear his hair out, but stopped, took a breath, and smoothed it back. "Well, guess what? In this town, there'll always be someone richer than you, no matter how successful you become."

The two detectives continued to quarrel. When they raised their voices to a dangerous level to hear each other over the live band, he suggested they split up.

Babs inched closer and pretended to skim through her notes. From what she could gather, the countess desired her own dog. Sponsoring this prestigious show was the perfect opportunity to compare various breeds in order to decide which one would be the right choice.

Guy returned after wandering around taking pictures. "Look, here's our chance. She's alone."

He took the countess's hand and offered a kiss, reminding her they'd met at the Rathbones' recent party.

"Dahling...who's your cute little friend?" she asked.

Guy made a brief introduction. The countess gave Babs a kiss on each cheek and ignored her afterward.

"How come you weren't taking photos at Basil's party?" she asked.

He explained the Rathbones invited him as a guest. "Please refresh my memory. What was your interest in coming to sunny Southern California?"

The countess, who was smoking a cigarette in a long, black-lacquered holder, exhaled and replied with a throaty laugh. "The movie industry, of course, but now, with the Fascist Party taking over in Germany, people are more interested in making propaganda films. Even Fritz Lang, one of our national treasures, has fled and come to Hollywood."

"You're an actress?" Babs asked.

"Doesn't everyone want to make a dramatic entrance?" the countess replied.

Babs was at a loss for a clever comeback. Instead, she asked, "What prompted you to sponsor this dog show?"

"For years, I've always wanted to own a dog. Lots of dogs. More than you could imagine, but my father forbid it. Once, I found a stray and snuck it home, but he beat me senseless. Said dogs were demonic, or something absurd like that. He locked me in my room with a pitcher of water, and I had nothing to eat for two days."

"How awful," Babs said, not believing a word of it. "Are you telling us you've never had a dog since you've been an adult?"

"*Aber nein*," she sighed.

Not allowing herself to get caught up in the woman's act, Babs played along anyway. "Do you have any idea what kind of dog you'd like to get?"

"I'm drawn to ones with exotic coats." Her head whipped around as a handler walked by with a striking Irish Setter. "The larger, the better. If you have any particular breeders you recommend, I'd love to hear all about it."

A roly-poly little man, whom Babs suspected had more hair on his back than on his head, came into the pool area, pinging a silver triangle musical instrument to get everyone's attention and to make an announcement. "The main event will start in forty-five minutes."

Babs realized she hadn't brought the proper business cards and came up with a white lie, saying she had given out her last one. She thanked the countess for her time and excused herself and her partner.

* * *

"Come, let's head over to the prep area," she said to Guy as they crossed through the lobby. A security guard stopped them as they tried to go backstage, but the detectives flashed their press credentials. Once inside, she fished out her stenographer's pad, while Guy snapped away, giving the contenders plenty of winks and smiles. The two of them passed one man who was fawning over his pooch with baby talk. Guy bit his lip to keep from laughing out loud.

"If we had recordings of these conversations, we'd have a hit radio show," Babs remarked as they passed by another dog owner, who might as well have been wooing his Weimaraner with love songs.

They kept walking and noticed a woman wearing a large-brimmed straw hat who was fussing over her toy Chihuahua.

Babs gave her an envious sneer. "I saw this hat in the window of I. Magnin's and thought it would look perfect with my navy crepe sailor dress."

"Why didn't you buy it?" Guy asked.

"Do I have to remind you about my eviction? Well, maybe I was foolish, but after we received our retainer, I went back to the store, but it was gone. She was probably the one who bought it, and look, it doesn't even fit her." The oversized hat slipped over the woman's eyes. "Her damned hat is bigger than her dog."

Guy dodged a handler with his Rhodesian Ridgeback. "You're one to talk, after putting me down earlier for my fashion foppishness."

Babs scurried over to one judge with questions. "Sir, I'm by no means an expert, but how does a dog qualify to enter a show like this?"

"As long as the canine contestant is a healthy, purebred pup—has a tail at one end and a bark at the other—he is eligible for a prize."

"Would you say this is the premier show in the States?"

"The Beverly Hills Dog Show is the first of its kind. America's largest show is the Morris and Essex Dog Show in Madison, New Jersey. Over 5,000 dogs!" he replied.

"Let's suppose I'd like to buy a pedigreed dog and enter him in shows. Would you say many of these breeds are valuable?"

"Show dogs can cost their owners up to the thousands, and that doesn't even consider the extra investments made in grooming and training. Plus, the handlers need to get paid. Everything adds up."

Calculating her inquiries toward her ultimate aim of locating Asta, she asked, "Do many of these dog owners hope to feature them in films?"

The chatty judge, who seemed eager to get as much attention as the contestants, went off on a tangent. "Quite an interesting history behind the Morris and Essex Show. I'd be glad to tell you more if you like."

Babs explained her assignment had to focus on this show only.

Guy bailed her out. "Come, I see a party of puppy pointers, perkily posed for a perfect picture—a photo opportunity only a puerile plebeian would pass up on purpose."

She tried not to laugh as they left. "Those poor dogs…getting their hair brushed and curled. It reminds me of the torture when my mother insisted I get a permanent wave for my high school graduation. The beautician hooked me up to a machine, which made me feel like a prisoner going to the electric chair."

The egg-headed emcee with the silver triangle emerged again. "Contestants and their handlers report to the holding area," he shouted. "Guests, your ticket shows the number of your reserved seat."

"They should've given him a gong or a pair of cymbals," Guy joked as he gathered his equipment for transport. "I barely heard him over the commotion."

* * *

The grand ballroom transformed into a show arena. As a photographer, Guy had the full run of the place and could come and go as he pleased.

"Don't worry, I won't abandon you," he said to Babs, who realized she'd be sitting alone. "Make a few friends. Who knows? They may turn into clients." He went in search of last-minute closeups of the dogs and their handlers before they went onstage.

The announcer emerged using a bullhorn, "Ladies and gentlemen, welcome to the debut of the Beverly Hills Hotel Dog Show and, we hope, one of many fine events to come. First up will be the Hounds. Our judges will give points for carriage, gait, and ring temperament, and each breed has its own special standard for scoring."

Handlers came out one by one, holding their dogs' heads high. The judges made their slow and deliberate inspections of the dogs' teeth, eyes, ears, gums, gait, and movement. Trainers in the various groups presented their dogs to be narrowed down to the semi-finalists. A rust-colored Dachshund won as best contestant in the Hound Group.

Babs recognized the same woman with whom she was so envious earlier. This time, her fancy hat lay beside her on an empty adjacent seat. "Aren't you entering your dog in the Toy category? I think they're up next."

The Hat Lady looked around the adjacent seats and went into hysterics. "My Boopsie! My little Chikiboom. My Chihuahua…" The woman said her dog was right here, but he had vanished. "Please, someone…everyone…help me find him!"

Babs tried to concentrate on the show, but this dog owner's antics kept vying for her attention. "Isn't he with his handler?"

Her reply, sharp and bitter. "He snapped at one judge—who disqualified him!"

Surprised no one else offered help, she felt compelled to be the Good Samaritan. In a crowded ballroom, the tiny dog could get trampled.

"My baby, Boopsie, and I traveled all the way from Orange County," she explained. "I'd rather die than face the wrath of my husband if I return home empty-handed."

Babs was unsure if her dog's name was Boopsie, Chikiboom, Chilidog, or Checkbook, which wouldn't have been far from the mark. Prize money was at stake, and it cost a "countess's ransom" for the dog owners to be here. After hearing all its nicknames, she asked those seated nearby, but with no luck. She forced herself, despite personal prejudices, to be sympathetic and insisted the dog's owner stay calm.

Babs jumped to her feet. "Look! It's doing its own Mexican hat dance."

The frantic woman stared open-mouthed as the hat continued to circle to the left and right on its own. On the final counterclockwise turn, two itty bitty paws poked out from underneath. Guy, who returned from taking his last photographs, lifted the hat and revealed the woman's missing pup. They both laughed out loud. The woman showered her precious little prize with kisses and couldn't thank the two of them enough.

"Is there anything I could do?" the woman asked. "A reward, perhaps? You don't know how frightened I was."

You can offer me your handsome hat. Babs kept the thought to herself. "Don't be ridiculous. I'm sure you would've done the same for me."

A miniature Doberman won in the Toy category. "They don't look so tough when they're tiny," Babs said to the Hat Lady. The woman raised her chin and snorted. Babs figured she was upset her dog could no longer

44

compete.

Next up, judging for the Herding Group and a German Shepherd took the prize for the best in its category. When a Boxer won for the Working Dogs Group, the Hat Lady grumbled again. "Seems like the German dogs are in favor today."

"Isn't a Boxer an English breed?" asked Babs.

The haughty Hat Lady flaunted her expertise. "The breed originated in Germany. I don't know where its name came from."

Despite everything, if this dog show were a three-course meal, the Chihuahua calamity was the appetizer, and the main course was about to begin.

The master of ceremonies announced, "Before we have our contestants compete in the Terriers' round, I'd like to introduce three special guests."

Myrna Loy slipped through a curtain, dressed in a flowing, floor-length silk crepe designer gown, trimmed with ostrich feathers, and holding—Asta! More often than not, he exemplified the best of canine behavior. In front of this audience, he barked and was uncooperative. Joining her onstage was the countess, who remained quiet in the background.

Myrna fought hard to keep Asta secure in her arms as she stepped over to the mike.

"Good afternoon, on behalf of MGM and the *Thin Man* films. We'd like to endorse goodwill toward dogs worldwide. As your spokesperson *du jour*, I wanted to show our appreciation for the ASPCA and all the animal charities of Los Angeles.

"The ASPCA is a volunteer, non-profit organization, not to be confused with the City Pound. First founded in the late nineteenth century to fight against cruelty to carriage horses, they also helped eliminate rabies during our recent scare in Los Angeles."

She continued her pitch, but Asta refused to stay calm. When he broke free from her arms, stagehands and show officials scrambled after him while the judge escorted the women offstage.

The master of ceremonies tried to restore order. "Ladies and gentlemen, everyone is in safe hands. We shall return to our scheduled programming in five minutes."

Babs scanned the crowd. It took enormous restraint not to rush backstage.

Why was Myrna here and with Asta? Since when did someone find him and not tell me? Maybe that wasn't him—but a look-alike.

Five minutes later, over the loudspeaker system: "Attention. Because of an unfortunate incident, we'll have to suspend our show. Please, do not panic."

I don't like it when someone says don't panic. She climbed up on her seat to get a better view. When she lost her balance, she quickly sat back down.

Guy returned, clutching his camera equipment so it wouldn't fly off his shoulder. Both of them spotted a flurry of security guards trying to control the chaotic crowd.

Another announcement: "We need to evacuate the ballroom. Please obey our hotel staff. They will usher you over to several holding areas for questioning."

"Guy, why won't they tell us what's going on? It's something to do with Asta. I just know it."

"From what I could overhear, he escaped somewhere backstage, and some of the other canine contestants are now missing. This is an enormous place, and it might be as simple as a few dogs running away from their handlers. You know how excited dogs can get when they're around other dogs, but security is trying to lock down the hotel until the cops arrive."

"What a perfect opportunity if someone wanted to steal them. I can imagine the headlines of *Variety* now: *Doggone-It! Famous Thin Man Pup Lost Again.*"

"Babs, don't get yourself into a tizzy. We might slip out of here if we make for the parking lot and hold up our press badges where everyone can see them."

Cops from the Beverly Hills Police Department barreled into the ballroom. Babs wanted to rush over with questions.

Guy grabbed her by the arm and gave her the evil eye. "We're supposed to be working undercover. Do you want to get out of here, or do you want to be stuck here until midnight?"

Chapter Eight: Showdown

Guy told Babs if she stomped her feet any harder, she'd kick a hole through the bottom of his rusted car.

"Did you see where the countess went?" she asked. "What about Myrna? It would break my heart if she was responsible. Whoever stole Asta and maybe even Basil's dog might've been right under our noses, and we lost their trail."

"Babs, I think you're trying too hard to make this all fit in a neat little box. Myrna's dog misbehaved too much. Not for one second did I believe it was Asta. From far away, it would've been impossible to know his real identity."

"Yet, I didn't see any of his owners or the handler present."

"They could've been hiding offstage," he explained. "After all, they're used to staying out of the way of the motion picture cameras. Besides, no one was certain if anyone stole the show dogs. All I heard were speculations."

"It could've been an inside job, and someone had accomplices. Please tell me you got this on film."

Guy almost ran a red light. "I posed as a shutterbug and pretended to take photos in order to get closer to potential suspects. Isn't that what you wanted?"

Babs slapped her thigh so hard it hurt. "How could you have been so shortsighted?"

A souped-up convertible swerved into their lane and cut them off. Guy slammed on the brakes and demanded silence for the rest of their ride. She kept the rest of her thoughts to herself, upset they had accomplished little. He escorted her to the Rathbones' Bel Air mansion and gave her one last hug before speeding off to his digs in West Hollywood.

Gretchen, the Rathbones' provisional housekeeper, stared at her from the dark foyer, lit by a beam of late afternoon light spearing through a narrow side window. The woman stood steadfast, like an overlord, and said in a formalized German-British monotone, "Madame requests you no longer have your own key to her house."

Beside her, Moritza, Basil's German Shepherd, stood guard, excited by the scent of hundreds of other dogs all over Babs since she had just come from the show.

Babs' heart tapped so furiously it could've danced the flamenco. She would've sworn she walked into the wrong place. On the tip of her tongue, *How does Madame expect me to do my job?*

"The key," Gretchen repeated.

Babs needed answers. *Maybe Ouida's changing the locks. Made sense if she thought Leo might've escaped during a robbery attempt.*

She dropped her copy into the woman's icy hand.

Gretchen waited a few beats before she stepped aside and allowed her to pass, as if making her feel the pain was deliberate. Babs held out her hand to the German Shepherd, with caution, to signal she was a friend to be trusted, but Moritza growled, and the maid restrained the anxious dog by her collar. Leery about any other surprises in store, Babs hurried upstairs to her bedroom. She tossed her purse on her bed, kicked off her shoes, and drew a bath, desperate to freshen up after a harrowing afternoon.

When she searched for her robe, she realized one of their maids must have made a mistake. Instead of washing and returning hers to her room, someone had folded one of Ouida's dressing gowns and placed it inside her clean laundry. Upon further inspection, other obvious errors were a shirt of Basil's, more women's underwear that wasn't hers, and a baby bonnet.

Maybe there was an emergency, a crying infant, or a kitchen crisis.

Her mind went blank. New faces seemed to be the norm around the Rathbone household.

Babs was too tired to think straight, but this unspecified person left her without a single pair of fresh panties. She donned her hostess's dressing gown, gathered up the items that didn't belong there, and ran downstairs to the laundry room.

Ouida confronted her halfway. "Why are you wearing my robe?"

"Your help must've made some kind of oversight and mixed up everyone's clothes in my room, and—"

The two ladies argued loud enough for their voices to echo. Babs assumed Basil was out with the dogs. Otherwise, he would have overheard and split up the fight.

Ouida marched Babs into the laundry room and rummaged through both clean and dirty items. As soon as she uncovered Babs' underwear, she tossed it into her face. Using a few unladylike words, she told Babs to "Get lost!" before storming out.

Babs returned to her room, exhausted and frustrated, because she always went out of her way to gain favor with Basil's wife. She needed to lie down and catch a much-needed nap before the Rathbones expected her to join them for dinner.

When her alarm went off, she heard tiny paws from one of Basil's Westies vying for her attention. Gretchen went up and down the hallway, ringing a dinner bell, giving the ten-minute warning.

Babs brushed her hair with her fingers as she hustled downstairs. She had walked in on a dining-room conversation where Ouida took pride in her recent gambling coup at the Santa Anita Racetrack. Basil's attention was on a racing form, trying to analyze where he went wrong.

"Your methods are too methodical." Ouida bragged she was always better at betting on a hunch than her husband. "If you quit pretending you're Sherlock Holmes, maybe your horse will win once in a while."

He studied the racing stats. "At least you were a good sport and sprang for the drinks afterward."

Babs stood at the entryway, taken aback when she spotted table settings only for two. Basil tried to communicate with Babs using some kind of eye signal. She presumed he wanted to intervene but couldn't. Instead, he placed aside his racing form and worked on his Bouillabaisse.

Ouida patted her lips with a linen napkin and said, "Have your bags packed by ten tomorrow morning."

Jealousies came to a boil, including other accusations of stealing clothes. Babs, in her defense, said this was an easy mix-up since they were the same dress size.

Ouida accused her of capitalizing on too much of her husband's time, especially since an adopted baby had just entered their lives. She even confessed that she bribed her housekeeping staff to spy on them. Meanwhile, Basil remained mum and in no contest.

"Aren't you interested in finding your Cocker Spaniel?" Babs asked, wondering if Ouida orchestrated Leo's disappearance to prove some point with her husband long before she got caught in between their marital mudslinging.

"Do whatever you want regarding that stupid movie dog. He's not our responsibility, but we'll let the proper authorities take over finding Leo. At any rate, I owe you some credit for filing reports with the pound."

Babs didn't get an outright thanks. Ouida softened somewhat but laid down the law.

"Perhaps I also owe you a brief explanation. My husband invited you into our household without my permission. He never discussed it with me first."

Ready to take sides, the Rathbones' German Shepherd examined Babs with a sniff and a snarl. She and Ouida continued their catfight until their baby daughter, who'd been half-asleep in a bassinet beside her mother, woke and cried. Babs apologized and hoped her soothing tone would appease their vigilant dog. Basil still failed to come to her defense.

Ouida picked up her daughter and began rocking her in her arms. She clarified Babs wasn't welcome at their table. "If you want something to eat, ask the cook. There should be leftovers from lunch or breakfast."

Chapter Nine: Marching Orders

Babs wondered if her presence caused a singular incident, or if there had been an ongoing divide in an outwardly congenial marriage. She was also worried the Rathbones would demand their money back regarding Leo. Her head ached from thinking about it.

Not even hungry anymore, she returned to her room, but didn't know where to begin. Whether the laundry incident was a deliberate plot by Ouida to get her out of the house, Babs made a mental note to make sure she left nothing behind.

Later that evening, she received a knock on the door.

"Who is it?" Babs wasn't in much of a mood to talk to anyone.

"Basil. Do you mind if I come in? I don't want to speak through a closed door."

Concerned she might make matters worse, she hesitated before letting him in. Basil, wearing a smoking jacket and looking like he stepped off the set playing Sherlock Holmes, hurried in and shut the door behind him.

"I'm sorry," he said. "My wife has treated you like an unwanted stray."

Babs began to cry. He put his arms around her in consolation but stopped and backed off. If Ouida barged in and saw them embraced...

"Can I do anything else to help?" he asked after handing her his handkerchief.

Babs tried to regain her voice. She pointed to paperwork in disarray and spread all over her bed, desk, and windowsills. "If you can wrangle a few spare packing boxes, I'd appreciate it."

"Do you mind if I sit for a moment?" He pointed to an empty wingback chair.

"Be my guest." What she didn't expect was for him to bare his soul.

"Ouida has always suspected marital indiscretions on my behalf, but I'm embarrassed she and our housekeeping staff played a game of espionage."

Not one to argue a moot point, she stood there, hands on her hips, and mumbled to herself about the best strategy on how to pack on such short notice.

Basil took out his meerschaum pipe, looking even more like a caricature of Sherlock Holmes, and prepared for a smoke. "I want you to remain on our case."

"Regarding Leo?"

"Even if we have to keep this confidential. I will continue to pull whatever strings are necessary to ensure the safe return of *both* dogs."

He blew out a long, drawn-out puff of smoke. "I've always been passionate about dogs to the extent that my wife accuses me of paying more attention to them than our baby girl. If my acting career weren't so time-consuming, I wouldn't mind owning a kennel similar to East and his wife.

"Before we moved here and were still at our Los Feliz residence, we started out with three dogs, two Westies and the Springer, which soon grew to seven. Ouida surprised me with Leo, just a wee little thing when she brought him home. Next, a casual acquaintance dropped off a black standard poodle named Toni for us to watch while he was on vacation, but he never came back to reclaim him. Sad to say, Toni is no longer with us.

"Ouida couldn't resist buying a black German Shepherd puppy, who replaced a male we had who died of old age. His name was Moritz, so we named her Moritza in his memory. Finally, a white Bull Terrier wandered into our yard. For several weeks, we placed advertisements to find her owner, but when no one came to claim her, we adopted her and named her Judy. We've had quite a collection between the dogs, our cats Gina and Gita, and my wife's canary. At one point, we built a kennel in our Los Feliz residence, which led outside from a bedroom attached to the servants' quarters. Each dog had their own personal bed and separate pen with their name on it."

Preoccupied with her packing, Babs tried to sound interested.

He continued to muse upon simpler times. "Back then, I had a more relaxed work schedule, and contrary to most of my Hollywood contemporaries, we weren't the typical social butterflies. Instead, we took a break from the parties, kept a small circle of intimate friends, and spent a great deal of time either in our garden or poolside with our pets.

"So much about my ramblings," Basil said. "I'm sounding like a sentimental fool and keeping you from your chores. Although it's not much of a consolation, I came to your defense. It was all my wife's doing to force you out, not mine."

Babs sighed. "I guess I can no longer count on you posing as our detective agency's frontman."

"I am not your adversary. Although, you might have to take over and wear my deerstalker, even if it's a figurative one, for the time being. Given my production schedule, I'll do what I can. What I will promise is I'll follow up on Powell. With as many movies as he has done, I was aware of his influence in Hollywood, but we hadn't known each other until now. Not even as casual friends."

"Basil, I don't know how I'm going to continue working this case, or any other case, while homeless. This sounds strange, but I was just settling in over here, despite always having to be on my guard around your wife."

"Babs, you won't have to camp out in your office. I went through the phone book and made a few inquiries. The best of the batch seemed to be a residential hotel off Hollywood Boulevard near the Pantages Theatre. It's close enough where you could walk and save on bus fare."

He handed her a slip of paper, having circled that one as his first choice. Then he took his wallet out of his smoking jacket pocket and handed her a few extra bucks. "Contrary to my current circumstances, it would be false to assume I'd been born into privilege. My old man went through great pains to feed his family. I might've been one of the lucky ones who had lucrative work waiting for me when I moved to Hollywood. Many of my friends weren't so fortunate. The challenge of getting a name for yourself and compensation for what you're worth is quite real for many."

"Is this a loan?" Babs asked.

"*Shush.* Think nothing of it, but don't tell my wife. I've also prepaid the next two months in advance, but I'm sure you'll find both Asta and Leo long before then. Soon, you'll have plenty of prize money to set yourself up in a respectable place. Maybe even buy a car.

"If it wasn't so risky from my wife finding out, I'd set you up at the Beverly Wilshire. Like Hammett's place, but not a penthouse suite. The studio he's working for has much deeper pockets. This is the best I can do under these circumstances, and once again, I can't emphasize enough how sorry I am that it's come to this."

Chapter Ten: The Hotel Down and Out

The morning after, Babs took a cab with all the suitcases she could carry. To avoid a dogfight with Ouida or that woeful woman who stepped in for their regular housekeeper, she arranged with Guy to make a separate trip after she already left to load up his car. Certain boxes would go straight to the office. He would deliver the rest to her hotel.

La Dolce Vita. Sounded like a provincial Italian pleasure palace, or decadent like the Garden of Allah Hotel, famous for its uninhibited parties. In actuality, more like a fading starlet, desperate to survive past its prime. Basil meant well, but he thumbed through the phonebook and never had time to see it in person.

Babs felt the immediate heartbreak as she viewed its rundown lobby. Lit by a single dim bulb, the hotel's sole passenger elevator reminded her of a flashlight with a dying battery. The doors shut with a screech, and it lurched downward before making its sluggish ascent.

By now, she felt she should've been able to save enough of a nest egg to afford a cottage in the Hollywood Hills. One with a yard big enough to have a few cats and a dog, and why not? She had always worked so hard to make it on her own. Everyone warned her it was a man's world out there, and a "good gal" like her could have an easy life as some decent fellow's wife, but she swore she'd prove them wrong. Not that matrimony was unacceptable, but a marriage with a mean-spirited husband was for the dogs.

Babs needed a strong stomach to deal with the smell of cigar smoke and sauerkraut coming from one of the other residents. Even her office had a better view where she could see the comings and goings on Hollywood

Boulevard. If she cracked her grimy windows open, all she could see here were the shabby stucco walls of the adjacent building and hear those residents. Her rusty fire escape led to a garbage-filled alleyway. Looking up, she wondered if an intruder could climb in from the roof.

Thrills, chills, and daffodils. But right now, she didn't have the luxury of feeling sorry for herself.

Compared to the modest one-bedroom she had in West Hollywood before her recent eviction, this was more like the epitome of the minimalist movement in interior design. Either inspired by the avant-garde Bauhaus or the austere Bow-wow-house trend with a barebones kitchenette, a tiny icebox, and a two-burner hotplate with one working—a place not supposed to make anyone feel comfortable enough to consider it as a permanent residence.

Shower only, but it had its own tiny washroom and wasn't one of those places where you had to share facilities down the hall with other tenants. Her room was half the size of her old place and a quarter of the size of the guest bedroom at Basil's, and her bed folded into the wall. She had a Murphy bed with joints and springs, which screeched to high heaven and needed a lube job like the Tin Man from *The Wizard of Oz.* If Basil thought this was the best option, she dreaded to think of what the other places might've looked like.

Having had no time to read her resident's handbook, she shuddered when she heard a loud buzzer, unaware of the intercom system installed next to her front door. Guy needed her permission to come upstairs.

Shiny with sweat and with strands of hair out of place, he poked his head around a tall stack of boxes, which towered over his head.

"Did that rickety elevator fail to level up with the floor like it did for me?" Babs asked.

"When I tripped, your boxes flew everywhere. Hope nothing's breakable." Ignoring her look of horror, he asked, "Where should I put these?"

"Good luck finding room, but where are the others?"

"Your front desk clerk was kind enough to let me unload and put the remaining stuff in the lobby. I was double-parked and needed to move the car to a lot around the corner."

Guy excused himself to go splash cold water on his face. "Do you need help to unpack?"

"Why don't you go downstairs and retrieve the last ones? Some tramp might wander in and help himself to early Christmas presents."

"Yes, ma'am," he said before he disappeared out the door.

* * *

He returned with a borrowed cart piled with more boxes. "Hey, don't you figure you should call your mom and let her know you're no longer staying with Basil?"

Babs had already collapsed in a well-worn chair and reviewed her tenant's manual. "If I ring Mom from here rather than the office, there'll be an extra surcharge for long distance. She can wait 'til tomorrow. I'll also need to alert the post office to forward mail to the office."

"What if I open your personal stuff by accident?" Guy asked.

"What are you going to do? Sell it to the gossip columns? What's Louella Parsons or Hedda Hopper going to do with it? Before I've had time to settle in, I hope to be elsewhere. Besides, how could I invite anyone to this dump?"

"Are you expecting a potential suitor?"

"Who's had time to pursue love?"

"No chance of wooing Basil away from the shrew?"

"I'm not that kind of woman."

"Stuck with a place like this, I'm surprised you're not wishing for a dashing hero, like good old Errol Flynn, to gallop in on his steed for a swift, chivalrous rescue."

Babs flashed him angry eyes.

"Calm down. Just joking. Maybe you should get a roommate like I did to help with expenses, so you can get out of this mess sooner."

She shook her head. "I expect our business to be successful and independent of whatever happens with my personal life, and about Basil... How dare you!"

"Sorry. He's a handsome fellow."

"He's not available and off-limits and still our client in secret. Although I don't know how much more cooperative at this point."

"Don't want to sound clichéd, but all work and no play—"

"Foolish priorities won't pay our bills. Basil might've fronted us enough to keep our agency afloat for a while, but that won't last forever."

* * *

Babs took an atomizer from her purse and spritzed perfume around the room. "Cheap stuff. Toilet water, I confess, but it's better than Fritz's sauerkraut wafting in from down the hall."

She returned to her chair, which wobbled as she put weight on it. Guy took out his Swiss Army knife and tightened its screws. "Next time I come, I'll bring some glue."

Babs cracked an approving smile. Having someone around who cared was a plus.

Guy took two wrapped parcels out of a paper bag. "How about a sandwich? Got you extra tomatoes for your BLT…the way you like it. I assumed you wouldn't have had time to pick up groceries." When he couldn't find a bottle opener in her kitchen drawers for their two Nehi orange sodas, he relied again on his pocketknife.

"You'll get reoriented in no time," he said in between mouthfuls. "You always do. I've never known you unable to bounce back."

Babs asked, "By any chance, did you pick up today's newspaper?"

"If you're wondering about the dog show? Nothing more than we already know. A few lines about its shutdown, but nothing definitive. Why?"

"We know little about von Rache, who seems to show up whenever there's something important with dogs. Guy, we can't let her slip out of our hands."

"Hey, speaking of dogs, maybe you should get a loaner from Mr. East or Mr. West."

"Mr. West? You mean Weatherwax."

"West…Weatherwax…what's the difference?"

58

Here we go again...

"Babs, what I'm saying is it might be a good idea to foster a dog to appear more credible in our investigation."

She revisited the resident's handbook. "No pets allowed."

"Not even a guide dog?"

"You want me to put on dark glasses and pretend I'm blind? The front desk clerk already knows I'm not."

"Regardless, we need to follow up with some of those folks we met at the dog show," Guy suggested. "Especially von Rache."

* * *

After a sleepless night filled with clamor from the boulevard, Babs stopped by the pink post office on Wilcox, picked up a chocolate éclair at her favorite bakery, and headed to her office. She delayed the daunting task of unpacking and placed a long-distance call to the Bay Area.

"Mom, yes, it's Babs."

"Who?"

"Your daughter, that's who!"

"Oh, dear Barbara."

"I hate when you call me that."

"Any prospects for a new husband?" her mom asked.

"No, why? You never remarried after Daddy died."

"Cliff and I were happy and together for almost fifteen years, before the tragedy. Your ex keeps hounding me all the time. He asks when you're coming home to visit."

"Still? Well, if that's not dogged persistence. I thought he'd get the hint and back off by now."

"What's so bad about him, Barb? You need a husband."

"Mom, stop. Everyone else knows me as Babs, and I don't need a man in the house."

"I can't understand why you get so upset."

Why won't she listen? "Have you forgotten? Troy Ulsterman nearly killed me on the first night of our honeymoon. He forced me to have sex when I was too tired after our wedding reception. When I wouldn't comply, he slapped me around. Finally, he dangled me over our hotel room balcony—by my hair! I screamed until someone called the police.

"Did you forget, after I had our marriage annulled, he stalked me? That's when I ran off to LA and used a different first name, and for my last, I went by my maiden name instead of my married one. Common enough so he'd never find me, unless someone like you spilled the beans, without thinking."

Babs raked her fingers through her hair and explained she was no longer staying in Bel Air with her clients. Any correspondence was to be sent to the office. She often wondered if she'd ever be able to settle down and stay put for a while.

"Mom, don't...under any circumstances, give that cad my address, phone number, or any name I'm using! Do you want me to have to disappear and hide in Puerto Vallarta? Whose side are you on, anyway?"

"Babs, I just want to see you happy...and married. You're too young to think about a successful career."

Arguments were pointless. Babs realized her mom grew up in a different era. "Fight him off. Hit him with a broom and a dustpan. Crack an empty milk bottle over his head. If you care about my best interests, don't betray me. I don't want him or any of his friends to find me—ever again."

Babs tried to take a gulp of water but realized her glass was empty. "If Troy Ulsterman threatens you. Call the cops."

Chapter Eleven: Peeping Tom

William Powell yawned three times after another boring, late-night celebrity party. The third this week. Yet he felt the mischievous urge to reprise his role as private detective Nick Charles, but to solve a real case this time. Without Asta, the show *would not* go on. Who might want to sabotage their next *Thin Man* film? Such excitement gave him a second wind. A producer like Hunt Stromberg, who might have insurance in case they didn't make the film? After all, it wasn't so long ago since Wall Street crashed. Many were still trying to recover. Maybe One-Take Woody Van Dyke, the film's director, had a better project in the offing.

"Head over to 334 South Bundy Drive," Powell called out to his driver.

"Brentwood, sir?" asked the confused cabbie. "Not Whitley Heights?"

"Change of plans." He folded his arms across his chest and smiled.

* * *

Powell shivered, in part from nerves. Misty ground clouds had also crept in from the Pacific with a crisp, unexpected coolness. An ivy-covered stone wall surrounded most of the film director's property. If sober, Powell would've surprised himself if he scaled it without breaking a limb. Eliminating the gates, dense hedges, and a tree unsuitable for climbing, at last, he chose a patch of shrubbery, sparse enough that he might shimmy his way through.

After brushing off broken twigs and smelling like mulch, Powell smoothed back his hair and tiptoed along a row of stepping stones to get as close as he could to the Van Dykes' house. His focus: an upstairs window, the only one with the lights on. From what he could see, One-Take's wife, Ruth, opened a fancy gift box and revealed sexy lingerie.

One-Take put a long-play on his phonograph and opened a bottle of champagne. Ruth made a quick change and returned, wearing her fur-trimmed satin dressing gown. She swayed to the music and continued to seduce her hubby with her best impersonation of hoochie-coochie queen Gypsy Rose Lee. Kicking off her sandals. Peeling off her stockings. Losing pieces of clothing one by one, until she realized she hadn't pulled their window shades down.

Powell sprang to his feet. He imagined from her point of view, he was a faceless, fleeting, and alarming shadow—a coyote, a prowler, or worse—a hot-in-the-zipper pervert. Unable to hear a thing from that distance, he watched her scream and point right at him. His cue to exit—fast.

By the time the police arrived, they had to disentangle Powell, who got caught in the bushes trying to escape.

"Never...could anything...more hellish be conceived than that dark form and savage face which broke upon us out of a wall of fog," Mrs. Van Dyke told the cops.

Her husband apologized for her being so melodramatic and swore that sounded like a line from a Sherlock Holmes movie. He also made it clear if William Powell hadn't been one of his biggest box office draws, he would've fired him on the spot.

* * *

It was off to the pokey for Powell. He was more of an amateur sleuth, and his acting skills didn't transfer to real-life criminology. The police still insisted on booking him for illegal trespassing, intentions unknown.

Allowed one phone call, Powell persuaded Rathbone to bail him out. Basil arrived wearing his deerstalker. He looked his incarcerated companion straight in the eye and asked, "What passion of hatred can it be which leads a man to lurk in such a place at such a time?"

Powell massaged his throbbing head, the aftereffects of his hangover. He asked, "Where have I heard that before?"

"Watson's comment from *Hound*," Basil replied. "The detectives discovered a mysterious fellow lurking in the distant moors. The poor chap turned out to be the brother of one of the Baskervilles' housekeepers and an escaped prisoner. In the end, the dreaded beast mauled him."

"Woody's wife is accusing me of being a degenerate."

"William, I'd assume the same if I were a lady parading around in my unmentionables who discovered a strange man staring through my bedroom window. My wife would, too. Yours, as well."

"How auspicious to have a spare Sherlock Holmes hat in your overcoat pocket," said Powell.

"You're lucky," remarked Basil. "Either it's an extra my wife is always buying, or people give them to me for Christmas and birthdays. We must have a dozen or more around the house in various tweeds and colors. Compared to Nick Charles, perhaps Holmes is the better detective."

"I didn't realize you were keeping score." Powell sank down on a sagging cot.

"My usual complaint is how I'm so done in portraying Holmes. Now, the studio wants to cast me as the villain again in *A Date With Destiny*. They keep changing its title. I suspect it'll wind up *The Mad Doctor*."

"What's the film about?" asked Powell.

"It's a Svengali story about an evil doctor who murders his wives for their money. I'd rather be performing Shakespeare, but I guess it's my duty to spring you out of here."

Powell begged his friend to get him home in one piece and tell nobody else what happened.

Chapter Twelve: Blackmail and Monkeyshines

F rank Weatherwax invited the detectives to meet him at MGM. Being on the lots—the cities unto themselves—seeing productions in process and the hopefuls lined up around the corner for auditions in front of casting director's offices, Babs often wondered what it would've been like if she'd stayed in the business and hadn't become a private investigator.

Guy joined her and insisted on dressing the part. He chose a V-neck pullover sweater to wear over his white shirt. Instead of a classic necktie, he looked like a hotshot wearing a silk ascot. Underneath, he wore his favorite pair of high-waisted pleated trousers and polished it off with an oversized golfer's cap and brand-new wingtip shoes.

"Eager beaver for another audition?" Babs asked.

"Heck no. How about a chance to become one of the top bananas behind the camera?" he said as he drove up to the main gate. Security gave him a day pass and a map of the lot and showed the location for guest parking.

Further in, Guy made an observation. "Everything looks so classy and upscale toward the entrance. Then you come upon buildings that look more like factories. Others resemble army barracks."

"Wouldn't it be fun if we ran into one of MGM's contract players, like Norma Shearer or Zasu Pitts? Don't you just love her name—Zasu Pitts? I wonder what's her real one."

"Don't know why you're so obsessed over it. You changed yours."

"Because I didn't want my ex-husband to find me."

He double-checked their map. "According to this pamphlet, MGM covers forty-three acres, and there are three miles of paved streets. We need to turn left over here."

* * *

Weatherwax explained this would be a working interview. The detectives were free to fire away with as many questions as time allowed, as long as they didn't mind him training his animal actors. They asked many of the same questions which Babs had already asked East.

"So much happened before and after the day Asta vanished. My memory draws a blank," Weatherwax confessed. "Between the day-to-day commotion on set and the number of people present, it's been tough to pinpoint blame."

With all the runaround they experienced, she wondered if that excuse was too convenient. So far, nobody had given them much to go on. "You know, I might've forgotten to ask either you or Mr. East if anyone took out an insurance policy."

"On Asta? Looking back, maybe I should've," Frank said, "But I've always felt he was just—a dog."

"He's your cash canine and earns more than you or anyone on your staff," Babs argued.

"Compared to insuring Marlene Dietrich for her voice, our doggie's a minor player. Regardless, East told me you already put him through the wringer. Demoed a few stunts, too. What about his wife? Have you spoken to Gale?"

"Not yet. Why?" Babs replied.

"We've had our disagreements about coaching Asta. For different breeds, one size doesn't fit all. Producers don't like to waste time and film on animals who aren't clear about their assignments."

Frank led them to a kennel behind his office. "If you're going to launch your dog in a successful film career, it's vital he must do *what* he is told and *when* he is told."

Babs slipped in a fast one. "Talking about wasting time, is there anyone you can think of who'd want to seek revenge on your producer or MGM Studios by delaying your next film?"

Whether coincidental or on purpose, Frank ignored her question. He unlocked the pen and leashed Lucky, a Labrador retriever, and took everyone to an open field.

"Have the two of you considered that whoever took Asta didn't care one way or the other if the next installment of the *Thin Man* series went into production?" Frank asked.

Touché. Best not to assault him with too much at once.

She lightened her approach. "When I met your film director at Basil's party, he called himself One-Take Woody."

"He can be full of horse feathers. Even when you think you've rehearsed your scene to perfection, any trainer who's worth his salt knows to go for a dry run or two."

Babs fished a small bag of dog biscuits from her purse. "Mr. East told me dog treats work wonders in getting your dog to cooperate."

"Put those away," he warned her. "One of the major rules of dog training: unless you gave him permission, never let him eat anything from a stranger. In fact, let's put him to the test. Babs, hand him one of those biscuits."

The dog approached. "No! Leave it alone!" Frank said.

Lucky sat down, wagged his tail, and awaited his next command. Several more seconds passed. Babs looked at Guy, wondering why he tortured the poor dog.

"All right! You can have it," Frank said. He fed Lucky the treat, patted him on the head, and looked up at Guy and Babs. "Good boy!"

Frank spotted another trainer heading in their direction, who had a small monkey perched on his shoulders. He waved for him to come over.

"I guess films use all sorts of animals," Guy remarked.

"Anything from rattlesnakes to skunks. Let me introduce you," Frank said. "Promise me, don't touch him. I can't guarantee he won't bite or do something we'll all regret later. Babs, Guy, meet another one of my colleagues, Rennie Renfro."

Frank asked Rennie, "Do you mind bringing me an old newspaper? There should be one in my office."

"Sure thing." Rennie gave him a mock military salute and took off.

"So, as I was saying, when training a dog, it's important you call specific items by their names," Frank explained. "They're smarter than you think."

Rennie returned and asked the monkey to hand Weatherwax the paper. Captivated by the stunt, Guy got curious but too close. The little devil leapt from Renfro onto Guy and stole his hat. With prize in hand, he scampered across the lawn and through an alleyway in between stages. Guy and Renfro dashed after him, getting a healthy dose of exercise.

* * *

When they caught up with the bandit, Renfro wrestled him into a leash and harness.

Renfro handed Guy back his cap. "You're lucky you weren't wearing a straw hat. Gummo would've eaten it."

"Gummo?" Guy asked. "What kind of monkey is this?"

"He's a capuchin and named after the fifth Marx Brother, who you never see on film, because he's a talent agent."

Despite being leashed, the mischief maker explored everything within reach.

Wondering about this trainer's competency, Guy asked, "Are you just breaking into this business?"

"I'm self-taught, but usually work with dogs. A few pro gigs here and there, but I'm a nobody. Now, about you. Is Babs your wife? If so, you caught yourself a real humdinger."

Guy laughed when Renfro whistled. "Oh no, just my partner."

"I didn't know there was such a bird as a lady detective."

"Don't let her hear that. She's my boss."

"Any chance you're looking for extra work?"

"Why do you ask?"

"Some dame is looking to pick up a few dogs."

"Not sure why you're asking me. Private eyes go after hubbies cheating on their wives, missing persons…those who owe sizeable sums of money or are delinquent on payments…stolen property… Often stuff the cops will overlook or are too busy to handle."

"Even if she has deep pockets?"

"Well… Tracking down special breeds isn't all that different from skip tracing. Quit the games. You getting a finder's fee? Who are you representing?"

"Wealthy broad. No doubt—lots of dough, but a newcomer in town. Don't know much about her previous history…"

"Her name? I don't have all day."

"Whether it's legit, she goes by Countess Velma von Rache. Crazy name. Means revenge in German. I wonder if that's a clue to her personality."

"Are you German?"

"Nope, Texas born. Why?"

"Never mind. I've met von Rache. Do you know how to contact her?"

"Funny you should ask. I have her card in my pocket. Don't forget to mention my name."

He handed the business card to Guy, who sprinted back alone to catch up with his friends.

* * *

"What took you so long?" Babs asked.

"Just talking shop," Guy said. "Sorry, I guess we got carried away."

Frank looked at his watch. "Are we back to our agenda?"

Guy nodded and gave him the go-ahead.

Frank rolled up the paper and threw it across the lawn. "Bring me the paper, Lucky!"

Lucky played fetch, trotted back, and handed it to Frank, who gave him another reward. Frank told him to sit and stay, and Lucky obeyed.

"Sometimes we can speak audible commands when the cameras are rolling. There are other times when silent cues are a must," Frank explained.

"How does a dog memorize everything if it's a long scene?" Babs asked.

"Can't speak for others, but we do several rehearsals. Then, when we film the actual scene, the animal actor should be able to go through the entire action with the words, 'Do what I told you!' Always worked for me."

"Do you use a type of sign language?" Guy asked.

"Good point," Frank said. "The answer is yes, but you must be in the dog's proper eye line so they can see your command."

The two detectives returned with Weatherwax to his office.

"Here's our official contract. I apologize for its delay, but it required more signatures than the Declaration of Independence." He was about to explain the nuances of studio politics when his phone rang.

"Guess who's visiting me at the studio? *Ah...*you don't say. That's terrible. *Hmmm*, we'll have to look into it. All right then. Talk to you later."

"What was that about?" Babs asked.

"Someone's been threatening the Easts. I suspect it's a fan reacting to the announcements of Asta's disappearance. Our publicity department shouldn't have plastered the news all over the trades. If anyone took out their frustrations on our poor little dog, they deserve to go to hell."

Chapter Thirteen: Bringing Up Asta

The detectives followed up to see if the pressure against the Easts was real or not. They made an appointment to visit their kennels. Henry East wasn't there, but they met with his wife.

Gale set up a film projector in their private screening room. "You recall that Asta's real name is Skippy?"

"Of course," Babs and Guy said, both embarrassed, because they answered in unison.

She dimmed the lights. "My husband made this publicity reel about our star performer. Maybe you'll uncover a theme."

Babs said they were always open to suggestions. "Besides, we always enjoy taking the afternoon off to go to the movies."

"My husband told you we're firm about forbidding the actors to interact with him between takes. That can break a dog's concentration. At first, we were lax and made exceptions. Asta's so hard to resist. After he bit Myrna Loy, we had to put our foot down."

Gale continued. "If you include the short documentary made this year about famous movie dogs, Asta has been in twenty films since 1932, although he didn't receive screen credit in all of them. Don't laugh, but his first film title was called *Merrily We Go to Hell.*"

"He's been a busy boy," Guy said.

"All the way to the bank," Gale replied. "When he started earning more than what my husband made in the prop department at MGM, we realized he had talent, and this wasn't just a fad. On-screen, he's had names from Ragsy to Rex to Pom to Habeas in a legal-themed film, *I Am the Law,* and to Mr. Atlas in *Topper Takes a Trip*. Most of the stunts in *Topper* gave the audience the impression our little pup did all the work, but those tricks were done with wires. He did have one memorable scene where he showed off his skills.

"Constance Bennett, who plays the ghost Marion Kerby, comes back with her dog rather than with her husband, played by Cary Grant in the first movie. Kerby meddles in the affairs of Cosmo Topper and his wife, who thinks she wants a divorce, but a handsome baron, in league with a group of con men, tries to woo her away from her husband."

The three of them watched the scene play out where the female ghost stole the man's swim trunks while buried in the sand. Then the dog (or Mr. Atlas, in this case) dug in the sand and tried to expose him—naked.

"Besides the *Thin Man* movies, one of Skippy's most famous roles was when he played George in *Bringing Up Baby*," the narrator said. "He wrestled and played with the giant cat. One of his most important stunts was when he stole and buried a rare dinosaur bone of Cary Grant's."

"My favorite scene was when Cary Grant got caught wearing Katharine Hepburn's frilly robe, and the dog kept chasing and nipping at his heels," Guy said.

The Thin Man scenes came at the end. "He performed a variety of tricks from hiding his head behind his paws playing hide-and-seek to playing dead," Gale explained. "Our dog was so good at following directions, he rarely needed to do more than one take on a scene—another reason why everyone wanted to cast him in their films."

Gale turned up the lights when the short film ended. "I'm sure you know dogs live about twelve to fifteen years, depending upon the breed and its upbringing. Since Asta was born in '31, my husband and I considered retiring him in the next year or two. He's already sired puppies to take over his roles. Some have looked similar, but none of them have been as smart or cooperative."

Babs brought up their being in Weatherwax's office when Gale's husband phoned about receiving threatening calls.

"He never identifies himself, but he tries to coerce us into selling our dogs," she explained.

"Does he indicate why?" Babs asked.

"He's interested in purebreds, not mixed breeds, and the amount he quoted was far above their normal market value."

The phone rang. Gale raised her voice and looked worried.

"Who was that?" Guy asked.

"Someone with a German accent requesting certain hostile breeds that are hard to handle. They don't work well for films, so we avoid getting them."

"Didn't you tell them your movie dogs aren't for sale?" Guy asked.

"Of course, but they're relentless. They've called in the middle of the night and woken my husband and me at least twice."

"Has he or anyone else contacted you asking for a ransom?" Guy asked.

Gale hesitated. "For Asta? I hope it doesn't come to that."

"I'm assuming you've already filed the standard police reports," said Babs.

"Of course, but the cops are after sensational cases like the Fatty Arbuckle scandal, and the dog pound employees can't make arrests."

"I'm failing to see the comparisons between the two missing dogs— referring to the Easts' and Basil's," Guy said to Babs.

"With Leo, he's owned by a celebrity," Babs explained. "But with Asta, he is the celebrity. Quite a difference."

Chapter Fourteen: Bay of Wolves Canyon

Going down the list of those who had close connections with Asta, the detectives needed to branch out into secondary sources. Their next step: investigate Countess Velma von Rache. Anything they had picked up at either the Rathbones' party or at the Beverly Hills Dog Show proved inconclusive, but that's where a "so-called Asta" reappeared and vanished again in a flash. Guy accused Babs of being too quick to point a finger. He kept an open mind but was inclined to give the countess credit as a benefactor of the performing arts and champion of animal charities.

For a while, he had put off whether to follow up on Renfro's tip, a possible conflict of interest. He wondered if she had hidden motives about spying on the Hollywood elite, and locating the dogs would wind up much more complicated. He also heard the Feds paid informants who could give them leads on anyone involved in Un-American activities. Maybe that was the real reason behind Renfro's interest. Babs insisted they make an appointment to meet at von Rache's place on the Hollywood side of the hills, on a private drive called the Bay of Wolves Canyon.

* * *

"I wish you would've allowed me a few extra days to put my car in the shop," Guy complained as he navigated a sharp curve with his convertible.

With its top down and the wind strong, Babs clutched her hat and wondered if she should've worn a scarf.

"Maybe I'm low on steering fluid," Guy said, grinding his teeth. "Or my wheels need to be realigned, but it's been getting harder to steer, and I'm dead sure I need my brakes replaced."

"Sounds like you need a new car." Feeling queasy from barreling around all those hairpin turns, she worried he'd have to pull over to the side of a road with no shoulder to relieve her car sickness. He mumbled it served her right for always relying on coffee and éclairs instead of eating a more substantial breakfast.

They rolled up to a guardhouse and presented a telegram with their invitation. After the guard opened the gate, Guy drove through and craned his neck to peer off in the distance. "Must be one of those places where you drive a half mile to get to the primary residence."

He slowed down as a herd of deer crossed their path. His car choked, puffed, and stalled. She offered to put it in gear if he would push.

"I heard Douglas Fairbanks and Mary Pickford own a huge, sprawling estate like this," she said.

"Twenty-eight acres, if I recall, but I think their place is in Beverly Hills."

"Golly, property is more expensive there. One day…" Babs mused. "We'll stake claims in our own pieces of land."

"If we strike gold…or oil. Babs, as a PI, if you've set your sights that high, you picked the wrong profession."

He pulled up to a circular drive and checked to make sure his beat-up car wasn't leaking oil. They went up to a pair of daunting front doors almost twelve feet high with brass ring door knockers coming out of the mouths of mythical dog-like demons.

"I already feel welcome," Babs said with sarcasm. "What are those ghoulish creatures?"

"They resemble *nahuals*," Guy said. "Witches who have shape-shifted into enormous dogs. Maybe there's truth about the countess's father's claim that dogs were demonic."

"How do you know about such things?"

"By feeding my intellect in the library when business is slow. As opposed to you, who goes window shopping for things you can't afford." He looked at his watch. "Right on time, just as Renfro warned us."

"Who's Renfro, again?" Babs asked.

"The monkey trainer we met at MGM. He's got some connection with the countess."

"What'll happen if we arrive late?"

"They'll feed us to the wolves," he joked, but with ominous overtones. "Or toss us into whatever bay or canyon they named this road after."

* * *

A statuesque manservant with a blended Eastern European and German accent opened the door and invited in the detectives, then excused himself to retrieve their hostess.

Babs almost gagged. "This place has the ever so slight smell...of old seafood."

"You think the countess is a fishy character, is that it?" Guy asked.

One obvious answer stared them in the face. The countess's striking grand entrance hall, with its two serpentine staircases supported by orange and black marble Grecian columns, became overshadowed by the three-ring circus. Exotic animals roamed free—mostly dogs and all without restraints. The menagerie, smiling and content with intoxication, languished on the cool marble-tiled floor.

At last, he remarked, "Babs, since when have you ever been to a zoo that smelled like a rose garden? Tell me if I'm wrong, but I got the impression when we spoke to her at the dog show she *considered* getting a dog but didn't own any at the time. Renfro had conveyed little, but unless she acquired all these animals since then—"

Guy stopped mid-sentence. A female leopard emerged from behind the staircase and sauntered toward Babs. She stopped at her heels, sniffed her hand, and rubbed against her leg like an overgrown house cat, except she made a Great Dane look like a Pekingese. This time, Babs reacted to an unrelated odor. The countess had snuck up from behind, smoking a cigarette.

Dressed in yet another outlandish fur ensemble, she paraded down the

75

left-hand staircase.

"Don't worry. She's tame."

Guy let the big cat give him her sniff of approval. He decided on a traditional handshake with his hostess rather than a formal kiss. Then he introduced Babs. It surprised both that von Rache gave no sign of their previous acquaintance.

"Will we also be meeting with your associate?" Guy asked.

"I have no associates," she replied with Garbo-esque intonations. "I prefer to work alone."

"Then who's Rennie Renfro?" he asked, confused.

"Oh, him." She made a low octave laugh. "He's just an occasional hired hand."

She made a quick call on an in-house line and explained she rang her butler to take Baby away.

While she dialed another extension, Babs whispered to Guy, "I wonder if this is the same cat from *Bringing Up Baby*, the film with Katharine Hepburn and—"

"Cary Grant," Guy said. "Who knows? Maybe she's her owner."

* * *

Countess Velma seemed eager to usher her guests outside and opened the French doors leading to her backyard garden. To the left: gated tennis courts. The stone steps on the right led down the hillside to the pool area.

"Once we head down below, it'll become clearer, but the architects had to get skillful with the property's uneven terrain." She pointed to her expansive view of other hillside estates in the distance.

"One could have a lot of fun with a telescope around here," Guy said.

The countess made a shameless confession. "I love spying on my neighbors when they're sunbathing naked."

She led them toward the tennis courts. "Despite lessons, I'm a pathetic player."

"Then why go to the trouble?" Guy asked.

"You'll see," she hinted with a tease. She opened the gates and welcomed them inside to find more dogs having free rein. She grabbed a racquet and a bucket of balls and served them over the net. The dogs, eager for a game of fetch, had a field day running after flying tennis balls.

When Countess Velma announced she was tired of tennis, she locked the gate and insisted on taking them to her pool. Babs couldn't comprehend how that woman walked with ease while her own heels caught and scraped against the rough and uneven surfaces. Making a brief detour, their hostess pointed out how stilts supported her tennis courts from underneath to accommodate the steep drop of the landscape.

"Wasted space, in my opinion, and the downside of the property, but the surveyors and architects told me otherwise. Drunken guests could lose their balance and tumble into the canyon. Animals have surer footing. Guess that's why I do most of my *human* entertaining in my garden."

Babs refrained from bringing up earthquakes with a suspended tennis deck and couldn't understand why there wasn't any protective fencing. She leaned over as far as she could to view its treacherous and steep drop.

Countess Velma escorted them to the pool area, explaining how she turned her resort-like pool into a canine country club.

"*Voila!* This attraction appeals to my swimmers."

Any dog unafraid of the water frolicked with glee after she tossed toys into the water. She claimed it was the best playground in the world.

Babs changed the subject. Her intention: information gathering. "I bet some of these places have gigantic walk-in closets, bigger than my entire residence."

Guy played along. "No one would own that many shoes or clothes. I'd like just one person to show me and prove me wrong."

They milked their mock argument like a rehearsed script, but to no avail. If their hostess had anything of the sort, they'd never find out. She took what seemed to be a circuitous route and led the detectives to her roof deck patio, which had its own garden of potted plants, including pygmy palms, in geometrical patterns encircling a Spanish stone fountain. To provide shade, a canvas open-air tent housed an intimate array of white wrought-iron chairs set around a table.

Von Rache insisted her guests take a seat. Using another extension of her telephone-like, in-house intercom, she ordered refreshments.

"Aren't you worried the vicious Santa Annas will upend your tent?" Babs asked, referring to the relentless winds that roared through Southern California. "High, exposed areas like this are vulnerable. This shelter could fly around the world in less than eighty days."

Countess Velma failed to respond except to her butler, who arrived with cocktails.

Resolved it was pointless to fight nature's fury, Babs unpinned her hat and held it tight in her lap.

"Mint juleps. I hope you like them," said the countess.

Babs worried the alcohol would go straight to her head. Drinks and socializing. They went hand in hand, but often were her weakness.

"I'm assuming you don't invite many children up here to play," Guy stared at the low, hazardous open railing. "You're not concerned about your pets?"

She seemed more interested in reveling in the ocean breeze than answering questions. Sunset crept over the Pacific like a rash of German Expressionism with explosive, rebellious colors. Velma approached the roof's dangerous edge and gestured for her guests to join her for the breathtaking view.

Babs tripped when her heel broke off her shoe. Guy caught her by the arm and helped her hop back to her seat. He plucked her drink from her jittery hand.

Velma phoned her butler and demanded someone fix her shoe right away. Babs suggested they should be going. Velma insisted they wait in the first-floor garden.

Babs excused herself to go to the restroom before their drive home.

"This place is rather large," the countess said. "Do you need help to find the closest one?"

"I have a pretty good sense of direction," she replied. On her return, Babs took an alternate route and stopped. *Did I just hear whimpering dogs?* She put her ear to several doors, but the noises seemed too far away. Then she heard footsteps. Her heart pounded.

Guy's voice echoed, "Babs, did you get lost?"

"I'm fine. Where are you?"

He instructed her to meet him at the top of the stairs and handed back both shoes.

"Hurry, I'd like to get home before the sun disappears. Almost no streetlights up here, and I don't like the way my car is handling."

Chapter Fifteen: Book 'Em

Despite Guy's complaints about needing to put his car into the shop, Babs coaxed him into driving downtown to do research at the Central branch of the Los Angeles Public Library.

She stood in awe in front of its entrance. "This place reminds me of a cross between an Egyptian and Persian temple. Love the pyramid with the sun. I think that's my favorite part."

Guy loved to show off. "Designed by Bertram Goodhue, then finished by his associate after his sudden death in '24, the library combines eclectic styles mixed with Art Deco."

"Looks like you chose book-smart attire to match your attitude." Babs weighed in on his single-breasted, middle-of-the-road grey suit with a solid tie, conservative enough to blend in with the concrete. "Are you trying to pull a fast one and sneak into an audition during lunch?"

Guy broke into laughter. "Do you still think I'm going to abandon you at your bleakest hour? I worried you'd accuse me of resembling one of those straight-laced senators from the House Committee on Un-American Activities."

* * *

They entered the rotunda, which soared sixty-four feet above them, with another sunburst at its apex and a celestial-like chandelier resembling Earth and the solar system. The rotunda's walls boasted complex geometry in hundreds of colors, blended with figurative murals depicting California's history. Their feet echoed upon the puzzle-patterned marble flooring—a cooling reprieve from the stifling heat outside.

Guy realized he had walked on ahead and left his partner behind. "If you stop to gawk at the art, we'll never get any work done."

They found a table in the periodical section. "We need to find more information on von Rache, and maybe we can get the lowdown on Rennie Renfro in a back issue of *Variety* or *The Hollywood Reporter*," Guy said. "What else do you want to dig up?"

Babs felt like they were back in grade school and working on a school assignment. She filled out a stack of request cards to hand to the reference librarian. "Stuff on Sherlock Holmes."

Guy laughed too loud. He got shushed and received a round of angry eyes. "Babs, I always thought you were a bit off-kilter, but now you qualify for Camarillo."

"The mental institution in Ventura County? Thanks a lot. You need to be more trusting of my judgment. Look, it's been gnawing at me the entire time, but when I ignore my intuition, either I get in trouble or lose out on an important lead."

"Does this have anything to do with Basil?" Guy asked.

Babs bowed her head to hide her oncoming blush. "Well, kind of... Stick with me. I want to search out dog themes in detective stories, and we might as well begin with Arthur Conan Doyle's stories about Sherlock Holmes."

"Besides *The Hound of the Baskervilles*, what others feature dogs?"

"It's been a while since I read these stories, but that's why we're here. Maybe whoever took Leo...and Asta is taking their cues from themes in popular literature or films."

"Babs, you've lost your mind."

She fanned herself with her notepad, her body temperature rising to a slow boil along with her temper. "Are you with me or not?"

"Never argue with a lady. Especially if she's your boss."

A librarian wheeled over a heavy cart and unloaded a stack of their book requests.

"Reference material must stay in this section." She pointed to the periodicals and city guides marked with red rubber stamps. "If you want to check out the general fiction, you need to get in line by no later than 5:00 p.m. Doors close at 6:00."

Babs thanked her for her help.

"One more thing," the librarian said. "I hope you're aware there are four novels and fifty-eight short stories in the original Sherlock Holmes collection. You'll have more than enough to keep you busy—for now."

"Have fun," Guy said, snickering. "You're the one set on Holmes. I'm still convinced it's a ridiculous idea. Let me concentrate on the stuff we can't take home and work on later. Like the entertainment magazines."

An hour after she dived into her material, Babs said, "There are more references on dogs than I thought, but I concentrated on the ones most relevant to our case."

Guy twiddled with the pencil behind his ear. "For instance?"

"In *A Study in Scarlet*, Holmes tests out pills, one of which is poison and the other a placebo, on the landlady's terrier."

Guy shuddered. "A rather brutal experiment, don't you think?"

"The dog was old and sick. Someone would have to put it down, anyway," Babs said. "*Oops.* I forgot about Toby. Sherlock Holmes borrows a dog named Toby, half-spaniel and half-lurcher, known to have an acute sense of smell to track down the killer in *The Sign of Four*."

"Babs, isn't that the story where Holmes meets Doctor Watson?"

"See, you're more interested in these tales than you're letting on, but to answer your question, no. That's in *A Study in Scarlet*. *The Sign of Four* is his second novel."

"I wish you'd stop making me feel illiterate. Especially since I'm the bookworm in our partnership."

"As someone who's trying to establish himself as a professional detective, you surprise me, Guy."

* * *

Lunchtime rolled around. Babs spotted a street vendor by the park in front of the library's main entrance. "How about sodas and hotdogs?"

When Guy whipped out his wallet, Babs refused to allow him to pay. "Who's to say the boss can't foot the bill?"

He stepped aside and gestured. "Ladies first," and implied, "Be my guest."

After they found a place in the shade, Guy put her on the spot. "I bet you don't even have a library card."

"I assumed you already had one."

"What if I'd left it home by accident?"

"You're always organized and wouldn't have done that."

"Babs, I said, 'by accident.' When are you going to get that into your pretty little head?"

"Here we go, squabbling again."

"Very much like Nick and Nora Charles."

* * *

Midway through the afternoon, Babs pushed one of her stacks of books aside and sighed.

"So far, I've encountered—bull pups, a Bull Terrier, a Mastiff... Bloodhounds, foxhounds, and hellhounds. Even came across a dog I never heard of—a draghound."

"That's a term for a hound trained to follow a trail, scented on purpose," said Guy. "To narrow this down, maybe you should focus on those passages with Cocker Spaniels or terriers like Asta."

At closing time, Babs checked out the Holmes books, along with a copy of *The Thin Man*, which she could read over the next two weeks before they needed to be returned. As they retraced their steps through the library to head outside, she asked, "Did you find anything useful?"

"Just photos of von Rache posing with others at local society functions, but nothing worth crowing about. Her late husband seemed to be a minor player."

"What about Rennie Renfro?" she asked.

"He's a better actor than we're giving him credit for."

"How so?"

"He told us he was an amateur trying to break into the business. What a lie! He's a pretty big deal in this town and knows a lot of people. Frank Weatherwax, who we met at Basil's party, has a whole family in the business, and some of them have worked for Rennie Renfro Motion Picture Dogs. Renfro also trained Buster and other dogs in the Barkies."

"I love those short silent films with the dogs dressed and acting like people," Babs said.

"There's more: three years ago, Spooks, a Cocker Spaniel-poodle-terrier mix and one of Renfro's dogs, starred as Daisy in the *Blondie and Dagwood* film series. Penny Singleton, the actress who plays Blondie, plays Polly Byrnes in *After the Thin Man*. A connection? Maybe. The first with Spooks' combination breed involving both spaniel and terrier, and the second with *The Thin Man.*"

"Or pure coincidence," she said.

"Babs, I don't know why he downplayed his credentials, unless he didn't want us to think he had a tight relationship with the countess. Maybe he was just as wary of her as we were. Did you unearth any more terrier or spaniel references?"

"The bit with Toby as a tracking dog was a good start," she said, "But I'll need more time to reread the stories."

By the time they stepped outside the library, Babs noticed the same food vendor and made a beeline in his direction. "I wouldn't mind another hotdog. He's advertising an end-of-the-day special. Fifty percent off."

Guy ran after her. "Babs, maybe you shouldn't eat one that has been out in the heat all day."

As he tried to catch up, a vagrant snuck up from behind to snatch her purse. Babs and the bum played tug-of-war. Guy got hold of his shoulders, threw him into the bushes, and yelled for a nearby policeman.

"So much for your dogged insistence on independence," he said. "Sometimes having a man around can come in handy."

"Clobbering him on the head with my purse would've been just as effective."

Chapter Sixteen: Doggone It!

Ever since Basil moved from Los Feliz to Bel Air, he assumed he needn't worry about dangerous traffic. Bellagio Road was a sedate, residential street and, one would think, with respectable citizens, but he proved himself wrong. One day, while he was out for a smoke and walking his dogs, a motorist driving a sports car rampaged down the road and knocked him into a neighbor's rosebushes. Judy, his skittish Bull Terrier, ran off, spooked by the speeding car.

Basil unleashed his German Shepherd. "Get help!" he shouted and hoped she understood those commands.

The property's owner, prompted by Basil's screams, rushed to the rescue. Judy was on the loose—wandering and scared.

A tall, sturdy stranger gripped Basil's hand. Like a sportsman to his fallen opponent, he braced Basil and allowed him to regain his balance. "Need an ambulance?" he asked.

Basil inspected his snagged pullover sweater and soiled trousers. "Do I have a fellow Englishman for my neighbor? Which locality?"

"From Liverpool. My family co-owned a shipbuilding enterprise, but enough about me. Should I ring for help?"

"Thanks, I'll manage." Basil's tobacco pipe had flown out of his mouth and shattered on the ground. "Nothing is sprained or broken, except my meerschaum."

"Did you catch this daredevil's license plates?" the man asked.

"A madman with a fancy Mercedes. A stunt driver, I imagine," said Basil.

"I've heard complaints about some imbecile with plates of TRNR99. Must be some kind of trainer. Of what? I don't know."

The man's gardener caught and returned Basil's Bull Terrier. "What would I do if I lost you, too, with Leo still missing?" Basil said, scolding her.

"Are you the one who put up signs?" his neighbor asked.

"City officials kept taking them down," Basil explained. "They've threatened me with violating a ridiculous beautification ordinance."

"By the way, my name is Jack Stewart, but I hate formalities. Call me Jack."

"Ah, one of my best friends was a man named Jack," Basil said, reflecting on brighter times. "In fact, the dog pictured in those signs used to be his dog."

"You look familiar, like a famous actor, but I'm too stupid to put a name to a face."

"Rathbone," Basil replied.

"Oh yes, *Robin Hood* and *Captain Blood*. I loved watching those films. I used to be on the fencing team back in college."

Sherlock Holmes wasn't on the tip of his tongue, surprising. Such immediate recognition followed him around like an unwanted shadow.

"I'm flattered," said Basil. "Even more since I had a supporting role in those films and played a villain. Have you kept it up?"

"Fencing? In fact, I have. Keeps me fit and on my toes. I've hired an instructor to come over twice a week for private lessons. One of those fancy choreographers who trains actors in the movies. He does this during his off hours."

"Fantastic! If you don't mind giving me his number, maybe I should hire him. I have a film, *The Californian*, with Tyrone Power, slated to start soon. The studio warned me I'll need lots of practice beforehand."

"Why don't you consider practicing together? Please, join me in my garden for lemonade, or something stronger if that's your pleasure?"

"I'm afraid I'm not too presentable at the moment. Of all times, I had to dress in a white tennis outfit," said Basil, somewhat self-conscious.

"Nonsense. After what you just went through, it's understandable. Come. Your dogs are more than welcome. I have a Scottish Terrier out back named Toby. If my gardener hadn't been able to retrieve your pup, Toby would've.

His nose would be a fair match for any foxhound or beagle, although he would look odd with his short legs on an official hunt. Nevertheless, he would love to have a few playmates."

With his anxious dogs taking the lead, Basil followed his new acquaintance down the driveway and into his backyard, where he let his dogs off their leashes to play with Stewart's Scotty.

Jack explained he had nothing to do with acting or the entertainment business.

"Then what attracted you to Bel Air?" Basil asked.

"Business down at the shipyards in Long Beach. Often as a consulting engineer. The *RMS Queen Mary* just pulled into port. Part of my job is to ensure she's in top-notch condition for her upcoming journey to the South Seas. Mind you, not her normal route. Did you know she's bigger than the *Titanic?*"

"Let's hope she's also a sturdier ship," Basil said with a sigh.

"Also, takes a smarter captain. He should've never underestimated those North Atlantic icebergs."

After Stewart gave him his instructor's phone number, Basil put his dogs back on their leashes and headed home. Along the way, a memorable scene from *After the Thin Man* got stuck in his head. Asta came home to see Mrs. Asta, who was in a pen surrounded by a group of pups. A lone black one stood out from the others. Confused at first, Asta spotted a male Scottish Terrier poking his head from under a fence. Suspecting the Scotty had something to do with being the father of the darker pup, Asta barked and chased after the culprit. Basil, thinking it odd this came up all of the sudden, laughed it off as nonsense.

Yet, when he and his dogs slipped in through his back door, his irate wife confronted him. "You're filthy, and you've been gone a long time. What have you been up to?"

He told her about his close call and how it led him to a propitious encounter with one of their neighbors. He also mentioned the lead on his fencing instructor.

"Anyone call?" he asked.

"William Powell left a message."

"Anyone else?"

Ouida shook her head. "You're not seeing that *girl* on the side, I hope."

"What girl?"

"The nosy detective I kicked out of our house."

"How did she come up all of the sudden?" He wondered if Babs had someone call on her behalf while he stepped out. Maybe his wife was withholding information.

Getting run off the road was traumatic enough, much less this. To get his nagging wife off his back, Basil excused himself to shower.

Chapter Seventeen: Here Come the Crazies

Dry as the desert and getting warmer by the minute, this was one of those mornings where Babs would've rather been anywhere besides a dusty office weeding through a pile of library books at Guy's desk. To catch a cross-breeze, she cracked open both his front door and the one to her office. The downside: she had to contend with her janitor mopping the outside hallway; the astringent ammonia caused a strange aftertaste to her coffee.

The elevator chimed on her floor, accompanied by approaching footsteps.

"You're late," she said to Guy as he entered.

"I went to the garage to check on the status of my car."

"Will it survive?"

"By a hair, but there are more things wrong than the mechanics expected."

"Didn't you say it needed an overhaul?"

"Babs, why have you taken over my desk?"

She placed a bookmark in the story she was reading. "Someone needed to be here in case a client came knocking."

"I'm surprised you're not reading the *Times* or the trades."

"My library books need to be returned soon. To refresh my memory, I reread *The Thin Man*. Just like everyone said, the movie was close to the original. Except for the Schnauzer."

One book slipped from her arms onto the floor. He picked it up and handed it to her. "Don't expect me to give you a lift with my car in limbo."

"Then I'll take the bus, even if it takes the entire day to ride back and forth. A taxi from Hollywood to downtown will be a waste of money."

Guy rearranged his desk to his liking. "Did you find out anything else in those Holmes stories?"

"As I said before, there are way more references to dogs than I thought."

"Did you focus on the spaniels and the terriers like I asked?"

"I did, but if the countess has anything to do with the disappearances, she didn't specify any breed of dog."

"Babs, we aren't at the point of singling her out."

She ignored his remark. "So, I reread the stories and made a list. *The Sign of Four* was a good start with Toby, the spaniel mix, used as a tracking dog. Holmes borrows him from a friend to follow the scent of whom he thinks is the killer."

Guy raised his hand like a student trying to get his teacher's attention. "You said yourself when you first met her at Basil's party that *Rache* means revenge in German. What if the person stealing the dogs is a disgruntled author who's mad at the screenwriter for changing his story? For all we know, it could be Dashiell Hammett."

She took a deep breath, held it for a few seconds, and blew it out. "Any changes while adapting *The Thin Man* from book to screen would be too insignificant to consider committing a crime, and so far, Hammett wrote one actual book. *After the Thin Man* and *Another Thin Man*, the two films produced afterward used his characters, but these weren't from his novels. He might plan books in the future based on those films, but we don't know yet. If you can come up with a better argument, then let that be your homework.

"Anyhow, getting back on track with dogs in the Sherlock Holmes stories, *The Hound of the Baskervilles* centers on a dog-like theme. Mortimer is the close friend of the cursed Baskerville family. He contacts Holmes with concerns that Sir Henry, the new heir, will suffer a premature death. Jack Stapleton, who'd be next in line for the Baskerville fortune after Sir Henry, is the villain. I sure hope I didn't spoil the ending for you.

"In *The Adventure of Shoscombe Old Place*, Mr. Shoscombe breeds black spaniels. Ferguson, in *The Sussex Vampire*, has a crippled spaniel named Carlo. Someone tested an exotic poison on the dog, causing the ailment. He's not to be confused with another Holmes story with a different dog, a Mastiff named Carlo."

"Sounds like Conan Doyle either liked that name or owned a dog named Carlo."

"Not sure, but it doesn't matter. For terriers, there's a metaphor in *The Crooked Man* about something 'like terriers around a rat cage.' In *The Adventure of the Gloria Scott*, a Bull Terrier 'froze' on Holmes' ankle, which was Doyle's way of saying the dog bit him. Victorian English doesn't always mean the same thing to us.

"There's another reference in *The Hound of the Baskervilles*. When describing the terror stalking the moors, someone said it was 'larger than a terrier.' Then, besides the terrier that ingests the poison pill in *A Study in Scarlet*, which I mentioned before, there's *The Adventure of the Lion's Mane*."

"Are we now getting back to Leo the Lion from MGM and Leo the missing Cocker Spaniel?" Guy asked.

"Believe it or not, the lion's mane refers to a jellyfish. An Airedale Terrier and its owner fell into a tide pool. Both died from its venom."

"Well, Babs, it seems like you've been busy, but what's the relevance?"

Babs reexamined her notes. "Here's an interesting situation in *The Adventure of Silver Blaze*."

Guy leaned in, curious.

"The Scotland Yard detective asks, 'Is there any other point to which you wish to draw my attention?'"

"Holmes says, 'To the curious incident of the dog in the nighttime.'"

"The detective replies, 'The dog did nothing in the nighttime.'"

"And Holmes explains, 'That was the curious incident.'"

"Which means?" Guy asked.

"The dog didn't bark because a stranger wasn't present. Whoever committed the crime was someone in-house with whom the dog was already familiar."

"Are you insinuating Asta and Leo knew their abductors?"

Babs drew a few diagrams in her notepad, along with the names of Weatherwax, Mr. and Mrs. East, One-Take Woody, Stromberg, Loy, and Powell. "We might have to revisit that later. I betcha he did."

While they continued reviewing their notes, their phone rang.

"B. Norman, Investigations," Guy answered.

After a few "ums" and "uh huhs," Babs saw his facial expressions shift from inquisitive and upbeat to grave. She tugged on his shirtsleeve.

"Uh, no. No, you can't do that…. Not advisable…" Guy said.

Ready to grab the receiver, she needed to hear for herself. He placed a tight grip over her hand.

"Hold on a second." Guy muffled the receiver. "He insists on speaking with you, but trust me, you don't want to speak to him. Sounds like one of the *Looney Tunes.*"

She yanked the phone away.

"Barbara?" the man asked. "Why are you hiding out in Hollywood and not at home in San Francisco?"

Feeling unsteady on her feet, she braced herself on a chair and eased into it—slow and deliberate.

"Called your mom every day until she gave me your office number. Said you didn't have a permanent home number yet. This was the best place to reach you."

As she stared off into nothingness, Guy refilled her coffee cup and pushed it toward her.

"Hey! You there? I'm talking to you."

The voice came over the line so loud, Guy reacted and whispered, "Do you want me to pick up and take over the conversation?"

She shook her head. "How many times do I have to tell you to leave me alone?"

"You and me—God ordained us to be together as husband and wife."

"Hold it right there. I had our marriage annulled. No longer do I have to answer to you, or anyone else."

"You must come back to me, Barbara. I love you."

Her knuckles turned white as her grip on the phone tightened. "You think

92

you know love, but you only love yourself. Get it into your head. I never want to see you again."

She slammed down the receiver so hard the phone tipped over.

"Who was that?" Guy asked.

"Mom caved and spilled the beans."

"About what?"

"He must've threatened her."

"Who?"

"My crazy ex-husband."

"The one who tried to kill you, and why you changed your name?"

"Didn't disguise it well enough, I guess, by keeping Norman as my last name. Mom couldn't take his threats anymore and gave him our office number."

"Don't be so hard on your mom. Your ex could've checked her outgoing mail and found your address. All it would take would be a call to an operator."

Babs shook her head in disbelief. "Here we're worried about a dognapping, but now I get the impression he might want to come to town and kidnap me."

"He'd have to get past me first."

"How much do you weigh?"

"Maybe one hundred forty-five pounds soaking wet at five foot eight. Why?"

"Guy, I think you're exaggerating. He's a dangerous man. Capable of anything if he dangled me over a balcony on our honeymoon. Perhaps I eloped with Troy Ulsterman by choice, but I also took the legal initiative to get out of that awful mess."

After her tense ordeal, Guy couldn't help but break into laughter. She demanded to know what was so hilarious.

"His name—Troy. I couldn't help but think of you as Helen of Troy with the face that launched a thousand ships."

She started blushing. "I'm not that attractive."

"Of course you are." He gave her a quick peck on the forehead and put his arm around her to show he cared.

Chapter Eighteen: Three to Tango

Independent of the detectives, Basil started his own search. He made a few calls and went over to MGM, not realizing he was in for a surprise. When he inquired about "Leo," an animal handler surprised him by bringing Leo, but the wrong Leo—the MGM lion mascot! Fearing for his life, he jumped backward. The lion extended his claws in defense and made a lasting impression on his trousers.

At least his leg remained unharmed. Yet, despite this embarrassment, he ignored Leo's slashes and shuffled over to the studio's publicity department.

"Hello, my name is—" He didn't have to finish his introduction.

The secretary looked up from her typewriter. "Gosh, Sherlock Holmes! How can I help you?"

He tried to take the misnomer in stride, although he felt it had branded him for life. After all, he was assuming a detective's role. Basil forced a smile. "I'd like to speak with the top person in charge."

"Concerning what, sir?"

He hated repeating his story. She saw him in full view and noticed his ripped pants.

"I hope that was from a stunt, and you didn't have the chance to change out of your costume."

"Afraid not." He tucked in his shirttail and tried to make light of it.

"The boss is out, but I'd be more than glad to give him a message."

Just as she handed Basil paper and a pen, her boss walked in. Basil received instant recognition. MGM's head of publicity, Howard Strickling, welcomed him into his office.

"You've offered a reward for your canine star from the *Thin Man* series," said Basil.

"It's all over the papers," said Strickling. "This isn't a battle between studios, I hope."

"By no means." Basil's hands shook as he lit his cigarette. "Someone has also taken my Cocker Spaniel. This has gone on too long to be a simple matter of a dog running loose with a neighbor taking him in and failing to report it. I think it was deliberate, but I wanted to keep this away from the police, fearing negative publicity. They're more concerned with bigger crimes. Not recovering a celebrity's dog. They're more likely to come up with the excuse the cocker got run over by a car just to get rid of me."

Strickling looked at his watch and dived into a heap of paperwork. "Please get to the point. I'm busy with a big event tonight and need to cut this short."

"Next time you publish an announcement about Asta, I'd like you to include something about my dog's disappearance, as well. There could be a connection between the two. Once this is out in the open, perhaps someone will come forward. I feel like I'm running out of options." Basil knew it was a tall order to ask, but Strickling wasn't buying it.

"If I'm caught promoting anything to do with an actor affiliated with a rival studio, I can lose my job, but this is what I can do. Tonight, we're holding a private but sizeable fundraiser at the Coconut Grove. By invitation only. We're comping celebrities because they're the draw. Anyone who desires to mingle with the stars can pay the steep price. Proceeds from ticket sales will go to the Allied war cause." He pulled out two invitations and waved them in front of Basil's face. "They're worth a pretty penny. Why don't you and your wife attend and ask around on your own?"

Basil looked at the invitations. "Sounds reasonable, I guess."

"I apologize; it's such short notice. Can I get a confirmation for two? Security will check at the door, and you can't enter solo. Only in pairs."

"Of course," Basil replied, unsure whether his wife was available but knowing she'd be furious for not having time to buy a new dress or visit her hairdresser.

* * *

When he returned home to convey the news, his wife was less than thrilled.

"You look like some wild beast mauled you."

"One did, but let's not discuss it."

"Maybe I should fetch some antiseptic and bandages."

"That's unnecessary," he assured her. "I'm fine."

"You're in a rush. I can sense it. What's so urgent?" she asked.

"We have invitations to a formal affair this evening and must attend."

"Darling, my charity benefit is this evening."

Basil scratched his head. "For what?"

"The Red Cross—for the British war effort—your heritage unless you've become so Americanized you forgot where you came from. Roosevelt has reinstated the Selective Service in case we need to draft our boys to go overseas. By the way, things are going, it shouldn't be long."

"You'll have to cancel."

"Impossible. I'm the head of the planning committee. Everyone's depending on me. Honey, this doesn't have to do with our dog, I hope."

Basil sighed. "In fact, it does."

"I told you to have the local authorities take over."

"I know, but I don't trust they'll care enough to get anything done."

"Who's sponsoring this affair?"

"MGM, and I can't go alone." He reexamined his invitation and noted the caveat. "They'll only admit couples."

"Then call up William Powell. Since he's one of their favorite stars, he'll be attending. Maybe he knows someone you can bring in my place."

After Basil took a quick shower and changed, he gave Powell a call, who was well aware of the event and had already agreed to accompany Myrna Loy.

"Is it true I can't show up solo? Ouida is one of the co-chairs of an event she can't get out of."

"Beats me why, but I don't make the rules," Powell replied. "Why don't you invite Countess Velma? I got stuck in the same predicament for your party."

"Don't be absurd." Basil gnashed his teeth as he heard Powell cracking up in the background. "That's not even taking into account that I think she's an oddball. Besides, I can't ask anyone I don't know to fill in at the last minute."

"What about that detective lady? She's not liable to raise any eyebrows."

"How do you expect I explain to Ouida if she finds out?"

"The girl's a nobody. Your wife is more apt to find out if you brought someone with celebrity status like Joan Crawford or Bette Davis. Who'd even suspect you brought a PI in disguise?"

"You might be right. Thanks, I'll see if she's around."

Basil hung up and called her office. Guy answered and transferred him to her line.

"No time to explain. Babs, are you available this evening? I need to attend a special event and can't get in without a partner."

"What's wrong with your wife?"

"I forgot she had plans."

"Basil, aren't I in the doghouse, as far as she's concerned?"

"You are, but she'll never know. Do I have a yes or a no? Because you won't have much time to prepare."

"If this is formal, I have nothing to wear."

"Suppose I borrow one of Ouida's gowns. Aren't you the same size?"

"Basil, aren't you forgetting our recent laundry mix-up? What if she notices it missing?"

"She has more closets stuffed with her outfits than she can keep track of. Tell me, what's your favorite color?"

"Lavender, but she won't—"

"On the contrary. She has a Chanel I wish she'd get rid of because of that designer's sympathies toward Nazi Germany."

"How do you propose I try this on?"

"I'll call for a messenger and send it to your office."

"Better yet, drop it off at my residential hotel. The La Dolce Vita."

"Ah, the sweet life. I knew it had a contradictory name."

"Thanks to your wife and your pick from the phone book."

"Babs, are we going to waste time arguing?"

"You're right. I'll taxi home. Can't very well do my hair and makeup from here. About accessories... The complete outfit will be important, and I'll look naked without a fur stole or coat to match...and jewelry. A tiara might look nice. She must have one or two lying around..."

Guy entered, and she hung up the phone.

"Appearing naked?" he asked.

She refused to look him in the eye and concentrated on packing up.

"Oh, nothing. Just an expression."

"Babs...it's never *nothing*."

"You mean it's always something?"

Guy planted his hands on his hips. "Do I have to remind you we're partners? When we first started our agency, we agreed to always let the other know what we're up to, especially if we're working undercover."

"Someone I met at the post office. He asked me out." She lied. "Do I need your permission to go out on a date?"

"Go! Get out of here! Make up your face. Make sure you wear a pretty dress and tell the lucky bastard I give him my blessing."

* * *

Babs met Basil in front of the famous Coconut Grove restaurant at the Ambassador Hotel. When he helped her from her taxi, he claimed she looked like a goddess, ready for the red carpet dressed in Ouida's silk chiffon Chanel ensemble with a matching silk evening purse.

"Sorry I didn't include a tiara," he said. "This gown looks more Greco-Roman. Couldn't find anything comparable to a laurel wreath, but the imitation pearls look classy enough. If it's any consolation, I think the look suits you better than on my wife."

Babs made a full turn, modeling Ouida's dress. "I hope no one will realize this is from her collection back in '37."

"The gown is three years old? How do you know?"

"A fanaticism for fashion magazines, and in '39 her Parisian couture house closed except for the boutique at 31 *rue Cambon* selling her famous Chanel

N°5 perfume."

Basil inspected it closer. "Seems longer on you."

"Let's hope it'll cover the one thing we both forgot about—shoes. Mine are scuffed."

"What would be the odds you'd have the same shoe size? Well, there's no point standing outside all evening. Shall we go in?"

Basil presented his invitation. Inside the party room, he noticed Babs seemed overwhelmed. "I'm taking for granted by your expression you've never been here before."

"I feel you've transported me to an exotic Arabian palace. These palm trees look real. Should I be concerned a real coconut might drop on my head?"

He laughed. "Made of papier mâché. They're rumored to have come from *The Sheik*, the Valentino film. The monkeys in them are also fake, but this Moorish architectural design is impressive. My favorites are the ceilings, painted midnight blue and filled with stars."

They entered the packed ballroom. The house band was playing, and partygoers danced wherever there was room, even if it meant in-between tables. Being taller and able to see over people's heads, Basil held her hand and pulled her through the crowd.

She asked if he was looking for anyone in particular.

"Nick and Nora Charles, some of our favorite detectives." Basil's remark conveyed a slight tone of sarcasm as he cast an eye over the crowd. "Powell gave me a visual landmark where to meet him, as long as I can find it."

"So far, I've had no chance to question Myrna at length. This could be my opportunity. Do you mind?"

"You will do nothing of the sort. Tonight, you are to act as my impromptu date and nothing more."

Strickling's invitation gave them the chance to snoop around. Maybe part of him was weary. Such a fruitless endeavor. Perhaps what they both needed were a few drinks, and here was the perfect opportunity.

Less-than-sober dancers shoved and sashayed into Babs. "Too bad he couldn't have picked a less-packed location like the lobby. I'm worried about this dress. Chiffon is so fragile."

He dragged her through the last stretch to find William Powell, leaning against a pillar smoking a cigarette. Basil labored to catch his breath. "Getting past those revelers felt like training for the Olympics."

"Come, I'll show you to our table," Powell said. "You know how impatient Myrna can get under stress."

"I thought scenes like these were her natural environment," said Basil.

"As Nora Charles, perhaps, her lifestyle revolves around one big party, but in real life, Myrna is more private. She's quite talented at flipping a switch and putting on the Ritz when necessary."

Servers were already offering them glasses of champagne before they sat down.

"Myrna, you recognize Babs Norman, correct?" Basil asked. "You met at my party."

"Of course, sweetheart. Don't you look divine."

Basil gave Babs a look, suggesting she downplay the compliment. No one needed to know the gown's origin, or who its actual owner was.

"Not to put you on the spot, Basil, but I'm a bit confused. Where is your wife?" Myrna asked.

Powell jumped in. "You saw those tickets. He couldn't be a third wheel and needed a companion to get past the front door."

"Don't know who made up that stupid rule," Basil explained. "My wife is co-chairing a fundraiser for the Red Cross tonight and can't get out of it."

"What a noble cause," Myrna said. "I volunteer my free time for animal charities."

Babs glared at Myrna but remained silent.

"Well, I think it's wonderful she's patriotic," Powell said.

Basil addressed Powell. "Don't know about you, but I served in the last war. Tried to enlist in this one. Didn't get too far."

Myrna overheard and asked, "What happened?"

"I received a brief note, and in so many words, they said, 'Dear Sir, you are too old.' So that settled it. As an alternative, people have approached me to serve as president of the British War Relief in their West Coast division.

I'll probably accept, but getting back to my invitation, Strickling presented it at the last minute, and Ouida was busy," said Basil.

"How did you convince him to give you an invitation if you're not under contract with MGM?" Loy asked. "I've heard that he and his henchman, the general manager Eddie Mannix, can be as ruthless as mobsters when they want to control the publicity about Metro-Goldwyn-Mayer or their bevy of stars."

"They didn't get the nickname of 'the Fixers' for nothing," said Powell. "If there's a drug addiction or a murder, they'll do their best to bury the evidence."

"Well, I hope they aren't burying a bone regarding Asta," Basil said.

"Is that why you saw him?" Powell asked. "Talking about dogged persistence—"

"I hate to say this, but I haven't given up on him or my dog until I've seen a dead—Perish the thought! I pray to God that will never be the case," said Basil. "Who on earth would dare kill a dog?"

Loy flung back her hair and almost slurred her words. "Someone crueler than the worst film villain you could imagine."

"Or someone out for bucks," Babs mumbled.

Basil took a pause. "No one has ever contacted me about wanting a ransom."

"Come to think of it, I don't think anyone has approached the Easts or the Weatherwax family," said Powell.

"I can vouch for the Easts," Babs said. "My partner and I spent substantial time with both of them. They received a series of strange calls from people asking to purchase their dogs. Basil, have you?"

He leaned over and whispered. "Didn't I tell you not to bring up any business this evening?"

"You brought up the topic," Babs replied.

"Don't discuss the dog hunt. Isn't it apparent they just want to have a good time?" Basil offered her his hand. "On that note, shall we dance?"

He helped her out of her seat. Loy and Powell followed. The crowd had thinned enough for everyone to wiggle their way to the dance floor.

After a few songs, Myrna looked like she was acting her hilarious role right out of a *Thin Man* film. Myrna complained she was starving, so in between dances, she rushed over to the buffet, grabbed a plateful of snacks, and tried to jitterbug and eat at the same time.

"Would you put that plate down?" Powell said, getting frustrated but even funnier and sounding just like Nick Charles. "The band's about to play a slow number. That hard porcelain won't be too comfortable in my gut, and I'd rather see something other than shrimp cocktail find its way into my pants."

The next song involved a slow, sultry clarinet solo. Babs fell into Basil's arms, and her head couldn't even reach his shoulder. This had been a long day for him, and he could imagine it had been a frustrating one for her. Between the champagne and exhaustion, he thought they might fall asleep standing up, until something pulled him out of his dreamy thoughts, and someone ripped Babs from his arms, tearing her delicate gown.

"What are you doing with my husband, and why are you wearing my dress?" Ouida shouted, so full of fury, she threw her drink in Babs' face.

Shocked, Basil jumped into action and offered Babs his handkerchief. "How did you get in? They gave me the third degree about this event is for couples-only."

"Showed the security guard my driver's license to prove I was your wife, and you were already inside—and a bribe," Ouida said. "When I forked over more cash than he earned in a month, he became very cooperative."

"I begged you to come, but you declined," Basil tried to explain. "House rules dictated I had to bring someone, but I guess you bent them. With this crowd, I'm surprised you found it so easy to find us. I had a helluva time finding my friends."

"My custom-made Chanel! How about having a searchlight pinpoint its location? The designer gave me quite a fuss when I insisted on having mine done in lavender when it wasn't a hue in her season's color palette."

Ouida turned her rage on Babs. "I guess business has been profitable if you can afford to replace it."

He intervened. "Did your charity event cancel?"

"I got everything under control and excused myself early. Told them I had an urgent matter with my husband, who now seems to have been sneaking around with other women."

"You know that's not true," he said in protest.

Powell stepped in to ease the situation. "He's here on behalf of his dog—and our dog—our film dog."

"Don't think I believe it for a second." Ouida gave Babs a slap on the face for good measure before she exited.

Chapter Nineteen: Katzenjammer

Was there no chance of a truce between the sleuth and the shrew? If ethics weren't an issue, Babs would've preferred to pin Leo's theft on Ouida as a plot to get back at her husband for infidelities, real or imaginary, and not spending enough time with her and their daughter.

The following day would get worse. Babs arrived late to work, carrying a box with Ouida's torn dress and bearing the torture of a wretched hangover.

"Did anyone call?" she asked.

"Basil did. Three times." Guy buried his attention inside his paperwork. "He said to respond in a hurry before his wife returned. What's been going on between the two of you? Was he your mystery date?"

"It's not what you think." She closed her office door and called him back.

"Basil, it's Babs," she said in a hushed tone. "What's so urgent?"

"If I want my marriage to survive, I'll have to call it quits."

"Have you given up hope?"

"I'll continue whatever I can on my own to find Leo and see what city officials can do, but any association between your agency and I must cease. If it's any consolation, I'll send you one last gratuity. You'll do fine without me fulfilling the role of Sherlock Holmes."

"What about Ouida's gown? I planned to take it over to my favorite dressmaker—"

"Don't bother. Throw it out."

"Then I can't take your payment."

"Suit yourself. Tear up our contract and forget we ever met. I don't want it dug up as evidence if my wife decides on filing for divorce."

"She—what?"

All Babs heard next was the dial tone.

* * *

Babs propped her head in her hands. She and her partner were so focused on other matters that they never got to question anyone who might have leads about the dogs who disappeared from the Beverly Hills Dog Show. Too many details. So little time. She needed to hire a larger staff. What now?

Guy entered her office, holding a cheesy gossip tabloid. On its cover: a photo of Babs assaulted by Basil's wife, with Basil, Powell, and Loy as onlookers.

"Care to explain?"

Babs ripped it from his grasp and examined it closer. "Lordy, I wasn't even aware someone took our picture."

"You didn't see a flashbulb go off?"

She heaved a heavy sigh and shook her head. "Not if my eyes were closed. Ouida threw champagne in my face."

"I'm surprised that got past the publicity police force over at MGM. The indomitable Mr. Strickling is going to have to pay *mucho dinero* to make sure the photo doesn't wind up anywhere else. Perhaps you and I need a break from each other for a while. As it is, I always need to protect my social reputation. Others jump to conclusions about my personal life. I don't need additional complications."

"Guy, stop being paranoid."

"I have more to lose than you. One of these days, I hope to land the role of a lifetime."

"Then you'll quit my agency, anyway."

"Maybe…maybe not, but nothing's on the horizon now. That could be a long way off, if ever."

Babs took another deep breath. "All right, you're jealous I got into a fancy star-studded party and didn't invite you. As business partners, we're supposed to do everything together, or as much as possible, given the circumstances. Yet, you refuse to hear my side of the story."

He stood resolute, hands in his pockets, and biting his lip.

"Confess, Guy—you know I'm right."

"Babs, you're incompetent. You didn't think things through by accepting Basil's invitation. I could bet dollars to donuts you didn't ask around about those missing dogs. No, you took the evening off, had a grand ole time, let the booze go straight to your head, and wound up in a fight with our client's intolerant wife."

"Guy, what if someone set me up?"

"Consider this my resignation. Unless you need it in writing." He made an about-face and paraded into the anteroom.

If he was that shortsighted—good riddance. Part of her wanted to chase after him, but her head ached from last night's champagne. She needed a more understanding partner, someone sympathetic. What happened to her sidekick? Her bosom buddy? Was this all it took to sever their trusted friendship?

Guy packed in a hurry. He tossed his office key on his desk before heading out and left her speechless.

Chapter Twenty: Honeymoon's Over

"Rathbone here, returning your call," Basil said. "My wife said it was urgent but wouldn't tell me why."

"That's because I didn't tell her," said Powell.

"Any secrets kept from her create a firestorm of suspicion."

"After last night's brouhaha, I guess that's clear. Basil, the reason I'm calling is I'm going to have to bow-wow out of our dog hunt."

"How come?"

"You weren't the only one with a resentful spouse. I promised my new bride as soon as they wrapped her current film, we'd take our long-overdue honeymoon. We got married at the beginning of January and postponed this for months. That's why I had to bring that pompous German aristocrat to your Bel Air party."

"Come to think of it, did you ever get to know her better?" Basil asked.

"My wife? I can't believe you're asking me this question."

"No, Countess What's-her-name."

"Countess Velma von Rache from Lithuania, or Transylvania, or from somewhere across the deep blue sea. Never spoke with her after your event, and I've already told you everything I know. Why?"

"Heard she appeared at the Beverly Hills Dog Show. Bankrolled it, too."

"Basil, to be honest, Myrna and I already started rehearsing for another picture called *I Love You Again* about a con man with amnesia and a wife who wants to divorce him, but if I don't tend to the wants and needs of my current wife, she might decide to file for divorce.

"Diana desired a romantic holiday in Paris, but a cruise across the Atlantic and back will take too much time, and I don't trust what's happening with the war escalation in Europe. New York's not so bad. We can catch a few Broadway shows, and I don't think she'll complain about the shopping."

"That's before she empties your wallet. Ah, Broadway. My heart sings for thee," Basil sang, as if reciting lyrics.

"You like it there more than Hollywood? It gets so cold in the winter."

"I've always been more passionate about theater than making motion pictures."

"Basil, you can't compare the pay scale and, with film, as long as our contracts are solid, we get paid regardless of whether our film ever gets made. Thank heavens for an excellent agent and a shrewd lawyer. Expensive as the dickens, but often worth every penny."

"You can trade in your Oscar statuette to pay for them, but you are correct," Basil said with dismay. "On stage, if our show closes because of poor reviews or an understudy takes over, our checks will cease. I get the impression you don't care one way or the other if someone finds Asta."

"Trainers are already trying to find a substitute," said Powell. "For our unofficial contest, I guess you won."

"Contest? For what?" Basil asked.

"Sherlock Holmes must be a better detective than Nick Charles, who quit before solving his case, because his wife had the final say-so."

This was never about a competition, Basil thought. It was about finding everyone's dogs.

"Say hello to your wife, and give my regards to the Great White Way," Basil said with slight sarcasm. They said their goodbyes, and he hung up in a foul mood.

Chapter Twenty-One: Another Dognapping

Why was it always a constant struggle?

Babs cleared her throat with a gulp of cherry soda. "If Basil's no longer on my team, I'll have to prove I'm the better Sherlock Holmes."

It was never easy being on her own after she annulled her marriage. Now, she lived in a decrepit hotel and seemed to have lost all of her collaborators, but for the love of dogs, she wouldn't allow her investigation to crumble.

Starting out as one of those dreaded silent afternoons, the phone finally rang.

"This is Howard Strickling from MGM's publicity department. Is this Babs?"

"Yes, how can I help you?"

"I heard from the producers, director, and trainers on the *Thin Man* films that they've hired you to track down our missing pup."

"Correct."

"You must swear to secrecy about this, because if this leaks out, we're doomed. Our biggest animal star is also missing."

Bigger than Asta? "Who?"

"Toto, from *The Wizard of Oz*—the most sought-after dog in America. After our film's overwhelming box office success, every child in America has begged their parents to buy them a dog resembling the little critter. You, too, I bet."

"Sir, do you have any leads?"

"We don't. That's why we're turning to you. Since you've kept the Asta ordeal under wraps so far, we're counting on your discretion to do the same with Toto, who has a much higher public profile. Ask anyone on the street. They'll know his name and what he looks like."

Babs wasn't sure she should mention anything about losing her detective partner, or her prior, but tight-lipped, alliance with Basil Rathbone. If Guy was still around, she'd have no qualms about taking on this case.

"Please tell me more about Toto," she said.

"Toto is a female Cairn Terrier, and her real name is Terry," he explained. "Her trainer is Carl Spitz, who runs the Hollywood Dog Training School. He used to train dogs for the military during WWI. Toto did a few other films before *The Wizard of Oz*. We're willing to triple the offer we gave you for Asta if you decide to help us out."

"Three thousand dollars?"

"*Pennies from Heaven*, just like the Bing Crosby film, if that's your fancy."

Babs reached for her soda and forced the sweet bubbly liquid down her throat.

"Hello? Are you there?"

She hoped he didn't hear her burp. "Here's a question: where and when did you realize Toto was missing?"

"Lady, I was elsewhere and don't know. That's why I'm paying you to find out."

He's not being helpful.

"You might have to interview the entire cast of *The Wizard of Oz*, not just the major actors."

"Including the Munchkins?" *That could be quite a few.* She started to perspire.

"We'll provide everyone's contact information. They always need to be accessible. This is our second highest-grossing film, surpassed only by *Gone With the Wind*, and we're always quick to jump at any opportunity to promote it further."

"Understandable." Babs patted off her sweaty forehead with her handkerchief.

"How much of an advance would you need to get started? I can send over a messenger this afternoon with cash and a contract."

Not only do I need my partner, but I need the real Sherlock Holmes.

Babs came down with a case of the hiccoughs. Her brain took a back seat as her tongue did the talking. "Five hundred—*hic*—to start."

"Great! Then it's a done deal. I'll have our legal department draw up the paperwork. Expect our messenger sometime between four and five this afternoon."

She summoned false confidence. "I'll take personal responsibility to sign it in his presence, so he can return with everything in order."

"Perfect!" Strickling said. "Oh, and one last thing. A minor detail. We have a deadline for the return of our little star."

Suddenly, her mouth became dry; she took a quick swig.

"We need him groomed and picture-ready for all the press photographers within two weeks. Otherwise, the deal's off...and we'll expect you to return your retainer."

Babs spit her cherry soda all over her desk and paperwork.

Chapter Twenty-Two: The Babs Street Irregularity

Babs marked the deadline on her calendar. If she didn't want to return the fee, she needed a plan. But first, she took a wet rag and cleaned up the cherry soda. Knowing her luck, the building's janitor would've thought it was blood.

She felt the need to make an "unofficial trip" to the von Rache compound. The next step: figure out how and when the front gate security guard wouldn't be around. How would she pull this off and get away with it? Complacency wasn't an option, and time wasn't her friend.

By the time the MGM messenger arrived with her contract and cash advance, the banks were closed. She remained in her office late into the evening and panicked when she heard her front door creak open, realizing she had left it unlocked.

"Who's there!" she shouted. A feeble attempt to sound bold and authoritative.

"Housekeeping." The voice came from an older male.

"Wiggins?"

By now, the cherry soda-soaked papers had dried, but Babs didn't want to give the impression she was hiding evidence from a crime scene. Inessentials went into the wastebasket, buried beneath other trash. Anything indispensable, she tucked under piles on her desk.

"'Tis so, lassie," he replied. The front door shut behind him as he entered. "Whatcha doing here at this hour?"

She hid Strickling's payment in her purse. "Catching up."

"Don't you have a lucky man waitin' at home for you expecting his supper?"

She met him at Guy's old desk, making sure he went no further. "A husband?"

She realized much of her makeup had sweated off. Her disheveled hair needed to be brushed, and her bobby pins reset.

"All right, under *normal* circumstances, I can't understand why a bonnie lassie like you hasn't gotten hitched yet."

"You flatter me, Abel. Maybe someday, but I've been too busy to get married."

"Don't wait 'til you're an old maid. All the good ones will be gone."

"Let's hope not," she said. "Although, it's better to be alone than to make...a terrible mistake." She hesitated at those last words and wanted to say, 'a deadly mistake' instead. No more excuses. Troy was still at large. Purchasing a gun would be inevitable. She'd be an idiot if she continued to pretend he wasn't a threat.

Perhaps he was lonely, but Wiggins rambled on about his extended Irish family and how it was getting too crowded in their Echo Park apartment to accommodate the whole brood.

"How would you like to earn some extra dough?" Her shy voice had sly intentions.

"Don't entail breakin' the law, I hope. Never sure what you shamuses are up to."

If anyone got in trouble, it would be her, not him. "Not at all."

"Whatzit entail?"

She improvised as she went along. "How good of an actor are you?"

"Get me drunk enough, and I'll start reciting limericks 'til I'm green on St. Paddy's Day."

How do I put this into words? "I need someone, not me...a guy, who'd appear more credible than a young woman, to pretend he's in trouble." *I should've thought this out first.* "He needs to run up to someone for help. When the guy leaves his post to help him, he disappears, and the guy can't find him."

"*Aye, Begorra,* your tryin' to sneak into a studio lot for a big audition you can't seem to get, right?"

"Not in a longshot. When I started my private investigation business, I kissed my acting career goodbye," Babs explained. "What this entails: I need to sneak onto someone's private property and get past a security guard."

She opened her purse. She plucked out two Federal Reserve Notes with Alexander Hamilton's face on them. "Would you be willing to distract him for a bit of...cash?"

Wiggins' cautiousness transformed into a smile that stretched from one ear to another.

"For that amount, I'd be willing to dance drunk and naked if that's what it took to get the sap to leave his post. When do you need this?"

"Saturday—after dark."

"Two nights from now, *hmmm*. Lucky for you, I have the evening off."

* * *

Realizing she couldn't put it off any longer, the next day, Babs planned to visit a gun shop. Thrifty by habit, she took several buses all the way from Hollywood to Culver City.

"I want to buy a small revolver and need your help on how to use it," she told the shop owner.

"Got the perfect thing. Better than a revolver," the gun seller said. "A 1930 Colt: model 1908, hammerless vest pocket pistol. It's a sweet little number—.25 caliber, featuring a two-inch barrel, fixed sights, a six-shot magazine, and checkered, hard rubber grips. Used, with a ding or two, but otherwise in great shape and for a fair price."

"You'll have to speak in plain English. I know nothing about firearms," Babs confessed.

"Have you ever fired a handgun?"

"My daddy let me fire a shotgun a few times when I was little."

"Do you recall getting thrown backward after you pulled the trigger?"

"My feet flew out from underneath me, and I fell smack on my can, crying."

He laughed. "That's the kick or recoil you felt. This gun is a good choice because it has minimal recoil for a lady your size. Fits right in your purse or pocket if it's deep enough. See for yourself."

Babs hesitated. "Is it loaded?"

He shook his head. When she realized how portable and concealable it was, she took out a wad of cash and handed him her PI license. "Is this sufficient?"

"You're the first female private detective I've ever encountered," he said.

She tried to make light of it. "There aren't too many of us. Haven't met any of the others."

"If there are others." He took extra care to count the money and checked for counterfeits. "You're in luck. The previous owner sold it to me with its instruction manual. Helpful for care and maintenance. I don't suppose you want this gift wrapped?"

When she looked at him funny, he apologized for the joke. She was about to say goodbye when she noticed an unusual object on a shelf behind his counter.

"What's that? It reminds me of Mickey Mouse ears."

He took it down to show her. "I collect and sell a variety of antiques and collectibles besides weaponry, par for the course if you acquire a lot of your inventory from estates and not just trade-ins. This is a relic from WWI. Once air combat and dogfights became popular, the Germans invented this contraption to pick up faraway sounds of approaching enemy planes. Looks funny as hell, but it's the perfect spying device. Here, try it on."

The man was already strapping the helmet-like getup on her head before she declined. Babs pulled a mirror from her pocketbook. "Don't I look ridiculous."

"Let's test it out." He adjusted its leather chinstraps and showed her how it worked. Then he walked over to the far end of the store and whispered. "You'd never be able to hear me under normal circumstances—"

"*Yow!* It sure amplifies the sound." She hurt her own ears the moment she spoke.

He returned to help her take off the rig.

"Come to think of it," she said. "This might come in handy. Too bad there isn't a way to prove the sounds are legit. All someone can do is take my word for it."

"Someone like who?"

She explained, "If I needed to present evidence in court or to the police."

"Hold on," he said. "I might have just the thing." He pulled another box off a shelf which contained a crude recording device. After connecting a few wires, his makeshift rig worked.

Thoughts bounced in Babs' head. "There has to be another way this stuff works without plugging a cord into the wall if it's used out in the field."

"Both devices hold a charge if you plug them into a regular electric socket for an hour before using them. Works for me."

"How much? For all of it."

"How about I give you a generous discount since you just purchased the pistol?"

Babs agreed to his more-than-reasonable price; he packed the recorder in a spare box and the spying device in its military-issued steel carrying case.

"Are you sure it's legal to possess this stuff? Even though I'm a professional PI with a license, I wouldn't want to be under suspicion for any home-grown espionage. A lot of folks are worried about the war intensifying overseas."

He shrugged but was quick to pocket her payment. "Beats me, but it was a pleasure doing business with you, miss."

Now, since she'd be carrying a gun and peculiar war salvage, she dipped into her advance to take an expensive cab ride back to Hollywood.

Chapter Twenty-Three: A Third Dog Named Carlo

Babs needed to contact the K-9 training center of the police department to find out more about using the services of a search and rescue dog. Their dogs had already tracked down missing children. If their sense of smell was that keen, maybe they could track down the familiar scent of another dog like Asta or Toto. Lucky for her, she could make an appointment right away.

Everything fell into place until she received a call on her in-house line.

"Miss Norman, this is Ferguson from the front desk," he said in a softened voice.

"Speak up. I can't understand you."

"Might be difficult. There's a gentleman in the lobby who's pestered me for the last ten minutes. He claims he's your husband. I told him you're not married. Should I call the cops?"

She froze in panic.

"Miss Norman, are you there? What should I do?"

Darn! I need to get out of here. A quick lie. "He's a crazy client. The bastard thinks he's my husband and needs to be in an asylum. Did he put his hands on you?"

"He grabbed me by the collar. I thought he'd yank me off my feet and pull me over the counter. Like a saloon brawl in one of those Western movies. For a while, he paced the lobby, cursing to himself. Right now, he's chain-smoking hand-rolled cigarettes and standing guard by our front entrance."

"Call the police. Report him on grounds of physical assault and harassment. Do it now!"

He must've followed me home.

Babs slipped her new pistol inside her loose-fitting jacket. Realizing she should avoid the obvious—the elevator, she noticed a rear window at the end of the hallway. When she leaned out, her fear of heights took over. She passed on the idea of climbing down the fire escape.

The next obvious place Troy would look would be the front or the rear staircases. With little time to spare, Babs hopped a ride on the freight elevator carrying garbage straight to the alley and bypassed the lobby. She ran several blocks to seek refuge inside a drugstore, where she used their payphone and called a cab.

Another close call. She prayed Ferguson followed through and contacted the police. If she requested a restraining order, what were they going to do unless he committed an actual crime? With her being a private detective, they'd laugh and say she should have been able to handle him. Maybe she needed a guard dog besides carrying a gun.

* * *

When Babs arrived at the police kennels, the canine handler introduced himself as Officer Jefferson Hope. He introduced her to his dog.

"Miss Norman, meet Carlo, my partner." Then he said to Carlo, "Miss Norman is our friend."

"Just a warning. Don't give him a hug or an approach like a regular dog. Stay put, hold out your hand to show you're friendly. Let him come to you first, but on my command."

The dog drew near and tickled her legs with his wet nose.

"I assumed your K-9 trainee to be a German or Belgian Shepherd," she said. "What kind of dog is he?"

"Carlo's a Giant Schnauzer."

"I've never seen one this large," she said.

"Most people are familiar with the standard or miniature ones," said Hope. "These can stand close to twenty-eight inches and probably outweigh you."

"If he ran after a squirrel, he'd pull me down the street."

"We train them to behave so they won't. Tell me, Babs, why are you so interested in our dogs? Are you thinking of doing this as one of your PI specialty services?"

She gave him a coy smile. "You never know, but often, I felt the need for protection, and a well-trained dog would serve that purpose. Getting back to your Giant Schnauzer, officer, what gives this breed an advantage over the other more common, smaller ones?"

"During the First World War, the German military employed them to sniff out explosives. Also, for police duties and apprehending criminal suspects."

Once again, Babs consoled herself with the famous words of wisdom from Sherlock Holmes, "Education never ends…"

He put Carlo on a leash, and they went to a nearby park. "We like to take our K-9s here, because it's separate from our training facility and simulates real-life situations. Our dogs need to be exposed to distractions, whether those are other dogs, sounds, people, wild animals, or scents."

Officer Hope showed her two pieces of fabric. "While I'm exercising Carlo and warming him up, why don't you hide one of these? Don't make it easy. When you come back, we'll see how well he can retrieve it."

He put on gloves and explained he needed to hide his own scent. Then he handed her a pair of tongs. "You need these, so you won't contaminate this fabric sample with yours. After you hide your piece, I'll allow Carlo to sniff the scent on mine. His job will be to locate yours, which has an identical smell. If you and I tried to take a whiff, we'd never be able to smell anything except the slight odor of dirty laundry."

They couldn't have picked a day with more ideal, balmy weather, and a much more pleasant way to spend an afternoon rather than fretting about Troy or cooped up in her stuffy office. Once she reached the hilltop, from that vantage point, she took in the panoramic view of the sprawling City of Los Angeles from all directions.

From there, she spotted a rock wall and chose that location to bury her test sample under a pile of loose stones. Her actions attracted the attention of two curious stray mutts. The female appeared to be in heat. The male stared at Babs with a bone in his mouth.

"*Shoo!* Go away!" Babs said in vain. "Are you spying on me?"

She headed back downhill. They tagged along, wanting to play.

"Looks like you brought along some company," Hope said as she approached.

"I didn't plan on it."

"People who don't know what to do with their pets, let them loose in the park," he said. "They're afraid someone will put them down if they take them to an animal shelter. Same thing with Easter bunnies. Kids love them as presents, but soon they tire of them, or they realize they make too much of a mess. Enough about that. Did you find a good hiding place?"

"I hope so."

"Let's find out." He allowed Carlo to sniff his fabric sample and gave the command for him to find its match.

Carlo headed up the hill. The strays insisted on joining the search.

"It looks like they don't want to give up their new playmate," Babs said.

The dogs gained a lead. From a distance, she perceived the male stray wanted to give his bone to Carlo. Hope shouted instructions to Carlo, who became distracted and went for the bone, abandoning his master for his new companions.

"Back to kindergarten for Carlo," Hope said, beside himself. "All that training time wasted, and I thought he'd soon be ready to report for duty."

"Shouldn't we go after them?" Babs asked.

"We don't know a thing about those feral dogs," he said, exasperated. "They could have rabies, and I'd hate to put you at risk."

"Nonsense," said Babs. "I have an idea. Do you mind lending me your scented fabric?"

Using the tongs, he gave it to Babs, who let the male mutt get a whiff. "Go get it!" she shouted.

Despite the mutt's lack of formal training, he upstaged the K-9 with his natural-born skills and retrieved its hidden counterpart. Carlo seemed more interested in pursuing his new love interest.

While caught up in the excitement, Babs forgot what Officer Hope told her about not petting Carlo like a normal dog, and when she did, she bent over, and her gun fell out of her jacket. Taught to defend his master if a civilian displayed firearms, he leapt and knocked her down and bit her leg in defense. Hope reprimanded him and dug into his carryall for a first aid kit.

"I don't know what I was thinking," Babs said. "He looked so gentle and harmless."

"I'm sorry this happened." The police officer applied a bandage. "You can't treat police dogs like regular pets. How do you feel now?"

"Sore, but I'll survive." *Is he going to give me grief for why I'd brought a gun?*

The feral male seemed protective of Babs and barked when Carlo got too close. She gave him an affectionate pat on the head, and he licked her face. "Seems like this guy is more cut out for search and recovery than yours."

"Maybe you should take him home," Hope said. "He appears to have taken a shining to you."

Calling it a day, Babs and Officer Hope headed back to the kennels, where he returned Carlo to his pen. The feral female lost interest and remained in the park, but the tenacious male insisted on accompanying Babs like a bodyguard.

When she tried to board her cab, the mutt surprised her by hopping in first.

"Is he yours, missy?" the cabbie asked.

She stared at the mutt in disbelief. "Looks like he wants to be."

"Make up your mind, lady. My meter's running."

The dog gave her a big, slobbery kiss on the nose.

"Has he got a name?" the cabbie asked.

Good question. She thought of names from some of the Sherlock Holmes stories. Baskerville was too long. Sir Henry, the heir of the Baskerville fortune? A possibility.

"His name is Sir Henry. Let him stay." She turned to the mutt. "Suppose I give you some supper and clean you up before taking you to the pound tomorrow?"

Sir Henry gave Babs the sad eyes.

"Poor baby. Think of it more like a lost-and-found. I'm sure someone misses your licks and cuddles."

Chapter Twenty-Four: Into the Leopard's Lair

Lucky for Babs, she was off the hook for her concealed weapon, but she worried about how long she'd be able to conceal a dog in a residential hotel that didn't allow pets. For the time being, she bribed the custodian into using the freight elevator and coaxed him to teach her how to use it when he wasn't around.

She had twelve days left to recover two dogs. Her next step was to get an object embedded with Toto's scent, since she already had Asta's toy rabbit. She called Strickling. He sent a messenger to bring her a scrap of Toto's favorite blanket.

Next on her agenda: Sir Henry needed a briefing. She filled her pockets with dog treats, snuck her new K-9 partner out of the building, and took him to the nearest grassy area to practice.

"All right, you Mongrel of the Baskervilles. Let's hope you're not a hell hound like the one in the Conan Doyle story. We need a miracle—and fast. Give me a repeat performance of what convinced me to adopt you."

They spent two hours together and practiced for tonight's big event. Afterward, Babs snuck Sir Henry back into her hotel and fed him lunch. The heat and all the running tuckered them out.

When her furry friend jumped onto her bed and insisted on snuggling, she pinched her nose. "*Oooh.* You need a bath."

She didn't have a tub, and Sir Henry was terrified of the shower. Babs had to improvise and used a sponge.

Big and hairy, he reminded her of a K-9 Irish stew—part Irish Wolfhound, part Irish Setter, Irish Soft-coated Wheaten Terrier, and maybe some Irish Water Spaniel thrown in for good measure, and he ate like a monster who escaped the Irish Potato Famine. With Irish stew on her mind, she ordered that for dinner. Sir Henry gobbled the leftovers.

Nightfall approached, and she needed to finalize preparations. Babs had no choice but to trust her luck in choosing Wiggins to carry out his plans and hoped he didn't bungle it along the way. They met at her office to go over last-minute details.

"Of what I recall…when I went over there on official business," she explained, "the guard booth had two phone lines—one connected to the main house and one outside line where he could call the police."

"Don't worry, lassie. I'll keep him busy long enough where you can pass through unnoticed. Are you taking the dog, too? The last time we met, you didn't say a word about him."

"He's my new partner," said Babs with a quick answer, which was as good as any.

Wiggins rested his chin on the small end of his mop. "Not that gentleman I always see at your front desk?"

Babs shook her head. "Sir Henry has an amazing talent for retrieval. He's also the perfect alibi if I'm stopped and questioned. I could always say he wiggled through the gate, and I had to chase after him. Even if it's on private property."

Wiggins gave her a peculiar stare. "How come you're dressed in black from head to toe? You look like a cat burglar."

"Even though it'll be dark, I still can't risk anyone seeing me. Trust me, I have no plans to steal anything." *Only to bring back dogs someone else had already stolen.*

"All right, I'll be heading along. Guess we won't see each other again until the workweek begins." Before Wiggins left, he handed her a tiny green plant.

"What's this?"

"A shamrock. For good luck," he said and shut the door.

With nowhere else to put it, she stuffed it inside her bra for safekeeping.

Everything else, she packed inside a rucksack. For the dogs, she brought collars and leashes, treats, and the scent items. For her, she included black leather gloves, a thermos filled with water, a pair of binoculars, flashlights, the makeshift recording device, and the "Mickey Mouse ears" or German amplification rig, but she took it out of its military-issued case because it looked like a housing for a bomb. Upon one last inspection, she realized she needed to include her handgun.

After Wiggins left, she finished putting together the rest of her outfit. To appear as inconspicuous as possible, Babs tucked her hair into a black, crocheted snood and pinned the collar of her dark-eggplant-colored sweater to stand up rather than lie flat to camouflage her pale neck. Despite the looseness of her Marlene Dietrich-style black trousers, she kept tugging and adjusting them to feel comfortable.

What Babs didn't realize was how difficult it would be to find a taxi driver willing to transport her with a dog. When she found one, he pulled up, looked her over, but was hesitant to let her in. She assumed he was more leery of her outfit than about Sir Henry.

"We're in a theatrical act together. I need to disappear into the shadows during a blackout—a magic show thing," she said, improvising. Awkward, but it worked.

* * *

Whatever Wiggins had planned, he pulled it off. At the predetermined time, Babs approached the unattended guard booth. Sir Henry squeezed through first, and she followed, but had to take off her rucksack to pull it through the narrow gap in the fence.

The two intruders galloped over to an area where she could make last-minute adjustments. She smudged charcoal on her face to obscure her features even further and washed the excess soot off her hands.

Sir Henry let out a woof of excitement.

"*Shush!*" Babs warned him. "Promise me you'll be as quiet as possible."

Much good that's going to do, she thought. I've known this mutt for less than twenty-four hours. Will he listen to my instructions?

Next, Babs dug out Asta's and Toto's scent objects, but realized Sir Henry could only follow one scent at a time. She let him sniff the scrap of Toto's blanket, stuffed Asta's toy rabbit into her backpack, and sent him on his way. After his departure, she put on her Mickey Mouse ears and hooked them up to the crude recording device, which she wore strapped across her chest. She took out her binoculars to see what damning evidence, if any, she could pick up from inside the house.

The only other time she tested the audio enhancers was in the gun seller's shop. When she turned it on, the fluctuating sounds reminded her of when she was a little girl and her father fine-tuned the right frequency on his ham radio.

Babs realized she might've been wrong in assuming the countess was guilty. Yet von Rache seemed to have the means and the opportunity to commit these crimes. What Babs couldn't fathom was her motivation.

Compared to the ease the merchant had back at his gun shop, Babs had great difficulty operating the spy equipment on her own. Maybe the operator's manual could answer some of her questions. Just her luck. All the instructions were in German.

Her contraption also picked up a lot of background noise. From what she could make out, it sounded like a conversation between a mature woman, whom she *assumed* was the countess, and a male, who she believed to be her butler. Both had unmistakable accents.

Butler: "Why do you bring in more dogs? They are taking over our house, and we are running out of room."

Countess: *Static...* "It does not matter."

More squelch. *What doesn't matter?*

Her equipment fizzled. *I thought this was supposed to be charged.* She slapped the side of the contraption like burping a baby, and it sputtered back to life. *Maybe it has loose wiring.* She worried about what part of this conversation she missed.

Butler: "You have—en-dan-gered species. That leopard, for ex-am-ple. When you appear in public—"

Countess: "What about my public appearances?"

Butler: "You always wear fur. May give others wrong ideas."

Countess: "*Harrumph!* How dare you! Consider yourself an endangered species."

Who was she planning on killing? Her butler? Not the dogs. The leopard? What's with this interference? Unable to get a clear signal, Babs was ready to pack up and call the whole thing off, but she couldn't if her pup partner was still on the prowl.

Her sound quality was awful. Using her binoculars, it looked like the woman left the room and the man or butler was alone, but she couldn't tell for certain. Maybe he was using the phone. Whoever this was, they had their back toward her, and all she saw were shadows.

Someone: "On the *Queen Mary*... Hiss. Crackle... We will fool the officials..."

Her contraption powered down for good, and her backup recording device jammed.

A foolproof plan? What about the Queen Mary?

Everything seemed to malfunction. Babs yanked off her heavy Mickey Mouse headphones, now useless. She hoped to rely on her binoculars, but they fogged from the brisk night air. Unaware the countess installed a newfangled security system, Sir Henry's proximity to the house activated a piercing alarm. Someone opened the front door, and the leopard escaped to pursue him.

"Sir Henry, come back!" She soon realized she might alert someone to her location if she continued to shout. If her *Hound of the Hollywood Baskervilles* was worth his weight in kibble, he'd get out of there—fast.

In trying to escape, she twisted her ankle. Her bandages tore off, reopening her wounds from yesterday's dog bite. She feared the leopard would discover her hiding place, attracted by the smell of fresh blood. While on the ground, re-wrapping her dressings, Babs felt a wet nose. She looked up and discovered a reddish Cocker Spaniel.

"Leo?" It was hard to make out his exact coloring in the dark, but she'd seen enough photos of Basil's and assumed this was his dog.

She snapped her fingers. "Leo—come."

The dog allowed her to pet him and wanted to lick her wound. When Babs felt she'd gained the cocker's trust, she leashed and collared him.

Maybe I can also regain Basil's confidence, she thought.

Sir Henry came barreling from the house. Babs put him back on his leash and ran the best she could with a hurt ankle and the two dogs toward the front gate. Search party flashlights closed in.

A Great Horned Owl swooped down low, spooking Leo, who bolted and dragged Babs, but soon broke free. In trying to catch up, she and Sir Henry got tangled in the underbrush. As she fell, her gun went off, not injuring anyone, but it signaled her location.

The search party made a swift retreat. She assumed someone, upon hearing the alarms and the gunshot, might've alerted the cops, and the countess's staff backed off, not wanting to reveal any illegal goings on in the main house.

Police arrived. Babs felt defeated. The one good thing: she recovered Basil's dog, who must have escaped on his own. Despite her plea that she had seen and overheard incriminating evidence that warranted further investigation, the police took her into custody. Babs spent the rest of the night in jail. Since they refused to let Sir Henry remain in the cell with her, they sent him to the pound.

Chapter Twenty-Five: The G-Men

I*t's always a man's world...* This played over and over in Babs' head.

"Rise and Shine." The warden flashed his gun. "No funny business, you hear?"

Babs rolled over, rubbed her eyes, and reoriented herself. She'd forgotten she slept the night in a jail not used to female prisoners. Her jailer mentioned something about the "hen pen" or the women's detention facility being under construction, and they had to detain her at a jail designated only for men. Not until she saw her reflection in the cracked wall mirror did she realize she still had the charcoal smears on her face used for camouflage. When she noticed the exposed urinal, she asked if someone could escort her over to an actual ladies' room.

He led her over to an area set aside for civilian visitors and stood guard outside the door. "Just so you know, there are no windows in case you were considering an escape."

"If there's no way to air the place out, it must smell terrible." Babs realized a snide remark wouldn't earn her a merit badge. When finished, he brought her back to her cell.

"Any way of getting a cup of coffee around here?" she asked.

"Breakfast will arrive soon," he said in a monotone. "Looks like you didn't get any shuteye."

Babs tried to make sense of her matted hair and felt like she'd woken in the drunk tank.

"My purse?"

"That rucksack didn't look like a dame's pocketbook. We confiscated it, along with your mutt."

"Oh, my poor puppy. Where did you take him?"

"To the pound. We couldn't risk him peeing on the floor."

"I had two dogs. What about the Cocker Spaniel?"

"We matched him up with photos on file. Some married couple offered a generous reward to the officers of any Los Angeles or Beverly Hills precinct who could bring him home safe and sound. With that kind of incentive, their case got preferential treatment."

I bet it did. "Did they come to the station to retrieve him?"

"Nah, one of our guys drove him to their house in a squad car."

"Do you mind if I call them?" *They probably wouldn't even answer.*

"They wanted to remain anonymous and explained why they were hesitant at first to report their missing dog."

She tried not to flip her wig. "That's because I was the one who insisted on filing the reports. No point in keeping this secret any longer. The *Rathbones* were my clients."

"Lady, I'm a bit confused. First, you tell us you're a PI. Now, you consider yourself a professional dogcatcher?"

"As a private eye, they paid me to find their dog. Somehow, their Cocker Spaniel found me—long story, but that's what led to my arrest. I also have reason to believe the person whose property I was on stole their dog."

"When our boys picked you up for trespassing, you didn't look like you were trying to rescue any dogs. Not dressed like a cat burglar."

Her objections went nowhere. Another officer arrived with her breakfast. The coffee—lukewarm and instant. Stale, compressed biscuits passed for toast, and a watery concoction which she suspected were leftover trench rations from the First World War comprised the meal. She scarfed it down and knew her stomach would regret it later.

Babs felt as dingy as a dog that had just rolled in pig slop. Something tickled her chest. She reached into her undergarments and pulled out a wilted sprig of green, realizing she'd forgotten about Wiggins' *lucky* shamrock.

"Hey, you never gave me a chance to make a phone call last night. Don't I get to call a friend...or a lawyer?" she asked.

"Not with possession of illegal spy equipment. We need to bring in a few experts and ask you a few questions first."

That's not how the law is supposed to work, she thought, figuring someone wanted to play hardball.

She was about to feel sorry for herself and worried they'd take her private eye license away for bending the rules too far, when her thoughts turned to her K-9 companion. *My Irish stew hound.* As it was, she'd taken a risk smuggling him in and out of her residential hotel.

She looked at her bare wrist. They swiped her watch, as well. "Have you any idea what time it is?"

"The cock crows at 6:30 a.m.," her jailer replied with a hard, sardonic smile.

Babs groaned. *How did I wind up in this predicament? Wait, this should be no surprise. Illegal trespassing and dressed like I could rob the place.* She could go down the list, and it was a long, incriminating one. Not to mention the firearm, which she never had time to register.

"I don't suppose there's a way to clean up around here," Babs said.

Another officer entered, holding folded clothes, a towel, and a bar of soap. "I'll escort you back to the restroom. Wash up. Change clothes. We'll bag up your dirty ones."

"This looks like a prison uniform," she said upon closer examination.

"What do you expect? Coco Chanel?" He laughed so hard that he coughed up phlegm and spat it on the floor.

* * *

Several hours later, a different officer unlocked her cell. He handcuffed Babs and led her to an interrogation room. Two men in suits instructed her to sit on the opposite side of the table. Armed guards stood by the door. Expedient introductions revealed they were special agents from the FBI.

"I don't understand," Babs said. "Why the Feds?"

"We'll ask the questions. You give us the answers," said the man with glasses and thinning red hair. He flashed his ID, Special Agent William Wright. The other man presented his badge, Special Agent Sherman Lockwood.

131

"Why were you in possession of German spy equipment?" Wright asked.

"Bought it from a gun dealer in Culver City, assuming it was a castoff from the last war and fair game. You should ask him where he got it and why he had it."

Wright: "Are you a Nazi sympathizer?"

Babs: "Heavens no."

Lockwood: "Where were you born?"

Babs: "In San Francisco. I'm as American as apple pie and major league baseball." She felt smug and smart, but it didn't seem to amount to much in their book.

Wright: "No Germans or Russians in your family tree?"

Babs: "My parents told me we're distant relatives to an impoverished British earl, impressive in title only. Why are you so worried about Russians?"

Wright lit a cigarette and blew it in her face. "Are you a member of the Communist Party?"

Lockwood interrupted. "I wonder if she rubs elbows with that Russian Nazimova?"

She coughed and tried to swish their smoke in another direction. "Madame Alla Nazimova from the Garden of Allah?"

Lockwood: "Yeah, from that den of debauchery near Crescent Heights off the Sunset Strip. I hear it's one of Errol Flynn's favorite haunts. Police are always putting the collar on doped-up deviants over there."

Babs: "Shame on you! I can't believe you're pairing me up with that crowd, but now, I'm confused. Are you interested in Fascists or Communists?"

Lockwood: "They're all enemies of the United States. So, are you?"

Babs: "Am I what?"

Lockwood: "Sympathetic to either cause."

Babs: "Of course not, and I'm glad it looks like FDR will go for an unprecedented third term."

The two G-men continued to put the screws to her until they realized further queries on her personal background and affiliations were useless.

Finally, she brought up the countess. Babs uttered a lie with no proof of her outrageous statement. "What if I told you I'm an animal lover and contribute to animal charities, and Velma von Rache is beating and torturing poor creatures on her property?"

Lockwood laughed. "We're not the ASPCA."

"We'd say you made that up to get out of jail," said Agent Wright.

Drat, he saw right through me. "If you'd be so kind as to retrieve my backpack, I have a recording you might find useful."

"Nothing was salvageable from that hunk of junk," said Wright.

I can't believe they were already on it.

"We can't use any German spy devices to present evidence in court," Lockwood said.

Even worse, she'd seen moving shadows with her binoculars, unsure whose conversation she actually overheard.

Babs sighed. "Please tell me this. Do you know of anything big about the *Queen Mary*?"

Lockwood turned her inquest into a mockery. "Outside of her being the mother of the current sovereign of England? Big? Does our British bigwig need to go on a diet? Too much tea and crumpets, eh?"

Babs thought she'd burst. "The ocean liner—the one bigger than the *Titanic* and sturdier, I hope. It's docked at Long Beach Harbor."

"There are unsecured sections of the harbor where we suspect Fascist sympathizers have been smuggling money and weapons and exchanging information about our military installations," Wright said.

Her words seemed to bounce off the walls. "The person I was *spying* on mentioned something about the *Queen Mary*, and *authorities* were powerless...to do something before my equipment went kaput. Maybe she could smuggle what you're looking for onboard the ship."

Lockwood added, "There could be Nazi spies right under our noses living in Hollywood. While we had the countess under surveillance, our men also spotted you sneaking around her property."

They've also considered her a person of interest.

After an hour of wasted time and much frustration, the Feds let Babs off the hook but warned her they'd still be monitoring her.

"Say hello to J. Edgar for me," Babs said as they started to leave.

"How do we know your PI license isn't a fake?" Agent Wright asked. "I've never even heard of a female private eye."

Agent Lockwood reexamined her credentials. "Either she's employed an excellent forger, or this is the real McCoy, but I wouldn't consider a private dick on par with any member of the law enforcement community."

Babs replied, "Better to be on your side than the wrong side, don't you fellows agree?"

As the Feds exited, she overheard Lockwood calling her a damned dame, and Wright called her a bitchy broad.

* * *

Next came her police interrogation. Not much different from what she just went through with the FBI, save the accusations about being a political dissident. Once it was all over, they advised her never to sneak onto someone's private property without permission again, unless she wanted to risk the suspension of her PI license. When they asked if she had a husband or a local family member able to take responsibility for her good behavior, she reluctantly gave them her ex-partner's phone number.

"His real name is Gary Brandt, but he goes by the name of Guy for obvious reasons not to be confused with Cary Grant."

Her captors, dismissive. For all they cared, she could've recited the theory of relativity to an orangutan.

She hated reminders of how much she distrusted the male establishment. When she was a youngster, they promised to help find her father's killer. They didn't. Now, they thought she was a criminal, but she wasn't, and they're still treating her like she needed to grow up.

An hour later, Guy arrived with bail. They returned her watch and ruck-sack, minus the contraband Mickey Mouse ears and recording apparatus. She pleaded with Guy to present his ID and investigator's license and vouch that he was (and still is) her business partner. After he signed off on the paperwork, they let him take responsibility for her handgun. Babs figured their leniency had something to do with the fact he was male, and they wouldn't have been so cooperative if she had requested it on her own.

"I'm always at odds with bureaucracy," Babs mumbled.

"The cops or the Feds?" Guy asked.

Babs gave him a look like he shouldn't have asked.

"You and me, both. As a queer, every cold-hearted person in power yearns for the chance to ridicule or arrest people like me for no particular reason."

She put her hand on Guy's shoulder. "Why?"

He grimaced. "Because they know they can get away with it."

Together, they headed outside and into the visitors' parking lot. "Does this mean we're back as a team?" she asked. "I hope you understand…you're the best friend I've ever had."

Guy grumbled and didn't seem to be in the mood for further discussion. He walked toward a motorcycle, straddled it, and put his key into the ignition.

"What's with that?" she asked.

"The old wreck kept breaking down, and the longer I postponed the inevitable, I was lucky not to wind up in an accident. I traded it in, but a motorcycle was all I could afford. You had all of our retainer funds in your bank account."

"How are you going to take me home?"

"Hop on the back."

"What about Sir Henry?" By now, Babs was in tears. "My dog! Who's going to rescue him from the pound? If he remains too long and we don't claim him, they'll put him down."

"Our dog now, I guess, with no choice but to bring him over to my place. They don't allow pets at yours. How did you sneak him in and out?"

"Made a deal with the freight elevator operator, but after spending a night in jail, I can't risk any more trouble. Sir Henry's liable to bark and alert a neighbor. How do you expect to get him home?"

"Guess I'll drive down there, fill out the paperwork for his release, and stall for time. Maybe I'll pick up a sidecar, even if I have to rent one. Either that, or spring for a cab. Aren't you glad there are now two brains working on this case?"

Babs gave him a hug and thanked him, once again, for bailing her out. "Guy, you're the only G-Man I'll ever need. Don't you forget it."

Chapter Twenty-Six: The Switcheroo

Dander didn't have time to fall on this dame's shoulders. With ten more days to go, Babs needed to regroup with Guy and figure out what was the big deal about the *Queen Mary*. The following morning, he arrived back at their office with boxes of personal effects and admitted he felt somewhat nostalgic. Guy brewed the coffee and asked Babs why she still insisted on targeting the countess.

"Something is up, and I know it. I overheard pieces of a conversation and have a feeling she's behind the crimes of the missing dogs. Just like the popular jingle you hear all over the radio, I heard enough snap, crackle, and pop on that German amplification device to drown out a bowl of Kellogg's Rice Krispies."

"You had the Feds on your back?"

"When we have time to catch up, I'll fill you in."

Guy plucked the pencil from the back of his ear and scratched his head. "Maybe we should make a fresh start."

"And do what?" she asked.

"Drop this case. Basil's no help. We have no guarantees from the *Thin Man* crowd. I borrowed from my roommate to bail you out. Oh, I kept that on the Q.T. until now. Come on, Babs, this seems to be more trouble than it's worth. Do you have any idea how I got by after I quit your agency? Sure, I went on a few auditions—nada. Not even a single, lousy callback. Jobs were harder to find than I thought."

He concentrated on reorganizing his desk. Moments later, he broke the silence. "There are things a guy like me can do when they're strapped for funds. Stuff on the sly, which can land me in jail, or worse. I didn't want to go there. Life's tough enough."

Babs reached over and firmly clasped his hand. "Sorry, I didn't know."

Guy moved his nameplate back to its usual spot. "No time for melancholy, I guess."

"A perfect title if you ever write a script. *No Time for Melancholy*, right?" Babs said, in an eye-opening shift of tenor. "If neither of us has a boyfriend by then, you can take me as your date to the Oscars."

Unable to hide being over-sentimental, his eyes misted over. "You don't give up, do you?"

"Did you know I auditioned for the Columbia Girl?"

"The Torch Lady?"

"You got it. The woman who holds the beacon of light, heralding Columbia Pictures, for the film you're about to see. Didn't get the part. I was too young for the original, but they considered revamping their image. For heaven's sake, I want my Hollywood ending. What else is there to look forward to? An abusive ex-husband?"

Babs rose to her feet. "Guy, what about you? Would you dare to settle as a stock boy at your pop's general store? Out of sight, because he's too ashamed to have his homosexual pride and joy scare off his skittish customers. Quit being such a softy. The prize is more than money. The prize is keeping our dreams and maintaining our dignity."

Guy also stood, but he clapped and shouted, "Bravo! Bravo!"

"Okay. Getting down from my soapbox. No one's giving me an Academy Award for this pep talk." Babs hung her head, now embarrassed. "Both of us have a lot of figuring out to do."

"Chin up, as the Brits say." He cracked a smile and apologized for his bad accent. "Talking about Brits, doesn't Basil owe you reward money for finding Leo?"

"From what I gather, he already gave it to the police department. I suspect, however, he gave them the amount posted on his original flyers and not the amount in our private agreement. Whatever the cost, I'd never be able to get past that rabid guard dog to collect it."

"His German Shepherd?" Guy asked.

"No, his wife."

Guy laughed. "Why don't I act as your Archie Goodwin? Let me do your legwork. She's not concerned I might seduce her husband."

"Be my guest, but don't say I didn't warn you. She can be vicious and full of unpleasant surprises."

While they addressed dealing with Basil's irritable spouse, she digressed. "You rescued Sir Henry from the pound, I hope."

"The big furry monster gave my roommate quite a surprise when he trotted through our front door."

"How did you get him home?"

"Took a cab both ways. If I waited to buy a sidecar, it might've been curtains for the poor pup. Seems like they put animals down over there."

"I didn't enjoy balancing on the back of your scooter." Babs reached into her pocketbook. "If I advance your salary, would this be enough to pay for a used sidecar or a rental? Sir Henry needs to go to a vet, and I never had time to take him."

Guy thanked her and said he'd look into what options were available.

Meanwhile, Weatherwax called asking about Asta's status. Babs didn't want to get into a song and dance about having to continue the hunt on her own because of her short-lived separation from her partner. Summing it up, she said she had a hot lead, but the timing would have to be perfect to make her next move.

"The producers and I are having a stand-off. They want to reassign the actors to a different project. Others, like me, want to plow ahead with our original plans. Tomorrow, we'll start screen tests on the next *Thin Man* installment."

Weatherwax explained the studio heads pressured the producers to use a replacement. Not only did he have concerns the substitute's performance wouldn't be equal to Asta's, but the dog wasn't identical. He worried others could tell the difference. "I'd like you to come to the studio and see for yourself. Maybe your presence will convince the producers to stall the production."

She accepted his invitation. Guy agreed to meet her at the soundstage after making a stop at the Rathbones' to collect the reward.

* * *

Babs taxied over to the studio in Culver City. A busy hair and makeup team surrounded Myrna Loy and fussed over constant adjustments. Powell found all the hustle and bustle boring and sat off on the side reading the *LA Times*.

Weatherwax was working out positioning and camera angles with the director of photography, so he could hide offscreen and still be within the dog's eyeline to give commands. They were about to roll some test footage when a woman wearing a groomer's smock rushed toward them, holding a wire-haired Fox Terrier looking almost identical to Asta. She held on to her dog's leash while he gave the dog a quick inspection.

"I hope no one pays attention to what's under her tail and realizes this one's a female," he said with a laugh. "Otherwise, she looks passable, but the actual proof will be when we see how she behaves."

Babs came in for a closer view. "Is this the dog you're trying to swap out for Asta?" With Myrna out of earshot, she considered asking if this was the same look-alike she used to deceive the audience at the Beverly Hills Dog Show, but tact was critical.

"Our director suggested makeup or a non-toxic impermanent dye on her fur," Weatherwax explained.

The groomer took out an atomizer and spritzed a light spray of water on the dog. "Look!"

The temporary dye ran and stained Weatherwax's arms. He shook his head and handed the dog back. "Tell *Mr. One-Take Woody* I won't even waste my time testing her ability to perform tricks."

Babs asked if he had heard anything connected to dogs and the *Queen Mary*.

He shooed her away. "What does that have to do with our next production?"

She was curious whether dogs like Asta or Toto might feel antagonistic toward their captors. Weatherwax was too busy and no longer gave her his attention.

* * *

Guy's detour to Bel Air caused his delay. He bumped into Renfro again on the studio lot as he tried to catch up with Babs. This time, Renfro wrestled with a determined Pit Bull Terrier, who insisted he was in charge.

"Hey, you…Mr. Detective guy," Renfro called out. "Sorry. Forgot your name."

"Guy Brandt. What's up?"

"Did you ever follow up with that dame looking for dogs?"

From his prior experience with the monkey, Guy stood beyond the dog's range. "My partner and I checked her out. Don't know why she'd need our services or anyone else's. She had more animals than Noah's Ark."

Renfro's dog seemed to be the one in control. "Oh, I wouldn't know. Was hoping the hot tip might pay off."

Guy backed up to make even more distance. "Looks like you've got a little rascal."

"Actually, I do. He's Petey the Pup from *The Little Rascals*. Retired, for the most part, and without his makeup."

"I wondered if he'd been born with the cute little circle around his eye, or if they faked it."

"Most don't recognize him without it," Renfro explained. "Someone needs to keep watch on our former doggy star. Bunch of folks coming to me asking about pit bulls and other aggressive dogs. Petey's a gentle fellow. Many are not."

Guy caught up with Babs as she was about to leave. He'd encountered the wrath of the Rathbones while trying to retrieve their reward. Ouida gave him a tempestuous welcome and ordered him off their property.

Chapter Twenty-Seven: The Unexpected

At eight days and counting, the detectives needed to brainstorm. Babs felt more confident now that she wasn't solving this case alone.

"Take out your notepad. What do we know so far?" Thoughts popped into her head. "The basics: she—the countess—loves showing off. She's obsessed with fur, that's clear from her wardrobe. Regarding Renfro... Guy, did you ever hear from him?"

"Bumped into him at MGM. Gave me that lead about von Rache, but she laughed him off. According to the information I found at the library, he's much more established than he claimed."

Babs continued. "Velma's love of animals appeared genuine, but she evaded our questions."

"Yet, she showed sympathy by fixing your broken shoe," Guy added. "Maybe this was just a chance to size us up. Wouldn't you think she had enough for a dame who said she didn't own a dog?"

"She acquired a lot in a brief span of time," said Babs.

"Let's suppose whoever has been stealing dogs has no connection with the countess," Guy said. "As a hopeful actor, I want to give her credit for all the charitable things she's done in the film and theatrical community."

Babs: "Have you forgotten all about my arrest and interrogation by the FBI? They've also had her under surveillance."

Guy: "Sounds like they've got tabs on everybody in town with a questionable accent."

Babs: "If von Rache is so innocent, how would that explain finding Leo on her property?"

Guy: "I'm not so sure Myrna Loy is off the hook. She's been less than cooperative since we met her."

Babs: "Unless William Powell's excessive friendliness is hiding a deception, neither the Easts, Weatherwax, nor Strickling has been able to clue me in to any pertinent information about what happened on the days their star-studded mascots vanished."

* * *

Babs took the newspaper and got comfortable on her couch. Ever since Sir Henry entered their lives, Guy got into the habit of bringing him to the office every day. The loyal mutt rested his head on Babs' lap while she paged through the *Times*.

"Sir Henry," she said while scratching his head. "Did you know the price of gas is up to eleven cents a gallon?"

He just panted and slobbered. Guy replied instead. "Glad I don't have to refill my tank as often with a motorcycle. When are you going to consider getting your own car?"

She opened the paper to the page with expensive automobile ads, shook her head, and closed it right away. "When we get our reward and don't have to worry about giving anything back if we don't make our deadline."

An unexpected visitor appeared at B. Norman Investigations. "I hope I'm not disturbing you," William Powell said.

He entered with his hat and coat in one hand and a dozen pink roses in the other. "I'd hate for these posies to wilt long before their shelf life. With such a pretty lady on the premises, I suppose you receive flowers all the time and must have an appropriate vase."

At such a taxing time, Babs needed to hear a few kind words. In the private eye business, surprises meant guns or knives. Not the gift a suitor would present as a token of affection, or one a satisfied client would deliver with a thank-you note. She tucked into her office and reemerged, improvising with her emptied trash can, the contents of which she stuffed inside her desk drawers.

"Silly me, I broke the one I had…from Tiffany's," she said, concocting a story. "This'll have to make do. Please excuse me while I fill it with water."

Babs took the roses out of their wrapping and did her best to arrange them with finesse.

"Shouldn't you be doing more rehearsals this afternoon?"

Powell tried to explain. "A dog swap on such short notice was nothing shy of a disaster. MGM muckety-mucks, who had the final say-so on production, put a halt on our project. Until we can find a better solution, they decided Myrna's and my next film will be *I Love You Again* instead of *Shadow of the Thin Man*.

"The problem is…I love that pup. Almost consider him like a son. You know both Myrna and I have fought over buying him from his owners."

"They told us several times," said Babs.

"Let me assure you I didn't steal him because I wanted him for myself." He reached for his wallet, counted out a stack of bills in a neat pile on Guy's desk. "It's not just money. Anything, within reason, of course, I can do to assist you in his recovery."

He scribbled something on a piece of paper and handed it to Guy. "Please call me. Any time." Powell headed out the door.

"Wait! Before you go," Babs shouted. "I have to ask you a question."

"What's that, my lovely?"

"You're plugged into Hollywood stuff, which we outsiders don't always know about. Any secrets you're hiding about the *Queen Mary*?"

Powell delivered a quick comeback. "Was I supposed to be having an affair with her? If so, nobody told me about it."

It took everything Babs had not to laugh out loud. "The *RMS Queen Mary*. The famous ocean liner… Do you know anything…anything at all kept from the public?"

Powell shrugged. "I'm one of the last fools to be kept in the loop. Why don't you call them and find out? Look, I must be going. Bring back Asta and put the cash to better use than blowing it at the racetrack."

The glass in their front door rattled as he slammed it behind. The detectives were at an impasse. Babs gave it her best shot to beautify her bouquet, even in her wastepaper basket.

"Babs," Guy called to her attention, "I hope you haven't overlooked the obvious."

"About making phone calls?" She groaned. "More than I care to admit. Including the newspapers. If there's something happening, everyone's buried it far away in Poughkeepsie. Perhaps you should try."

Puzzled at first, it took a second for Guy to catch on. "You've always had a more seductive phone manner. When prying for information, strangers are more likely to cooperate with you, not with me."

"Maybe the FBI circulated a memorandum, and I'm on some kind of watch list, 'cause whatever I've been doing, it's not working, and Guy... What's this about a racetrack? You almost quit for good because I kept secrets from you. Is there something you're not telling me?"

Chapter Twenty-Eight: "Doctor Watson, I presume."

D ay seven. With a copy of *Variety* in hand, Babs demanded Guy's attention.

"*Bingo!* Finally, someone mentions something about the *RMS Queen Mary*! There's talk about drafting the *Queen Mary* and the *RMS Mauretania* ocean liner to be put into service as troop carriers. Have you heard of the latter?"

"The *Mauretania* is a sister ship of the *RMS Aquitania* and the *Lusitania*, the famous one the Germans sank, which caused the U.S. involvement in WWI," he replied.

"Aren't you worried if our president declares war, you might get drafted?"

"Babs, if the army drafted me and I had no choice about the matter, it wouldn't be the worst thing to travel on one of those luxury cruise ships."

She needed a windfall once in a while and treated herself to a second chocolate éclair and a fresh cup of coffee. "Listen up. I think I might've found another useful lead. Here's an article about plans for Basil Rathbone and Nigel Bruce to do a fundraiser. They'll perform in a Sherlock Holmes-themed radio show—on the *Queen Mary*. There's more. It says William Powell and Myrna Loy will also do a radio drama based on the *Thin Man* films."

"They have a recording studio?" Guy asked.

She read the article out loud. "It started out as a music studio with a grand piano near the Observation Bar back in '36. On the floor are clef signs and music notes inlaid on the customized wood floor. They'll broadcast these shows at a later date, because it's not yet capable of producing live radio broadcasts."

"I guess they don't want to interfere with the ship's radio frequencies, but who am I to say? Sounds fancy-dancy to me. Does it mention a date?" Guy asked.

"Looks like it's happening in five days. The *Queen Mary's* usual route is between New York and Southampton, England. They're docking in Long Beach for repairs and renovations pending its next long journey. Soon, it's scheduled to sail to Sydney to carry Australian and New Zealand soldiers to Britain."

She continued to skim through the article. "They'll be filming a documentary. Their guest list includes cast from *Gone With the Wind*, Mae West, Bette Davis, and some of *The Wizard of Oz* crowd."

"Toto is on our missing canines list," he said.

"We have to figure out a way to get onboard."

"Babs, don't expect to get an invitation from the Rathbones."

"Are you a detective or not? Contact the Screen Actors Guild. Find out who Nigel Bruce's agent is and call him."

"How should we present ourselves?" asked Guy.

She retrieved the press badges from her desk they used for the dog show. "These are generic and should work. We're journalists working for a new publication—the first issue, but he must keep it a secret and tell no one, since we've chosen to interview him before Basil."

"On what angle?" he asked.

"Somewhere, I read, he's got royal blood in his lineage, and that's why he's got first dibs."

"What'll be the name of this publication, Babs?"

"*American Sherlock Holmes*—ASH, for short. Why not? Their main office will be out of New York, like most magazines, but we're the local columnists covering the Hollywood beat. Sounds plausible, right? Now go to it!"

* * *

Later that afternoon, Guy arranged for them to meet with Nigel Bruce at the Hollywood Cricket Club, an upscale retreat for former members of the British Empire transplanted to Southern California. Lucky for them, Nigel knew that Basil, also a member and cricket player, was otherwise engaged, with no chance of him interrupting their secretive meeting.

He popped a roll of film in his Rolleiflex camera. "Just so you know, I had to promise Mr. Bruce a real photo session, not a faked one."

"Whatever it takes. Consider yourself a better actor than you've given yourself credit," said Babs. "At least you mentioned it would be in our magazine's first issue. That would cover our tracks in case he expected us to give him a sample back issue on such short notice."

Guy was too embarrassed to drive his motorcycle with Babs sitting in his new sidecar, so the two detectives arrived by taxi. The moment the cabbie dropped them off, she spotted Laurence Olivier helping Joan Fontaine get out a Rolls-Royce Wraith.

"Hide your camera," Babs warned her partner.

"Did you think I was going to ask for their autographs or expect them to pose for our phony publication?" he asked.

Babs announced their arrival at the front desk. While the concierge went to find Mr. Bruce, Guy peered into their guest book.

"Ah...Boris Karloff, David Niven, Olivia de Havilland, Elsa Lanchester ...they've all visited. Looks like they've had both the Frankenstein monster and his bride as guests."

The club's gatekeeper returned, and Guy closed the sign-in register.

"He's in the garden enjoying afternoon tea and requests you join him there. Said something about it being a conducive backdrop for photographs. Please, follow me."

The concierge led the detectives behind the clubhouse. Babs braced herself to admit something embarrassing.

"Mr. Bruce, you'll probably recognize me as the woman from Basil's party who peeked, by accident, inside your cabana while you were dressing. Once again, I have to apologize for my actions."

"Please call me Nigel, and for heaven's sake, I can't seem to recall the incident, but that's neither here nor there. I enjoy a surprise once in a while. Breaks up the monotony and predictability of life. Please sit down. Order whatever you like. It's all on me." He snapped his fingers for a waiter.

"That's very gracious of you, sir," Guy said, making his introduction. "This is the first time I've been to the Hollywood Cricket Club. How do you like it?"

"We Brits are birds of a feather, and we like to flock together. We enjoy the same humor, the same food and drink, and often the same pastimes, like cricket and rugby rather than baseball. Although everyone enjoys golf on both sides of the pond."

He made one of his signature on-screen chuckles to himself. "In a town that's full of artifice and theatrical hijinks, it's refreshing to get a taste of home every so often."

Nigel knocked over his cane by accident. Guy picked it up and handed it back. "For my leg wound from the bloody first war. Just like the fictional Doctor Watson, except it confined me to a wheelchair afterward."

"You've bounced back, however," Guy said.

"Did so back in 1919, following my discharge. Took ten years after that for my lucky break on Broadway. The theatrical production of *Springtime for Henry* in '31 led to reprising the same role on film in '34. That was my entrée into the lovable, bumbling British fool most people know me for."

"You did a string of films before partnering with Basil for *The Hound of the Baskervilles*, correct?" Babs asked.

"Yes, and last year in '39, don't forget to mention we did two Sherlock Holmes films, *Hound* and *The Adventures of Sherlock Holmes*, for Fox. However, I'm afraid Sir Arthur Conan Doyle wouldn't approve of my performance."

"In what way?" asked Guy.

"His Doctor Watson is a much cleverer individual. I'm afraid he'd be rather upset with my portrayal as more of a comic relief or a companionable sidekick rather than a contributor to solving Holmes' cases about crime."

"I wouldn't put yourself down," Guy said. "The box office receipts speak for themselves."

"So true, I guess. I shocked some of my critics when they discovered my family comes from a line of British aristocracy. For my formal education back in England, I attended the Grange School in Stevenage and Abingdon School in Abingdon-on-Thames. By the way, most people don't know my full name is William Nigel Ernle Bruce. Close friends often call me Willie. If you didn't know already, despite my gray hair, Basil and I are only three years apart, and he's the elder."

Their host enjoyed talking about himself, and as observed by the detectives, he also talked to himself.

"Overall, life has been good, and it has blessed me with a marvelous career, which I hope will continue. Enough about my boring life. How can I help you?"

Guy cleared his throat. "We heard you and Basil will do a radio show on the *Queen Mary.*"

"Indeed, we will. Not a live broadcast, mind you, but a recording to be aired later on many radio stations all over the States. Maybe in England as well. Soon, the *Queen* will transport troops to the Land Down Under. This is part publicity and part fundraiser for the Allied war effort and to boost the soldiers' morale."

"My partner and I need to get on board the evening of your performance," Guy said, "But we can't ask Basil for an invitation."

"Bear with me if this comes out awkward—" Babs tried to hold her teacup steady, but her hand shook.

More sure of himself, Guy took over. "Look, I called your agent to arrange this meeting. I must confess, we weren't entirely upfront about being journalists."

Nigel appeared upset and sat up straight.

"Please hear us out," Guy said.

Babs could see by the look on Nigel's face, this situation needed a feminine touch. "Nigel, we're private investigators. Basil had hired us to recover Leo, and that's why you saw us at his party."

"Who I heard someone found," Nigel said.

"Thanks to Babs' bravery and substantial risk," Guy said.

"Along with a night in jail," she added. "No matter whose version of the story you heard, Basil's wife has been at my throat. He and I are no longer on speaking terms."

"This isn't the first instance where she gave an alluring young lady a hard time," Nigel said.

"Gee, thanks," said Babs. "All the same, we can't pose as journalists as long as Basil and his wife are present. Ouida will make sure we get the boot."

Nigel took a pause. "What are you planning to do?"

"We think someone will commit a crime, behind the scenes, while everyone else is celebrating," Guy said.

"Who's hiring you?"

"Quite a few people connected with Metro-Goldwyn-Mayer," Babs replied.

Guy cut in. "Babs, we might as well come clean with Mr. Bruce and tell him we also suspect the people behind this are the ones who stole Basil's dog. Although we recovered his Cocker Spaniel, two other high-profile dogs we know of are missing: Asta from the *Thin Man* films, and Toto from *The Wizard of Oz*. There might be even more."

"Oh my," Nigel exclaimed. "That's awful. But let me get this straight. Are you asking Basil and I to play Holmes and Watson upfront to the public while you assume their roles, or your roles as detectives behind the scenes?"

Babs cracked a cunning smile. "Could be one way of looking at it, but I need a buffer or distraction, so Ouida doesn't find out."

"I guess I can have my wife keep her occupied. There must be a spa or a pool or bowling alley onboard. I'll check into it if you like."

"Making sure she has a few strong drinks wouldn't hurt either," Babs said.

"Meanwhile, my partner and I will figure out what to do on our end," said Guy. "If you can get us on the invite list, even if we have to go under assumed names and physical disguises to get past security, at least we'll get onboard."

"Do you mind me giving you my opinion as, *uh hum*...Doctor Watson?" Nigel asked.

Guy and Babs looked at each other.

She answered, "Why not?"

"Have you considered since no one demanded a ransom or other compensation, whoever is behind these abductions has no intentions of returning the dogs? Basil's dog knows how to sit and stay, but he's not trained in the same capacity as Asta. How are they comparable?"

"Leo is a top-notch purebred dog, and he's owned by a well-known actor," said Guy.

Nigel nodded, and Babs continued. "Maybe the dognappers plan on selling them to the highest bidder? I can't believe none of us, not even the police, have come up with that possibility until now."

"What would they do? Hide the stolen dogs in their house?" Nigel asked. "You'd think their neighbors would turn them in. After all, there's a hefty reward."

"I agree," Babs said. "What if they smuggled them out of town? The dogs would be impossible to track, and I bet there are plenty of wealthy buyers who'd love to own a piece of Hollywood, even if they can't be upfront and brag about it. A dog star from the movies? Another purebred owned by a popular star? There could be a significant demand."

She needed to think of something fast. "Are you a dog lover, Mr. Bruce?"

"Why, of course, I adore dogs. In fact, my agent handed me a script where I'll play a rich baronet who shows dogs. The character is heartless but makes a turnaround in the end. Quite the opposite of the sort of fellow I am in real life, but the script looks like it might be a winner."

Nigel gave a sigh of relief. "We might be on to something." He pulled a whiskey flask out of his jacket and poured some into his tea. Without even bothering to ask, he poured a generous amount into Guy's and Babs'.

The booze rushed to her head. "Pretty please? For the love of dogs?"

Raising his cup, Nigel made a toast. "By George, for the love of dogs!"

152

Chapter Twenty-Nine: Arresting Circumstances

S ix days until the radio show, and everything would need to go like clockwork. Blueprints for the *Queen Mary* lay on Babs' desk. Guy's cluttered work area now included dog toys, since Sir Henry was their new unofficial partner. Even Wiggins, their janitor, fell in love with their mascot and made a point of bringing him extra knuckle bones from his butcher.

Everyone was on edge, including their mutt, who moped about the office as the detectives were running in their own circles. Basil's on-screen partner and long-time friend, Nigel Bruce, promised the detectives he'd get them on the guest list. They could only hope he and his wife, Violet, would devise the perfect plan to distract Mrs. Rathbone. Babs still had to figure out how to make a truce with Basil. Meanwhile, the detectives needed to decide what guises to assume in order to operate incognito.

Guy groomed his furry friend. "I want to bring Sir Henry."

"Here, we are worried about getting in, and you want to sneak an enormous dog onboard?" Babs asked.

"You said he could track scents better than a K-9 police dog."

"True, but—"

"The *Queen Mary* is a colossal ship. It will be crowded with partygoers and who knows how many crew members, and we'll be hunting for other dogs."

"How do you expect to pull it off?" she asked.

"What if I posed as a blind man, and Sir Henry was my seeing-eye dog?"

Babs tried not to burst out laughing. "Sounds farfetched. Aren't most seeing eye dogs German Shepherds? Not mixed breeds like our lovable mutt."

Sir Henry lowered his head and whimpered.

Guy reassured him with a pat on the head. "I'll make up some kind of excuse. Like he scored higher on their obedience tests than any of the others. He seemed more suited for search and rescue than Officer Hope's dog."

"Woof!" Sir Henry agreed. He rolled over and begged for a vigorous rubdown.

"If I wear a pair of dark-tinted welder goggles that wrap around on the sides, no one will know my eyes are open, and I can still see like a normal person," Guy explained. "Then I'll carry a cane and do a few practice runs with Sir Henry, but I'll need a credible profession. Nothing that'll depend on sight, but posing as someone who has a keen sense of hearing."

"Like a music critic for our fictitious *American Sherlock Holmes* magazine? After all, whoever's sponsoring the event will promote a radio show."

Guy grabbed a sheet of paper and sketched the idea forming in his head. "Add a bit of gray to make me older—"

He arranged excess dog hair from Sir Henry's wire comb on his drawing to create a fake goatee and glued it down before showing the illustration to Babs.

"Can't grow this type of facial hair to save my life, but I think we'll wind up with a distinguished gentleman who looks nothing like me."

Sir Henry gave him another "woof" of approval, and Babs laughed. "All right, you've got your disguise. How about I pull off a slick Jean Harlow number?"

"With a platinum blonde wig and a slinky, sexy dress?" Guy asked. "You don't plan on plucking your eyebrows, or do you?"

"I'll have to make do with what I was born with. We'll just have to forewarn Nigel and his wife in case my disguise is too convincing. Not the best getup to hide a weapon, but there's always my purse if it's large enough."

"Since when do you need—"

Sir Henry barked a warning before Guy could finish his sentence. No clever disguise would save Babs from the one person she hoped to avoid at all costs—Troy Ulsterman, who walked through their front door unannounced.

Babs needed to appear brave on the outside, even if her stomach was doing flip-flops.

"I told you to get lost!" she shouted.

Guy came to her defense, but with a clumsy delivery. "You're not wanted here, ever. Go back from wherever you came—Oakland, or Monkey Island at the San Francisco Zoo—the gorilla cage, you big ape! So quit swinging on vines on Hollywood and Vine. You're no Tarzan, and she's no Jane."

Troy stepped forward and forced their door shut. "What you need is to have some sense talked into you," he said, addressing Babs.

She was defiant. "Don't you suppose it should be the other way around?"

"A wife is supposed to obey her husband."

Guy stepped between Babs and the beast. "What kind of malarky is that?"

Single-handedly, Troy flung him aside. Guy fell on the floor, slamming his head against her desk.

"I'm not your wife anymore and have divorce papers to prove it!" Babs yelled. "Now, scram!"

Guy rubbed his head and struggled to sit upright. "Our mutt has more sense than this cad. He understands our commands."

Babs took her handgun from her desk drawer and pointed it at Troy.

"Guy, quick! Call the cops on your phone."

Troy ridiculed her. "Hardy-har-har... You don't have the guts to fire that weapon. I've seen how you are with animals. You couldn't hurt a tick—or a flea—or whatever's the saying."

"You wanna bet?" She fired a hole into the trashcan holding the roses that William Powell had given her. Water poured out, and a puddle formed on the floor.

Troy lunged for Babs and tried to seize her gun.

"Do something!" she shouted to her partner.

Guy scooted toward the door. "Come on, boy. Attack!"

Sir Henry sprang forth and gripped Troy's leg between his teeth.

Wiggins overheard the commotion and stormed in from cleaning the hallway. Seeing the brute wrestling with Sir Henry on the floor, he planted his boot on Troy's back and pinned his head in place with his wet, soapy mop.

The police arrived, cuffed Troy, and hauled him to jail.

Chapter Thirty: The Game's Afoot

The Rathbones' feisty Bull Terrier found a new boyfriend. She fell in love with Toby, the Scottish Terrier owned by Jack Stewart, who came to the rescue when a motorist ran Basil off the road and into rosebushes. Since then, every time Basil passed his house during their walks, she'd insist he pay a visit. When Jack confessed how much he enjoyed Basil's swashbuckling films, he invited him to join him for fencing lessons. His private instructor turned out to be Ralph B. Faulkner, a former Olympic champion and Basil's fencing master on *Captain Blood*. Soon, these sessions became a regular habit, forging a friendship through kismet.

Basil and Jack, both wearing traditional fencing gear, practiced on their own while waiting for their instructor's arrival. Their two dogs flirted like lovers, with Judy taking on the role of the aggressor.

"The lady calls the shots," Jack joked. He wiped off his neck with his handkerchief and reached for his glass of iced tea.

"Seems to be the same way in my household," Basil remarked, in part tongue-in-cheek. "Anyway, I've always preferred taking the dogs all together. Saves time," Basil explained. "Judy must have a sixth sense and wants nothing of it. If she suspects I'll pass this way, she'll want to monopolize the opportunity and be the only one accompanying me. She insists on having playtime with Toby all to herself."

They barely had time to catch their breath when their instructor *du jour* came walking down the driveway.

In respect, Basil greeted him with a deep bow. "My word—the *maestro* himself!"

"Of course, you know Frederic Cavens," Jack said. "Too busy to make house calls to teach us peons, but today's an exception."

"What did we do to warrant such an honor?" Basil asked.

"Your teacher had a family emergency," said Cavens. "I promised I'd step in and substitute, but just for the day."

"Did you sample the bottle of Scotch I sent you?" asked Basil.

Jack interrupted, in part to taunt them. "Is there something going on I don't know about?"

"Something I've asked him to keep secret," Cavens explained. "I've started training Basil for one of his next films. The studio's original title was *The Californian*, but you know how everything changes in this industry.

"Everyone wants their say-so. Between producers, directors, publicists, and screenwriters, and the original novelist where the script adaptation came from, I suspect its title will change to *The Mark of Zorro*. Basil needs to be in tip-top shape. Don't want our young whippersnapper to turn him into a shish kebab."

Jack couldn't follow their conversation. "Who's that, may I ask?"

Cavens pointed to Tyrone Power, already dressed in his fencing attire, with mask and foil in hand. "The gallant gentleman joining us right now."

"We're all going to practice together?" Jack asked.

"Why not? But beware, Tyrone is turning into a worthy opponent," replied Cavens.

"A great honor, no less," said Jack.

Cavens addressed the two actors. "Even though official production hasn't started yet, I've seen your preliminary test footage. What a remarkable performance! You kept a perfect distance the entire time. I loved the part when Tyrone lunged into the bookcase, breaking its glass—a good example of destroying the set for effect." He turned to Jack and explained, "We've wanted this sword fight to be so perfect that we've hired cameramen to document it for training."

"It's always refreshing when my adversary isn't an amateur," said Basil.

"Don't want to reveal too much before the film hits the theaters, but my son Albert will perform Tyrone's more dangerous stunts," said Cavens.

Power remained modest. Cavens continued his praise. "That being said, Tyrone has proved to be the most agile man with a sword I've ever faced before a camera. Far better than Errol Flynn."

Jack asked, "Do you expect your project to be better than the earlier film where Douglas Fairbanks played Zorro?"

"That remains to be seen," Basil replied. "As long as audiences crave these kinds of movies, the bar for such performances will continue to be raised. Enough of the accolades. Shall we carry on?"

* * *

A female Basset Hound ambled in from the neighboring yard. Judy and Toby ran from their play area and cut a path between the fencers. Jack withdrew his sword, almost striking Judy before he stepped backward. Basil leapt onto a piece of lawn furniture. For someone whom the instructor praised as being quick on his feet, Tyrone stumbled over a lawn ornament.

Judy continued to bark at the intruder until she alerted its owner, who scooped up the hound in his arms, apologized, and promptly left.

Jack made light of it. "Judy is rather possessive, don't you think? Looks like she wants my Scotty all to herself."

Basil's response, somewhat bittersweet. "Comparable to my wife."

"A handsome gentleman like you?" Jack asked. "How could she not sense competition might lurk around the bend?"

"I guess you're right," said Basil, "But living with it year in and year out gets tiring."

Tyrone joined in on the laughter. "Isn't that why they call them the opposite sex? Care for some manly advice?"

"Words of wisdom are like pearls from the ocean," Basil said.

"Then listen up, Sherlock," said Tyrone, "Because you'll need all hands on deck."

Basil's wife sallied forth at a quick pace, holding the rest of their dogs on leashes and with a stern scowl on her face.

Basil rose. "Dearest, what's the matter?"

159

"Someone called. Several times, in fact. He said he must speak with you right away."

"Didn't you take a message?" Basil asked.

"He refused to leave one. Said it was confidential."

"He didn't leave a number?"

She shook her head. "Maybe you should give Nigel a ring. He might know what's so urgent. My guess is it has something to do with your next Sherlock Holmes project."

The dogs tugged at their leashes, pulling tiny Ouida behind.

"Unhook them, dear," Basil said. "No sense preventing them from playing with Judy and Toby."

He helped her release the dogs. All ran off in another direction when Cavens tossed a ball.

Ouida looked at the four fencers. "It doesn't appear like you're practicing. What kind of conversation did I interrupt?"

"We had a rigorous workout until another bitch wandered into our yard," said Tyrone.

Basil observed the radical change on his wife's face.

"That's a crude and disgusting term to call a woman," she replied.

"A female Basset Hound, to be exact," Basil clarified. "Judy became overprotective of Toby and wouldn't let the newcomer get away with it."

Ouida turned red. "Then, pardon me. I assumed—"

Basil finished her sentence. "Your devoted husband had eyes for another lady. Shame on you! How many years have we been married? You've been even more clingy since we had our baby daughter."

Ouida bowed her head. "Please don't rub it in."

Basil asked for the time. He gave his wife a kiss and said, "I think our session has ended, anyway. Cavens, always a pleasure. Tyrone, I'd suggest ice for the nasty bruise you'll discover tomorrow. Jack, once again, thank you for your hospitality. I hate to put an end to our dogs' fun, but, Ouida, let's round them up and head home."

Chapter Thirty-One: Dinner at Eight

"Dinner at Chasen's?" asked an unidentified man on the other end of the office line.

Is this some kind of joke? "Since when can I afford to eat at one of LA's most expensive restaurants? Who is this?" asked Babs.

"'Tis Powell, mademoiselle."

"Pardon me for not recognizing your voice right away."

"I'm inviting you and your right-hand man to meet me there at eight. My treat, of course. If I were a woman, I'd assume I was pregnant, but I'm having this terrible craving for their famous chili and can't shake it off."

He's such a prankster. "Not that I don't enjoy a fine meal when offered, but Guy and I are running out of time to recover the stolen dogs. Our plans are far from solidifying."

"Have you narrowed it down?"

"Can't say yet."

"Now I need to make amends," said Powell.

"For what?"

"Rathbone approached me about joining forces in your dog hunt, but I pulled out for personal reasons. However, I'm the one who suggested he bring you as his date to the Coconut Grove. If I hadn't made that blunder, the two of you would still be on speaking terms...but you've always had Guy to rely on. Correct?"

"Not after my picture wound up in the tabloids. Until he sprang me from jail, I was on my own, and the main reason we're so behind schedule. Speaking about trust, I'm not so sure about your partner."

"Not my wife?"

"Myrna...Mrs. Charles... Whatever you want to call her."

"Babs, didn't I promise I'd do anything to help?"

"So far, she's done nothing but push us away, which makes us believe she's supporting our adversary."

"Then you need to reach out to her. She sees too much of my ugly mug, both at social events and on-screen. Thus, I require your presence."

"Maybe I'm saying too much, but all along, I've felt she's been hiding something."

"All we can do is give it the good old Boy Scout's try. Girl Scout for you, I guess. I'm the one sticking my neck out and orchestrating this. Will you join us?"

"I don't know. Guy and I can't afford to take the night off. If we screw up this operation because we're unprepared—"

"A gal's gotta eat, right? How much more persuasive do I have to get?"

"Fair enough."

"One more thing. Don't forget; dress snazzy for the occasion."

* * *

Babs still had to run home to change into proper attire when the phone rang again.

"Nigel here. I think I found your solution."

"Please make it quick."

"Someone just delivered the script for the Sherlock Holmes radio play. Basil and I will read selections from *The Hound of the Baskervilles*. Not the entire story, but an excellent choice. We just released the movie and are already familiar with it. Short-sighted, for sure, but no one considered the need for voice actors for the other parts. The producer who adapted this version insisted Basil, and I only read for Holmes and Watson, as expected. He suggested Tyrone Power handle the other younger male parts, such as Sir Henry Baskerville and John Stapleton. For the older male voices like Dr. Mortimer, Barryman, and the coroner, he wanted Groucho Marx. When he wants to, Groucho's capable of being a serious actor."

"What about the female roles?" Babs asked.

"That's where I stepped in and insisted they hire a talented young actress by the name of Eileen Adlon."

"Who's she? Sounds almost identical to the Holmes character of Irene Adler."

"Why you, of course, and yes, I made that up—on purpose."

"Well, before I moved to Los Angeles, I used to sing jingles for radio commercials. From time to time, they'd ask me to take part in a radio play or allow me to serenade with a live orchestra."

"Fantastic, then you have radio experience."

"Why should Sherlock—I mean Basil want to cooperate? After all, I found his dog. He has nothing more at stake and everything to lose by getting involved."

"He'll comply because I say so. He can't play Holmes without his Doctor Watson, and that's settled. Besides, he'd do nothing so low as to walk out on his obligation. Any anger toward you, even if it appears to come from him, comes from his wife. I'd bet on it. Doll yourself up like a femme fatale, and you'll fit right in. Besides, my wife said she'd collaborate with Groucho to keep Ouida occupied. You'll be free to do whatever you need to do."

"Funny you mentioned a femme fatale. I planned to disguise myself to look like Jean Harlow."

* * *

Guy and Babs took separate cabs to Beverly Hills and met out front under Chasen's awning.

She gave her partner an inspection. "Don't you look spiffy this evening?"

"How did you rustle up that *très chic* get-up on such short notice?" he asked.

"Being a common size can be helpful when modeling but can work to my disadvantage when picking up something last-minute from a secondhand store. Those are the first sizes to disappear. Since I needed something right away, my dry cleaner lent me a dress, which had been in his shop for a while, and no one claimed."

"Convenient. He can always clean it again in case it gets soiled."

"Not all stains come out. Red wine is notorious."

The maître 'd led the detectives to where William Powell and Myrna Loy were already enjoying cocktails at a high-backed leather upholstered booth too large for four diners. They scooted toward the middle to hear each other better.

"You'd think whoever made the seating arrangements misjudged how many members are in our party," Babs said.

"No mistake at all," said Powell. "I invited a guest who should join us any moment."

"I hope it wasn't J. Edgar Hoover," Guy said. "I thought I recognized him sitting at a table eating Chasen's famous Hobo Steak."

Babs shuddered. "Head of the FBI? What's he doing here? After my arrest, the Feds grilled me like I was a juicy sirloin."

"Honey, he comes here all the time," Myrna said. "Maybe he likes to keep Hitchcock under observation. You never know. He might use his movies to cover up real crimes."

Powell leaned closer to Babs. "Don't listen to her. Hoover's here because he enjoys the food. Simple as that, but you know…I should order a bottle of champagne."

"William," Myrna said, "Shouldn't you wait for your guest? Open it now, and it'll get flat."

"Well, I'm as dry as Death Valley," said Powell. "What's everyone drinking in the meantime?"

Babs thought about her borrowed outfit. "Maybe someone can recommend a Chablis, though not my usual choice."

"Be more imaginative," Guy said. "Celebrate the occasion with a cocktail."

"All right. I'll go with a sidecar." Babs gave him a wink, knowing he just purchased a sidecar for his new motorcycle.

Every time a group of notable personalities passed by their table, William Powell lifted his chin and acknowledged their presence with a smile, a nod, or a peculiar glance.

When asked, he explained, "That's what I call giving them the eye."

A dazzling woman whom Babs didn't recognize waltzed across the room. This time, he exaggerated his response, raising his eyebrows up and down and sucking in his lips with all sorts of clownish mimicry.

Babs tried not to laugh too hard. "You look like you're trying to pick up on someone's scent. Like a dog."

Myrna took out her compact and powdered her nose. "William, come on. Who's your mystery guest?"

"He'll be here soon enough. If you're so anxious, why don't you order another drink?"

"But I don't want another drink. I've had enough already."

Powell explained to the detectives, "It's a tough act when the public always expects you to act like Nick and Nora." He turned to Myrna. "Order one anyway and pretend you're drinking it."

William Powell tilted his chin upward and gave that *look* to signal his surprise guest had arrived. "Babs Norman, Guy Brandt, please have the pleasure of meeting the one...the only...Dashiell Hammett, the visionary genius behind the *Thin Man* films."

Hammett kissed Babs' hand, but surprised everyone when he said, "Are you going to behave? I don't want a lot of monkey business out of you."

When Myrna asked what that was supposed to mean, Hammett laughed. "Babs and I have already met. Her partner, too. I wanted to get a kick out of everyone's reactions. Besides, any chance to kiss a pretty dame's hand is always welcome."

"Might as well get started on the liquid libations," said Powell. "We delayed placing our dinner orders until you got here."

"If you don't mind holding off, I've also invited a companion," said Hammett. "That's why I insisted you reserve a larger booth."

"Mr. Hammett already knows that a handful of people at MGM hired my partner and me to find Asta," Babs said.

"Where's your Sherlock Holmes friend?" asked Hammett.

"Basil Rathbone had agreed to help us, but reconsidered," she explained.

"To be honest," Guy said, "we had a falling out because of his wife—"

"Who insisted on wearing the pants in the family," Babs replied. "It's unfortunate, but right now, we can't count on his cooperation."

"We're assembling a search and rescue team," Guy said. "We'd love to have your participation. Dashiell, this could also wind up as a hot topic for your next best-selling novel."

Myrna pushed one of her untouched martinis toward Hammett and insisted he put his claim on it. He took a sip and said, "I've been as bad an influence on American literature as anyone I can think of, but I'm wide open to fresh ideas. Right now, I've tired of cranking out the same old detective stuff."

Myrna's stomach made such a growl that all eyes turned toward her. She tapped her fingers on the table and toyed with her silverware.

To kill time, Powell made a joke about Claude Rains' character in the film adaptation of H. G. Wells' *The Invisible Man*. He said to Hammett, "Maybe we should order. For all we know, he's been sitting here the entire time, but we ignored him."

"Didn't he become insane because of a serum he took to make him disappear?" Myrna asked.

"We're waiting for a she, not a he," Hammett replied, "and she's being tardy just to make us sweat."

Babs tried to read into that as she nursed her drink. Guy was already on his second.

William Powell dramatized lines from the film while his friends bided their time. "An invisible man can rule the world. Nobody will see him come, nobody will see him go. He can hear every secret. He can rob, and wreck, and kill!"

"Ah, there she is." Hammett got up to greet his guest and gave her a kiss on the cheek. "Meet my partner-in-crime, Lillian Hellman, who just came in from New York. She's one of the biggest playwrights on Broadway."

"For *The Children's Hour* and *The Little Foxes*," Guy said.

"With many more masterpieces to come," Hammett said with pride.

Lillian gave everyone her greetings and scooted next to him. "I've never met a real lady private detective. I've always pictured gumshoes like the ones Dash makes up."

Babs secured her napkin. "Well, you've met one now."

Powell insisted on sharing a large platter of Chasen's spare ribs. He wouldn't hear anything of it when Babs refused on the grounds they were too messy. After he persuaded her to try them, she got sticky sauce on her borrowed dress and broke down into hysterics.

"Soda water lifts stains," said Myrna. "There'll be no short supply from our bartender. It's always worked when I've spilled stuff on carpets."

She hailed a waiter who fetched a glass. Babs took the miracle solution and headed to the powder room. Her tears caused her makeup to smudge, and she worried that her dress was beyond salvaging. Along the way, someone asked her an outlandish question.

"Ah, a beautiful woman... Will you marry me? Do you have any money? Answer the second question first."

"Well, I—" Without the exaggerated eyebrows and mustache, it took Babs a few seconds to recognize him. "You're Groucho...Groucho Marx."

"Looks like you've been crying. Cheer up. If you find it hard to laugh at yourself, I would be happy to do it for you."

Babs did her best, but the stain refused to come out. She held her napkin in front of her dress to hide the huge wet spot and ran into Groucho again on the way back.

"Next time I see you," he said, "remind me *not* to talk to you."

* * *

Powell made a declaration. "Tonight, we're going to show Holmes and Watson, who are the better detectives. We'll all get to play Nick and Nora Charles, along with the writer who created them."

"I'm game," said Guy. "As long as Babs and I don't have to get married, and Babs, it would do you good to loosen up once in a while." He ordered her another sidecar and insisted she drink it. When she complained about getting drunk, he reminded her who was driving.

"Unlike Nick and Nora," Babs said, "we butt heads more often, rather than glossing over marital trifles."

The detectives needed to ferret out any notions that Myrna was cooperating with the top dog behind the dognappings. If she wasn't, would she agree to take part in taking the thieves down? They had to keep their cards close until one hundred percent certain. They also had to assume any disclosures would be first-time news for Lillian Hellman and, mostly, for Dashiell Hammett.

Halfway through dinner, Babs said, "We're running out of time, and I'm running out of ideas. Has anyone come up with any new leads on finding Asta?"

Myrna languished over her martini olive. "Not yet."

Powell, who was having difficulty not making sewage out of his chili, said, "Soon, our producers will have to make a tough decision."

"Like what?" Lillian asked.

"The studio execs are postponing the next *Thin Man* movie," Myrna said. "They've already prepared a substitute project."

Powell added, "Attempts at finding a replacement have come to naught."

Lillian lit her cigarette. "I've never understood who's in charge if an animal disappears. Is it the police or the city pound?"

"When Basil lost his dog," Guy said, "he hired us because he didn't care for how the city handled those things. My partner found his dog, but—"

"But not using a normal or recommended procedure," Babs said. "Dash, you have a Pinkerton background. Be our mentor. I'd love to hear your input."

Amused, he put his arm around his girlfriend. "So you want to put me to work, and that's why you invited me here? Or am I still being considered as a person of interest?"

Guy shrugged and feigned surprise. "Why would you believe that?"

"Because the movie dog wasn't a Schnauzer like the one in my original novel? You know how bitter authors can get when Hollywood butchers their original creations. Why don't we ask my detective characters for their opinions?"

"Nick and Nora Charles?" Lillian first glanced at her lover and then around the table at the others. "Looks like I came a bit late to the party. Sounds intriguing, but you're going to have to fill me in on this new film project you're planning."

"Sad, but true, it's the real deal," said Guy, who turned to Myrna for answers. "Suppose you were Nora Charles. What would you do to track down Asta?"

She protested. "Don't be ridiculous. I'm not a real detective."

"Use your imagination. As an actress who's starred in many roles, how would your on-screen persona react?"

Myrna gave a telltale upward glance to the ceiling. "My first guess would be to narrow it down to anyone who was nuts about dogs. What about the recent dog show at the Beverly Hills Hotel? That would be the first place I'd start."

"Sounds right on the money," said Powell.

"Get a list of all the attendees," Myrna said. "Smart idea, right?"

"I heard there were hundreds in attendance between the contestants and the spectators," Powell said. "Quite a task to narrow down."

"Ha!" Guy laughed. "We should've hired her at our agency. We couldn't even make a dent in that list."

Babs looked Myrna straight in the eye. "I was at the studio the other day when the animal trainers tried an unsuccessful test on another dog. Where did you get the terrier you took to the dog show?"

Myna cowered. "Were you there?"

"Far enough away in the audience where you would've never noticed."

"I'm sure the Easts told you their favorite star fathered a bunch of puppies."

"None of them were up to their papa's skill level," Babs said.

"Many of them are hard to tell apart. I borrowed one for a publicity stunt, and if you need to know, the little runt peed all over me afterward. Thank heavens that wasn't captured by any of the press photographers."

Guy tried to hide a sheepish grin. He posed as one of those photographers but never shot a frame of film.

Myrna wrinkled her brow. "Besides Asta's charm and intelligence? I can't think of any other quality a dog would have where someone would go out of their way to steal it. Their fur, perhaps? You don't suppose someone would desire them for their distinctive coats, do you?" Myrna shuddered. "God, no! Forget I ever mentioned that."

Once everybody resettled, Babs called for their attention. "Get wise. I'm convinced something big will take place during the big celebration onboard the *Queen Mary*. I wish I could disclose more, but I seem to learn new things every day. Something to do with smuggling those stolen dogs."

"How come I never heard of that?" Hammett asked.

Guy cut in. "You knew all about the stolen dogs from our visit at the Beverly Wilshire."

"Not that," Hammett said, "I meant the party on the *Queen Mary*. Neither Lillian nor I received an invitation."

Lillian added. "If the drinks are on the house, I'm all for crashing a party."

Powell offered to pull a few strings. "How can I not do a favor for the man who made my career?"

Myrna didn't quite get the point. "You were doing films long before *The Thin Man*."

"So were you. Flash back to the years when you hardly wore a stitch of clothing. What about the scene you did in *The Barbarian*?"

"Where I bathed naked in a bath of rose petals?" Myrna asked, blushing.

Powell snapped his fingers and danced in place. *"Va-va-va-voom!"*

"Sweetheart, why did you bring that up and embarrass me around company?"

"Of course, we made movies. Plenty of movies," Powell explained, "But most people identify us as Nick and Nora Charles. What about you, Babs? Guy? Do you need my help?"

"Nigel Bruce promised he'd get us in," said Guy.

Then Babs leaned in and whispered to Powell, "I hope you don't mind, but I was thinking along the lines of a Jean Harlow-like disguise. Considering the calamity at the Coconut Grove, I can't have Basil or Ouida recognize me. I'm sorry if that'll remind you of the time when you lost the love of your life."

He bowed his head. "You do what you have to do. I'm married to a wonderful woman now."

"Honey," Myrna said to Babs, "I have an elegant silver fox mid-length jacket. I've been dying to wear it, but my husband thinks it makes me look like a fuzzy barrel. It's large enough where I could stuff inside an evening gown, a wig, and costume jewelry."

She's being supportive. A good sign. "That's kind of you to offer," said Babs.

Everyone insisted on making their opinion known—pro or con.

In winding up, Powell told Babs, "You know what I do when I can't settle an argument?"

"What's that?"

"I punch the man in the nose. That shuts him up for a while."

"If you're trying to settle a score with a woman, what do you do then?" she asked.

"I'll kiss her on the lips, ask her to marry me, and if she won't—"

Myrna intervened. "All right, where's the punchline?"

Powell said, "If she refuses matrimony, then I tell her she's missing out on the best time of her life, excuse myself, and say, 'Sorry, but I'm going to be late to my own wedding.'"

Myrna said to Babs, "Isn't he just a fool? That was straight from our film *Manhattan Melodrama*...and the martini talking."

Chapter Thirty-Two: Ivan, the Not-so-terrible

The two determined detectives plowed through remorseful morning-after headaches. Boundless issues needed to be resolved before the big night. Each hoped their partner would come up with the easiest solution. Sir Henry seemed indifferent.

Guy tossed yesterday's paper and finished his coffee. He leashed the dog and announced, "We're going for a walk."

Babs failed to understand his logic. "Won't that be the third one he's had this morning? Please don't tell me he ate something from the garbage."

Guy shook his head. "I might've forgotten to secure the cover on my sidecar. Don't want curious onlookers poking around since it's parked in a public garage."

Babs asked to borrow his phone book and waved him off.

* * *

Guy returned full of pep and couldn't wait to tell her the breaking news.

"Babs, you won't believe what happened."

Desperate for an encouraging sign, she looked up from her paperwork.

"Here I was, checking on my wheels. Sir Henry jumped into the sidecar, expecting a ride. A man with a remarkable accent approached and startled me. Babs, remember Ivan Alexandrescu, the countess's butler?"

Their front door opened. A long-legged man with a prominent nose stepped inside. His face? Familiar. His name, not at all. She thought he resembled Arthur Treacher, the actor, the perfect Jeeves for Bertie Wooster. Her immediate knee-jerk reaction was, "What's he doing here?"

Instead, she asked, "How can I help you?"

Ivan came forward. "My status...here in the States,...not quite legal. I am a Romanian but lived in Germany. A ref-u-gee, fleeing Nazi oppression—"

"We've never worked with immigration and aren't in the habit of turning in our clients unless—" Babs hesitated. "Have you taken part in a criminal act?"

The man paled and broke out into a cold sweat. "My em-ploy-er. To keep my po-si-tion, she has forced me to assist her."

Babs got out her notepad. "Her accomplice... Not sure if this is the type of case we take, but go on."

"She has ordered others...many people besides me, but the countess... Countess von Rache stole dogs from movie stars. From famous films and an-i-mal people. She plans to smuggle them overseas. Sell to rich buyers."

Babs raised her eyebrows. "Are you sure?"

"Maybe she has Toto and Asta," Guy said to her in a whisper.

I just knew it. "Then I have a question for you, sir. Does the phrase, 'Authorities are powerless,' mean anything to you, and could there be a connection between that and the *Queen Mary* ocean liner?"

"Will you hear my story and...not call the police?"

Babs glanced at Guy. They both nodded. Maybe he could fill in the blanks where they failed to do so.

"The countess said law people were powerless once these animals were off Amer-i-can soil. She claims to know plen-ty of people. From her time spent overseas. They want to purchase these dogs. Lots of money."

"The *Queen Mary*?" asked Guy, "What's the connection?"

"To transfer her stolen dogs on the ship...which will sail far away. But she assigned others to handle. No turning back once the ship goes to sea."

What a shrewd plan, thought Babs. She wanted to know who would be involved. When she asked Ivan if the name, Rennie Renfro, rang a bell, he shrugged. "By any chance, you wouldn't know where these people will keep the dogs? I'm told the ship is larger than the *Titanic*."

Ivan shook his head. "My boss... She gets upset if I ask too many questions. Tells me what she thinks is nec-es-sary."

Babs rubbed her forehead. "So, you're not sure—"

Guy interrupted. "Did you go through an employment agency to get your job with her?"

Babs sensed where this was heading.

"No agency. People like me will do... any-thing to stay in this free country. Yes, a big price to pay. Es-pe-cial-ly if you knew my real back-ground and ed-u-ca-tion. You are so lucky you live here and not over there."

"Now, I'm curious. What is your background?" Guy asked.

"I have a PhD in Zoology...with a spe-cial-ty in an-i-mal behavior from Friedrich Wilhelm Uni-ver-si-ty in Berlin."

"A bit overqualified to work for the countess," said Guy, "but I can imagine she considered it handy given her obsession with animals, and you also speak German."

"Nazis burned twenty thousand books in our library. To quote the German poet Heinrich Heine, '*Das war ein Vorspiel nur, dort wo man Bücher verbrennt, verbrennt man am Ende auch Menschen.*' That translates to, 'This was but a prelude, where they burn books, they ul-ti-mate-ly burn people.' I had no choice but to flee for my life."

"I'm sorry. How do people like you make the connections to find work if they aren't here legally?" Guy asked.

"Word of mouth. Clubs, hotels, and places like those bars which sold *bees* during Prohibition."

Guy gave a half-suppressed laugh, so as not to embarrass Ivan by correcting his English.

"I think you meant *booze*, not bees."

"Ah, yes. *Booze*. I mix up words all the time."

Guy tried to get him on track. "You're referring to speakeasies, right?"

"We have un-der-ground networks of fu-gi-tives. No protection. Always danger for us."

"I've heard there are Nazis hiding in plain sight here in Los Angeles," said

Guy.

"People like...countess... They take ad-van-tage of us because we are outside...the law. I work as her chauf-feur. I was supposed to drive her to...upcoming event...at the *Queen Mary*. Errol Flynn... His driver will pick her up..."

"You have the evening off?" Guy asked.

Ivan nodded.

"Babs, what if what he's saying is true? We still haven't devised a plan for how to round up the dogs. In fact, we haven't even squared away our own transportation."

She took her eyes away from her steno pad and looked at Guy with one of those *what do you mean* stares.

"Do you mind stepping outside while we have a moment alone?" Guy asked Ivan before closing the door.

With Ivan out of earshot, he turned to Babs. "How do you think it would look if someone saw us when I'm supposed to be blind, but driving my motorcycle with you in the sidecar and Sir Henry on your lap?"

Babs countered. "How do you think it would look if the Feds thought I was conspiring with people who may or may not be Nazis?"

"You're missing the point. Ivan is trying to avoid political persecution, and he can drive our getaway car."

She took a deep breath and blew it out. "Open the door and let him back in."

Guy popped one of his slugs into the vending machine and offered Ivan a soda.

She disclosed their plan. "So far, we've determined my partner will pose as a blind music critic. Sir Henry will serve as his guide dog."

"For obvious reasons, nobody can see me drive my vehicle," Guy explained. "Someone else needs to get me there who also doesn't mind traveling with dogs."

"She has several cars. The biggest one is a Cadillac V-16 Limousine."

"Could it hold a lot of dogs in case we find the ones we need to rescue?"

"Many, depending on...size."

"All right, here's the deal," said Babs.

Her nose tickled. Unable to figure out what caused it, she tried to ignore it.

"Can't promise anything," she said, "But we can plead on your behalf to give you immunity from deportation and admit you played an important part in catching a criminal."

Guy asked, "Are you willing to work with us, given those conditions?"

Ivan agreed, but Guy needed to contact him. When he realized it would be too risky for either him or his partner to call over at the countess's, Guy suggested he check in with them instead.

"I think you found your *zauberkugel*," Ivan said.

Guy said, "What's that?" while Babs dug into her desk and pulled out a battered book.

"I picked up a German-English dictionary this past week, although I never used it until now," she mumbled, trying to look up the word. "Must've been nuts to think I could learn the language so quickly." She got lucky with guessing its spelling and found the right page.

"*Zauberkugel… Hmmm*, makes sense you'd pick a biology or zoology-type of word since that's your background. It translates to a magic bullet, a medicinal term for a remedy of natural antibodies, which come out of the clear blue and fly to their specific target in an unharmed fashion." She looked up at Guy and Ivan. "Okay, I'm not a science expert, but it sounds good to me. I guess you'll be our *zauber*—whatever."

Everyone shook hands, and Ivan departed.

* * *

Guy helped himself to another soda. He took one long, refreshing gulp and patted himself on the stomach. "I feel good about Ivan coming forward. We'll just have to figure out how you'll get there."

Babs had her reservations. "One step at a time."

"Our problem is we're running out of time," he said. "Didn't you also mention that Strickling expects his retainer back if we don't meet our deadline?"

She nodded, unable to hide the grave expression on her face.

Guy coughed. He set down his soda and pinched his nose with his handkerchief. "Babs, do you smell an odor? Something like seashells... covered with algae?"

Sir Henry barked and sniffed around the room.

She took in a deep breath. "Come to think of it, I do sense the slight scent of *Parfum de la Mer*..."

"Like Ivan picked up the catch of the day," Guy explained. "Straight from its source."

Babs clicked her tongue against the roof of her mouth. "Don't know about you, but let's hope he doesn't plan on using us as bait."

Chapter Thirty-Three: Bratwurst and Biergartens

"The press, Watson, is a most valuable institution, if you only know how to use it." Rathbone recited his quote from Sherlock Holmes— from *The Adventure of the Six Napoleons*, to be exact, and glanced at his pocket watch.

"Does that antique still keep accurate time?" Nigel Bruce asked.

"I can't wear a modern wristwatch and break my character, now can I?" Basil replied.

"Up for more merry-making?" Nigel asked. "Press conference parties can be so boring. We already gave everyone more than enough interviews."

Basil sighed. "Can't quite face the brat and the wife, but another beer or two might not be such a bad idea."

Noises from Nigel's stomach dictated their next course of action. "Speaking of another kind of brat, I seem to crave a hearty plate of bratwurst, and that would go well with beer."

"No bangers and mash?" Basil asked. "Where's your loyalty to the Union Jack?"

"Right now, this *Tommy Atkins, or former British soldier*," Nigel said, *sotto voce*, "is pledging his allegiance to his tummy."

"I caught the patriotic reference. What about our costumes?" asked Basil. "The publicists insist we wear them to all press junkets to promote Holmes and Watson. Got to keep the photographers happy, I guess. Shouldn't we change back into our *civilian* attire?"

"That'll take too long. Besides, could you imagine if showing up in character would give us the red carpet treatment?"

"Very well," Basil replied. "I'll hail a cab, and I'll answer to the scolding from our wardrobe department later."

Nigel gave unusual instructions to their driver.

"Downtown? Are you sure?" Basil asked.

"Heard it's a private social club. Anyone willing to spend money can get in. Recommended by some stagehands. Once in a while, Watson can make a few smart suggestions."

* * *

By comparing the obscure address Nigel provided with others across the street, the cabbie deciphered where to drop them off. Basil inspected its nondescript exterior, marked by a single black-on-black placard. One which someone could remove at will and hard to distinguish in the dark.

"*Wurst Haus?*" Basil asked. "This reminds me more of a hush-house, although Prohibition is over. Let's hope it's not the *worst restaurant* you ever suggested."

"Appears like there used to be multiple entrances," Nigel said, "Like one of those grand movie palaces, but all of them seem to be blacked out and shuttered."

"Except one." Basil pointed to the only open entrance, blocked by a motley crew of rabble-rousers. "A bit of action happening tonight. Is this what you were expecting?"

Despite straying from the norm by wearing their costumes, the supper club's goon squad paid no attention to the two actors. Basil noticed a newshound down for the count, bloodied forehead, crushed hat by the curb, and his press camera shattered. "Must be commonplace if no one gave us a second look."

Nigel peeped over his shoulder. After the crowd shifted, he spotted a low-key, almost imperceptible, public notice: No Kikes or Coloreds Allowed. "Rather disturbing, don't you think?"

Without further ado, Basil concealed his deerstalker inside his jacket pocket. "Promise me one thing. Don't make waves. If you weren't so dog hungry, I'd suggest we turn around and go elsewhere."

The club's high-ceilinged, combined auditorium-dining room reminded Basil of a converted dance hall—one where pathetic old men and randy sailors paid opportunistic women a dime a dance, if that much. Murals depicting quaint but kitsch German villages adorned the walls, giving a year-round Christmassy feeling. Several long tables lined up in rows at the far end, facing the stage. Smaller round tables dotted the perimeter, which left room for couples to dance in the center.

On stage, an oompah band—full blast with heavy brass. The males wore Tyrolean hats and lederhosen. Women braided their hair and dressed like typical "beer wenches" with peasant blouses and dirndl skirts with aprons.

Once seated at a vacant table, Basil pulled his signature curved pipe out of his pocket and packed it with fresh black shag tobacco.

"You came prepared," said Nigel.

The pungent odors of cigars and sausages, lager, and sauerkraut soon overpowered his smoking pleasure. Basil didn't see any menus. "Maybe we need to go to the bar and place our orders."

Nigel gave the crowd a once-over. A tall, solid-built man with a butcher's apron picked up his cue and plunked down enormous platters of food. Another server wearing a chemist's smock slid large mugs of beer toward them. Basil smacked his lips after he sampled his lager.

Nigel gulped his too fast. "Not bad for what's on tap. Looks like everyone's getting bratwurst whether they like it."

The two men did their best to tune out the band.

"Have you had time to read your script for our radio show?" Nigel asked.

"Not too worried about being unprepared. Has anyone informed you about the rest of the evening's agenda?"

"Supposed to be a fundraiser. The proceeds will finance the Allies." Nigel became tense. "All the same, we shouldn't jabber about that in here."

Basil lowered his voice. "Good point. These folks look like benefactors of the opposition party. Are you aware last April, the Warner Brothers declared their own war with Germany? Released *Confessions of a Nazi Spy*, starring Edward G. Robinson."

"Created quite a furor, especially with the Führer." Nigel chuckled, amused by his quip. "I remember the advertisement: They don't want you to see this picture!"

"In the film, an FBI agent exposed espionage activities by the German-American Bund against U.S. military operations," said Basil. "The studio and many actors received death threats afterward."

Nigel looked up and off toward the stage. "The band seems to have taken a break."

Basil picked at his plate like a finicky child. "Now, we can dine in peace, despite the crowd and company."

His attention shifted to a group of workers, who began stacking tables and clearing the middle of the dance floor. Afterward, they erected a sturdy, fence-like barrier.

"Maybe they're going to have a boxing match," Nigel said.

"From my recollections, flexible ropes surround boxing rings." Basil pointed out several musclemen who brought out weighty iron kettlebells and clamped chains onto them.

Every time the oompah band resumed playing, Basil cringed, but Nigel seemed to enjoy the voluptuous female performers, bouncing around with their accordions and flugelhorns. Between songs, officials made announcements in German mixed with broken English. Servers made their rounds with beer and pretzels.

Club members in groups of three, each holding a different colored basket, approached each table. The actors looked at each other, unsure of what was happening, except people started tossing money into them.

When the basket bearers approached Basil and Nigel, Basil shook his head and said, "*Nein.*"

The disappointed volunteers murmured among themselves but moved on.

"Not sure if that was the right response," Basil said. "Guess we'll find out if it wasn't."

"It would help if we understood more German," Nigel said. "What do you think they wanted?"

"Those looked like tithe baskets used for church donations," Basil replied. "To be honest, I suspect they are for placing bets."

"With three contestants?" Nigel asked.

"Not sure. My deduction: maybe two for the contestants and the third for those who don't want to gamble but want to contribute to whatever cause they're supporting. Someone's got to pay the rent in this place, and I'm sure the food isn't free."

* * *

Two human gorillas each dragged dogs on chains into the arena. Each of those chains clamped onto the restraints attached to the kettlebells. Their extended length was long enough so each dog was within reach of the other, but too short to leap the protective fence. The wretched animals looked half-starved and willing to kill—dog or man.

"I've heard of cockfights, but canine combat?" Nigel asked. "Those pathetic things will skin each other alive."

Cruel reality hit them like a sucker punch. Basil's stomach wrenched. The basket-bearers made another pass. The heathens tossed their life savings away—money for blood.

Basil sneered. *Basket-bearers... More like pallbearers.*

"Isn't this illegal?" Nigel posed his question to the air.

Basil's attention went elsewhere. He wanted to shout, to scream, to fire a pistol, even though he didn't have one. Anything to halt this atrocity. Yet it looked like his wish would come to pass. Close to fifty demonstrators stormed the auditorium. Many carried protest signs. The unyielding beasts thrashed at their handlers as they rushed into the ring, unhooked their tethers, and ran them into an adjoining room for safety. An outspoken dissident took center stage and stole the microphone away from the referee. *Das Deutscher volk* fought back, shouting anti-communist and racial slurs. The rebels countered with their own version of inflammatory rhetoric. Each swore they were the ideal Americans and patriots.

Club patrons reached inside their pockets for knives, guns, and other hidden weapons, as if choreographed. Uniformed police insiders bullied the agitators. The blood-thirsty minions cheered while they made arrests.

Bile rose in Basil's throat. He darted for the restroom, vomited in a sink, and splashed water on his face. Upon return, he passed a table he hadn't noticed earlier covered with circulars, in German, with evocative visual clues—images of Hitler and swastikas.

He reunited with his friend and pushed his unfinished meal over to the next place setting. "Next time, remind me never to take any of your nightspot recommendations."

"Was your food that awful?" Nigel asked. "You look green about the gills."

Basil grimaced. "I feel gutted. Their appalling behavior made me sick to my stomach."

Nigel looked concerned. "From the dog fighting?"

"Never theorize before you have data," Basil recited memorized dialogue. "Invariably, you end up twisting facts to suit your theories instead of theories to suit facts."

"Please... *A Scandal in Bohemia?*" Nigel faked a yawn. "You know, it makes me weary to hear you forever quoting Sherlock Holmes."

One server removed their empty glasses and replaced them with handouts.

"You jumped to conclusions way too soon," said Basil. "The dog fighting—revolting, to say the least. But you didn't let me explain. I discovered deplorable fascist literature while coming back from the men's room. Here's another. Look at this crowd. You spotted the handwritten abomination posted out front. We're both at fault for being so ignorant."

"I assumed people and threats like this were just a bunch of hooey," said Nigel.

Basil crumpled up the hateful propaganda and tossed it under their table. "I felt the same way when the First World War broke out."

Nigel moved his dinner out of the way and confessed he also lost his appetite. "We should report this. Not sure how, since the local police are in on it."

"We should leave, but we must be discreet," said Basil, "So not to get caught up in a riot."

"If I pull my cap low enough, none will be the wiser, but you? Security will be more vigilant now," said Nigel. "You're taller than most and too recognizable if someone spots us together."

Basil examined the crowd with caution. "I guess your hope for celebrity privileges backfired."

"I can't believe I was so foolish to suggest going here, but how was I to know? My world doesn't extend much further than the screen or the stage. I prefer it that way."

Nigel wiped his mouth with his cloth napkin, then raised a finger. "Basil, I want your cooperation. I have an idea, and it just might work."

"I shall be delighted."

"You don't mind breaking the law?" Nigel asked.

Aware of his partner's Conan Doylean references, Basil played along. "Not in the least… These Germanic fanatics must be breaking all sorts of laws."

"Nor running a chance of arrest?"

"Not in a good cause," Basil replied.

"Oh, the cause is excellent!"

"Then I am your man," said Basil.

Nigel concluded their playacting. "I was sure that I might rely on you."

He was also grateful Americans defied the rules of classic German cuisine and served ketchup with their bratwurst. He smeared some, along with traditional dark brown mustard, on Basil's napkin. "Let's hope this looks like dried blood." With another napkin from the empty adjacent seat, he took the soiled ones, tied them together, and wrapped them around his friend's head like a turban.

"Am I supposed to resemble a wounded soldier?" Basil asked.

"A victim from the street fight. I suppose you'll pass."

Unsure of their meal's cost or if it was on the house, Basil left a gratuity on the table.

Nigel grunted and pocketed the cash. "They don't deserve a penny, and we'll wind up as dog meat if we're not careful. *Holmes*, shall we depart?"

"Before we start a *Scandal in Bavaria?*" Basil said, pulling his leg.

'Move along." Nigel poked him from behind and prodded him toward the door. "No place for shenanigans, now. Hurry, hurry."

Chapter Thirty-Four: In the Queen's Secret Service

For their grand scheme to succeed, Babs and Guy needed to catch the countess in the act tonight and prove to those who hired them they could return the dogs by tomorrow. Thanks to Nigel Bruce, she had carte blanche to mingle with the VIPs. Myrna assured her she'd sneak in her Eileen Adlon outfit and leave it in the cloakroom. She even had the perfect platinum blonde wig left over from last year's Halloween party.

Abel Wiggins, her janitor, suggested Babs masquerade as a cabin maid to board the ship prior to her radio show. He knew the ropes of the custodial trade and secured a gig for that evening. Since she didn't own a car and couldn't have anyone see her arriving with Guy and Ivan, he offered her a ride in his pickup truck. Babs agreed to meet him at the office to avoid leaving her residential hotel while dressed like Tugboat Annie. She added padding around her waist to make herself even more unrecognizable and purchased a jumbo-sized brassiere, stuffing the cups with small bags of birdseed to simulate larger breasts.

On the drive down to Long Beach, Babs made a brief mention that she and her partner suspected the countess's house servants might've had a hand in abducting the dogs.

Abel had his own opinions. "Let the men with the badges handle it. Dig too deep, and you might get in over your head."

"Don't forget, I lost my entire team at one point," said Babs. "Basil? I can't vouch for what he thinks of me at the moment, but I reckon it's not too favorable."

* * *

Right after they pulled into their parking space, they commented on how the ship's maintenance crew had already repainted the *Queen Mary* for camouflage.

"Enemy ships won't be able to see her," Wiggins explained. "She'll disappear like a gray ghost on the high seas, shrouded by fog."

Babs spoke her mind and resented having to use the unglamorous service entrance rather than the red-carpeted gangplanks.

"Come on, lassie, I can't believe you haven't snuck into events through hotel kitchens and back alleyways before. Be thankful we're not cutting through a garbage dump."

He led her to an area full of clean staff uniforms. "We call this the mudroom where you're supposed to kick off your muddy boots after working the dockyards. Men's stuff on the left. Women's on the right. They sort everything according to size. Don't expect it to make you look sexy, but find something that fits."

"Change, again? I'm already in disguise."

"You betcha. Meet me outside the door over yonder when finished. It's rather common that every venue has its own uniform for its maintenance staff."

Always fit in. Always look like you belong, Babs thought. A motto that was like a mantra.

To navigate the enormous ship, he pulled out a small utility map and instructed Babs to follow him down a maze of never-ending corridors and blinds.

"Wow! I have to admit, this ship is more majestic than I had ever imagined—masterful woodwork, breathtaking at every turn," Babs said. "Some people nicknamed her the Ship of Woods, because designers used so many varieties."

He snatched her by the hand. "Lassie, you can admire the ship all you want after we retrieve the dogs. Time's a wastin.'"

By the time Wiggins picked the stateroom farthest away and in a dead-end corner, Babs complained about sore feet.

"High heels? Why on God's earth didn't you bring more sensible shoes?" he asked.

"Need to make a quick change. It's too much trouble to slip into new shoes and stockings."

Babs reached into a bag and dug out a ratty-looking chew toy.

"What's that?" he asked.

"It's for scent recognition. Sir Henry must've lost the scrap of Toto's favorite blanket when we tried to escape from the countess's, but Asta's toy rabbit remained in my pack. Everyone ignored it when they confiscated my surveillance equipment. A smart dog like Asta should be able to smell it if we're close by."

She knocked first. "Anyone home?"

When no one answered, she used her passkey. "Did I hear a bark?" Babs wiped the door handle clean of prints with her dust rag.

The two of them entered. A scruffy little dog sat on top of the bed, saying, "Hello," in his own special way and wagging his tail.

Babs asked in a sweet doggie-talk voice, "Would you be Toto?"

The dog barked again and turned around in circles.

"I think he's trying to say yes," Wiggins said.

Babs set the record straight. "Toto is a she. Her real name is Terry the Terrier." When she called out, "Terry," the dog also responded. Then she pointed to a damp spot. "Bingo! Strickling told me she's a carpet-wetter."

"Someone left the radio on to keep her company." Wiggins examined it. "It's tuned to the in-house station. Sounds like Nick and Nora Charles performing their *Thin Man* segment."

"That'll cue me when I need to head back and change into the guise of Eileen Adlon for our Sherlock Holmes sketch."

Another pup wiggled from under the bed. He gave a stretch and a yawn, as if he'd woken from a nap.

"Asta!" Babs cried.

"*Shush!*" Wiggins said. "We're not supposed to be in here. What if there's someone in the hallway?"

Without even thinking about how he'd react to a stranger, Babs handed him his rabbit, scooped him up in her arms, and gave him a hug. His little tail wagged like a motorized toy.

"He's more adorable than I imagined," she said while he licked her face. "No wonder he's captured the hearts of so many."

While she had her hands full with Asta, Wiggins capitalized on affection from Toto.

"I have to give our dognappers credit," said Babs. "I worried someone might've mistreated them. This might not be a luxury suite, but it's classy and far more comfortable than my place. Of course, they'd pick the stateroom the farthest away."

"Did you think the crooks would make it easy for us?" Wiggins said in jest.

"We need to find Guy. We can't sneak both dogs out in your water pail." Babs heard her thirty-minute warning, cued by certain lines of dialogue on the radio. "Myrna sent a note. She left my other disguise in the cloakroom. I'd better hurry."

She started for the door but heard the ominous sound of someone else's key. "We have to hide." She conveyed this in pantomime and hoped Wiggins could read her lips.

Their normal exit wasn't an option. Neither was squeezing through the porthole window and diving into Long Beach Harbor. They both ran toward the closet and collided. Between Wiggins' potbelly and the necessity of hiding his mop paraphernalia (a dead giveaway), the two of them couldn't fit. Babs had no choice but to roll under the bed. She prayed Toto or Asta wouldn't think she was playing hide-and-seek, otherwise they'd give her away.

Two people entered, both male. One sounded American. Familiar, but she couldn't place it. The other, a heavy German accent mixed with broken English. From Babs' vantage point, she couldn't see much past their knees.

189

American: "You're going to a lot of trouble to sell a bunch of dogs. There have to be easier ways to raise cash."

German: "Supply and demand. Prices as high as I want... *Sehr teuer...* expensive now since I have Asta and Toto. Our black-market op-er-a-tion has proved quite prof-it-able."

A pause, followed by the horrible stench of a cigar. The dogs whined. They didn't like it. She tried not to gag and give herself away. Toto ran over to the closet where Wiggins was hiding. She stood on her hind legs, barked, and pawed at the door, trying to get the men to notice.

No, Toto, no! Don't give us away. Babs hoped she could telegraph her thoughts.

Toto yelped and tried with all her might to pry open the door.

"Nothing in there for you, girl," the American said and kicked the door shut. From under her perch, Babs saw his hands pick Toto up. Still couldn't identify him, but prayed he wouldn't discover her hiding place. Toto wouldn't stop whimpering.

The man turned his attention back to his so-called partner.

American: "I resent being roped into this."

German: "You—no other choice. Do you want to die? Along with your friends?"

American: "Of course not, Cig. *Arrgh!* You burned me!"

Babs swore she'd heard his voice before. *Cig? Siegfried, the animal handler? Henry East chewed him out the day I visited him. Upset, he smoked cigars at his kennels.*

German: "Rich people will pay to own a piece of Hol-ly-wood. Imag-ine if you knew you owned something that belonged to Clark Gable or Bette Davis? Almost as good as sou-ve-nir from one of their films."

American: "Untie me, you thug. Think of the dogs. Let me give them more food and water. They might be stuck here a while."

German: "Skip both. *Hundescheisse...Wie kann ich es sagen?* How do I say? They might poop...or piss. All over. No good for bad smells. Ruin our plans."

Asta shimmied under the bed to check out Babs. Maybe to signal her to come to their rescue. Babs blew on his nose to get him to back off. He crawled out and dropped his toy on the one man's shoes.

The German picked it up. *"Was ist das?"*

American: "Looks like a chew toy, but I don't recall seeing it earlier."

The German's voice cracked in panic. "Could someone else come in here?"

"Housekeeping has keys. So does maintenance, but it could've been from a previous guest," said the American.

The German grumbled. "No one is supposed to be in here."

"Who knows how long it's been under there? This is not the first time anyone's brought dogs onboard," said the American.

Babs heard unintelligible sounds and moaning, as if the German had gagged the American.

German: *"Wir müssen gehen.* Go! Now!"

* * *

The two left, and the door shut. Babs gave it a minute and scooted out from under the bed.

"Psst, Wiggins. All clear. Get out of the closet."

Now, she'd be cutting it close to make a quick costume change and get to the recording studio on time.

"Find Guy," she explained, trying to keep her thoughts straight. "Tell him what we know, although it isn't much. Too bad we don't understand German, but this guy's got to be connected to the countess. Tell him to *get lost.* That's his signal. Sir Henry will appear to guide him in the wrong direction. In reality, he will sniff out the location of other dogs. Tell him to try this hallway first, although I didn't hear any other barking, which you'd assume would be a dead-sure indicator. If not, any place, out of the way, where others won't find them. If I don't leave now, I'll be late."

* * *

Who were those guys? Babs' brain did double duty as she bolted down the endless hallway to the cloakroom.

"A woman left me a parcel. I don't have her receipt, but it's under number 221B," she said, panting.

The attendant eyed her with skepticism after retrieving a pricey fox jacket. "This must be a mistake."

"Check the hanger. There should also be a smaller item. She might've stuffed it inside the sleeve so it wouldn't fall out."

The lady pulled out a peachy-pink, silk, envelope-shaped pouch, the kind upscale department stores would use for fancy lingerie from one's wedding trousseau.

"Mind if I look?" Babs asked.

The woman scoffed and gave her a mistrustful stare.

She's wondering why a cabin maid would rummage through such finery unless she planned on stealing it. Babs presented her with a cream-colored, unsealed envelope. It contained a handwritten note from Myrna, giving whoever was in charge permission to dispense the parcel.

Inside: a platinum-blonde wig, a luscious, long silk bias-cut slip dress the color of champagne, so alluring that it looked more like suggestive undergarments. Jewelry included a flashy top-quality rhinestone and faux ruby necklace with matching earrings, which would fool anyone except a bona fide gemologist. Also included, essential cosmetics to complete her new glamorous look.

"Goodness, Myrna thought of everything. Glad this is a floor-length gown. My run-of-the-mill shoes will have to do."

She flagged down the attendant. "Excuse me, do you have a pen I can borrow?"

Babs wrote a quick note on the flip side of the stationery: *Rache!* She folded the letter the opposite way, placed it back into its original envelope, and licked it sealed. With a single line, she crossed out her name and wrote: Nick and Nora Charles—urgent!

"Sorry to bother you," she said. "I need one of your stewards to track down Myrna Loy and make sure she gets this right away."

Once again, the cloakroom gal gave her a leery look. When Babs flashed a fiver in front of her eyes, the lady was more than glad to oblige.

Chapter Thirty-Five: A Night at the Observation Bar

Part I

In a corner of the semi-circular Art Deco Lounge, Captain Irving elaborated upon a group of gifted ceremonial swords to an audience, including Basil, Tyrone Power, and Errol Flynn, who had Countess Velma von Rache at his side, along with others.

"We hosted several members of the Spanish royal family on our transatlantic route from our port in Southampton to New York. One of them became ill—a combination of seasickness and food poisoning. Not from our kitchens, mind you, but from the so-called 'exotic African delicacies' he brought with him before he boarded. If you want to know, I think they were aphrodisiacs, but he would've died before confessing anything so embarrassing.

"His condition was touch and go for the longest time. He and his family were so appreciative of our crew and in-house medical staff. Not to mention a masseur who excised every ache and pain. As a token of his gratitude, he presented me with these rapiers from his royal repository."

Basil whispered to Tyrone. "I bet you anything he was referring to Spanish fly but was too shy to say it around the ladies."

"To me, they look more like épée blades on saber handles," Tyrone replied. "Except it's too impolite to correct him."

While the ship's captain enlightened the crowd about the history of the *RMS Queen Mary*, Basil inspected the swords in closer detail, and Tyrone followed.

"Here and now, how confident are you with your fencing skills?" Basil asked.

"How confident are yours?" The question repeated by an outsider.

"Jack Stewart!" Basil couldn't contain his surprise. "What are you doing here?"

"The *Queen* is my second home. Her engines are under my watchful eye. I might not be sipping champagne with the rest of you, but I'm on duty tonight," he explained. "She's docked right now, but I must make sure she's seaworthy at a moment's notice. Soon, she'll be transporting thousands of soldiers."

The captain warned Basil and his buddies to stay out of trouble. He didn't want to have to rescue anyone who got so tipsy that they fell overboard.

After making the rounds and introducing himself to his stellar guests, Captain Irving called for everyone's attention, "Who would be interested in an abbreviated tour of my ship?"

"When?" Basil asked.

"Right now," he explained. "I'm short-staffed tonight and can only focus on the highlights of the more luxurious sections. Who's on board?"

Ouida got excited. "Basil, this sounds like fun."

"Can't go, honeybuns. My show starts soon."

Nigel's wife, Violet, interrupted. "My husband won't be able to come, either. We'll do it together, but let's get a drink first."

Violet dragged Ouida over to the bar. Mae West, Mickey Rooney, and a few others took the captain up on his offer. Countess Velma clutched onto Flynn like a dog guarding her bone. They opted to stay behind.

Ouida returned with a tall, extra-potent drink in her hand. Basil kissed her goodbye and went on ahead to the recording studio. Tyrone, who wanted to make a few last-minute farewells, said he'd join him in a few minutes.

* * *

Busy technicians strung wires across the floor of the recording studio, readying for their pre-performance sound check.

"I find the blonde bombshell look quite flattering on you, Babs," Basil said in a subdued voice as he sat down next to her. "Or do you prefer to be called Eileen Adlon?"

Despite everything, Nigel assured her by the time Basil found out about her disguise, they'd never be able to find another actress. Especially one already familiar with the script, on such short notice.

"You're not worried my wife will declare war?" he asked.

She shook her head. "Bigger matters are at stake."

Besides resuscitating her acting skills, Babs had two preeminent concerns—the countess and Ouida. One step in the wrong direction, and her entire operation could fail. Tonight, she'd have to trust people she didn't know too well, like Nigel's wife, to handle things in her absence. Under ideal circumstances, she would've preferred to be more in control and leave less to chance.

Under his breath, Basil confessed, "I guess I owe you my gratitude."

"For what?" Each question made her more on edge.

"For finding Leo. Sorry, my wife insisted on giving the police the reward. I know you deserved it."

Babs grumbled. She and Guy needed to nail the countess—tonight. They expected challenges.

He changed the subject. "So, are you working a job, reviving your acting skills, or did you just intend to crash a fancy party?"

Her reply: "There's nothing more stimulating than a case where everything goes against you."

From outer appearances, she seemed to ignore him and hadn't answered his question. In fact, she had recited a line from his dialogue in the radio play they were about to perform.

Babs gave a wink to acknowledge Nigel Bruce, who entered the room.

"Oh, for heaven's sake! Don't I look foolish walking into the studio holding two cocktails," he said, laughing at himself in his typical disparaging manner. "My wife, I like to call her Bunny, her nickname. Anyway, Bunny had to run and take care of something urgent and asked me to hold her drink. She said the ship's captain was about to conduct a private tour.

"Well, I was so busy rhapsodizing with Olivia de Havilland that I forgot I was holding an extra glass, and for whatever reason, my wife never returned to reclaim it." He placed the unwanted drink on a small table and made himself at home.

"Really, Watson, you excel yourself." Basil pushed back his chair and lit a cigarette. "I am bound to say that in all the accounts which you have been so good as to give of my own small achievements, you have habitually underrated your own abilities... I confess, my dear fellow, that I am very much in your debt."

Nigel blushed. "Oh well, thank you very much."

"Not you, Nigel. I was rehearsing our script," said Basil.

Nigel turned an even darker shade of red. Babs (or Eileen Adlon) did her ladylike best to suppress her giggles.

Groucho Marx entered and took a seat. Babs took her script and made a last-minute review. She stopped to look up when she heard the mesmerizing words, "There's a light in a woman's eyes that speaks louder than words."

For a moment, Babs felt that had struck a romantic chord. A sorrowful reminder of one shortfall in her life. To her disappointment, it was Tyrone Power reading his part as Sir Henry of the Baskervilles.

Part II

After a successful recording of their radio show, everyone headed to the bar. The place was jumping and jiving by the time they arrived. Babs assumed Powell pulled the strings for Hammett's and Hellman's invitations. The couple sat at the counter, content to indulge in martinis and take an occasional glance at the rest of the scene. She figured snobbery was one perk of fame, which allowed them to choose their friends.

Babs pretended to have fun when she was busy keeping mental notes. Powell put on the charm. He and Myrna continued the antics of Nick and Nora Charles until, at one point, Myrna excused herself and said she'd return before long.

Among Babs' observations, Tyrone Power re-examined Captain Irving's collection of Spanish swords. He approached Basil and wanted to know why he brought up the subject of fencing earlier. "Were you thinking it would be a good publicity stunt to stage a duel?"

"Wicked thoughts, I guess," Basil said with a snicker. "I'd love to put that over-inflated hot air buffoon, Errol Flynn, in his place one of these days. Has that bastard any scruples? Between his brash behavior I witnessed firsthand at my party, and what I hear from Hollywood gossip, he seems perverted and shameless."

"Did I overhear my illustrious name?" Flynn asked, peering over Basil's shoulder.

While Flynn seemed to be engaged with Basil and Tyrone, Babs was within a stone's throw of the countess. Though she'd have to leave soon, Babs had to make the best of it—eavesdrop, ask around for other's opinions—whatever it took.

She envied von Rache's floor-length navy gown of silk crepe, which had a straight silhouette and plunging V-neckline. The bolero jacket she wore over it was the showstopper.

The jacket, silver mink trim all around the edges and cuffs. Long, tapered sleeves with exaggerated puffs where the tops of the armholes met the shoulder seams, with glittery rhinestone embellishment. Babs realized these were in the motifs of dogs, as if in an almost masochistic way, she felt an urge to give away her hand. On top of her head, a skewed velveteen hat, like an oversized button with netting, which veiled her eyes in mystery.

Momentarily star-struck, Babs snapped out of it and set the record straight: von Rache was a criminal and a clever con artist. To her, dogs were a commodity, a means to an end. So far, she'd given many people the impression she was innocent of any wrongdoings.

Without warning, von Rache was no longer in the spotlight. All eyes shifted to Myrna, who returned to the lounge. In her clutches, one obvious conversation piece everyone recognized, and a cream-colored envelope, ignored by all except Babs. No one was as gob-smacked as the countess when she spotted the whiny, but adorable wire-haired Fox Terrier in Myrna's arms.

Babs' crabmeat canapé tumbled off her tongue and back onto her plate. Not expecting the sudden curveball, she pussyfooted behind a group of revelers for camouflage but remained within earshot. The countess nearly fainted. Errol Flynn came to her rescue and helped her off her barstool.

A group of noisemakers corralled Myrna and her precious cargo. Myrna stuffed Babs' note into Powell's pocket, who nodded in acknowledgment. He read the note in a flash, squeezed through the crowd, and sidled up to where Hellman and Hammett monopolized the bar. He noticed a third, untouched martini between them and gave it an odd stare. Babs took this as her cue to position herself closer to their conversation.

"Please, join us on our booze cruise," said Hammett, who pointed to the untouched beverage. "I think the bartender mixed up another's."

"Don't mind if I do," Powell said. He winced; this drink was stronger than expected. "I considered proposing a toast to our success, but I'd rather propose a challenge."

"About what?" Lillian asked.

"Better take advantage of the fact that at this point I'm three sheets to the wind, because tomorrow I'll regret this. Here's the deal: I'll offer a cash prize to whoever comes up with the best detective story."

"Any particular angle?" Hammett asked.

"How we stopped Countess Velma von Rache from smuggling her stolen celebrity dogs overseas," Powell said.

"You believe it's her?" Lillian asked.

Babs, who'd been keeping them under surveillance the entire time, pushed past others and arrived at the moment of Powell's proclamation. She gave him a dirty look but had to cover his tracks.

"I'm sure of it," she said and hoped Myrna had also read the note before handing it over. "Don't ask me how I found out, but my partner and I plan to stop them."

Hammett tapped his pack of cigarettes on the countertop. He pulled out a fresh cigarette, struck a match, and gave it a few puffs.

The dog was already out of the bag. So, Babs played along. "Correct me if I'm wrong, but I think William is offering this prize as an incentive."

Myrna and "Asta" broke away from admiring fans and joined in on their banter. "Looks like you've been making merry. What did I miss?"

Babs volunteered to answer. "Your on-screen partner has devised a story competition. This could be a real turning point in anyone's career with a wild cast of characters. Think of it—an alluring foreigner, two famous writers, and two honest-to-goodness, bona fide detectives. Spice it up with two sets of on-screen detectives from popular films, and you have a winning formula. After all, Dash, how much do the studios pay you?"

"Top tier, I bet," said Myrna. "Fifteen hundred or two thousand a week on contract?"

"Sounds so tempting. I should throw my hat in the ring," said Babs. "Live in this town long enough, and writing a screenplay should be as second nature as breathing, right?"

Powell rubbed his head and looked like he was trying to sober up. "Nora, I mean Myrna, and I will each offer twelve hundred dollars to whoever can write the best script or novel based on this whole conundrum."

Myrna protested. "Thanks for helping yourself to my bank account without my permission."

"Confess! You tried to bribe the Easts into selling you Asta for that amount."

"My memory...too foggy," she said with a sigh. "I guess I'll have to take your word for it." Her troublesome terrier squirmed and scratched her arm. She almost lost her grip.

"I think there's an old Irish proverb that says, 'Money won is twice as sweet as money earned,'" said Lillian.

Powell suggested they tend to their disobedient dog. Both he and Myrna excused themselves and left the lounge. Groucho also looked like he was ready to take off. Not long thereafter, the other Marx Brothers, including Zeppo, made a swift departure. Babs knew they were up to something, but what?

* * *

Ouida wondered if Violet had undertaken some kind of conspiracy to keep her well-liquored. Throughout the captain's brief tour, when Ouida's drink needed refreshing, Violet poured some of hers into her glass since they were drinking the same thing.

At one point, Violet surprised Ouida and produced a skeleton key.

"Where did you get that?" Ouida asked.

"Does it matter? Come, let's break away and peek inside some of the first-class accommodations."

Lacking sense and sobriety, the two ladies took care to knock first, then tiptoed into several luxury cabins. To their delight, the two giddy gals plopped onto feathery-soft pillows, jumped on top springy beds like raucous schoolgirls, and tossed aside any reservations of propriety. They indulged in their unrestrained behavior until they encountered Groucho Marx in the hallway.

Groucho held his ever-present cigar and stared at them with his wall-eyed gaze, almost hidden by his glasses and Vaudevillian eyebrows. "Step right up and come on in." He eyed the ladies up and down as if inspecting a piece of merchandise. "With two of you, even better. I'll get two for the price of one."

Ouida scratched her head, confused. "You must be mistaken. We're not for sale."

"Then I get you for free—a real bargain. Looks like I'm about to empty my wallet once room service arrives with the hotdogs I bought for my pals."

He grabbed Ouida by the shoulder and shoved her into his room. Violet, who held on to her other arm, followed in tandem. Both ladies fell face forward and on top of Chico.

A knock sounded on the door. "Room service!"

"My friends all want hotdogs. Lots of hotdogs," Groucho said.

"And corn dogs," Chico said as he scrambled to his feet.

"That's right, and corn dogs," Groucho repeated.

"*Honk! Honk!*" Harpo squeezed his horn since he never spoke.

"And chilidogs," said Groucho.

Blup, plhfw-e-e-e-e... The deflated noise, which came from Harpo's horn.

"Goodness, what's that?" Violet asked.

Chico pinched his nose. *"Awww,* no. It's-a gonna smell in here," he said in faux Italian.

"Sounds like he might've used a whoopee cushion," said Groucho. "Waiter, he wants to make sure the hotdogs have no bones."

"But hotdogs never hava no bones," Chico said. "And I want to make sure they hava no dog in dem neither."

Ouida swung her head back and forth to make sure she addressed both. "Hotdogs don't have real dogs, nor do they have bones."

Groucho asked the newcomers, "While they're raiding the kitchen, what can I get you, pretty ladies?"

"Nothing, but thank you anyway," Ouida replied. She brushed herself off and looked around the room, which was much smaller than she imagined.

Inside were four out of the five Marx Brothers: Groucho, Chico, Harpo, and Zeppo, just like she'd seen in all of their films, or at least most of their films since Zeppo wasn't in every one of them. Ouida knew they had another brother—somewhere. Zeppo was more handsome than she imagined, although the vast amount of alcohol she consumed fueled those thoughts. She tried to tune out the clamor of Harpo's obnoxious honking every time she overhead Groucho, asking what kind of hotdog Violet wanted.

"Why didn't you reserve a bigger room?" Ouida noticed four large steamer trunks stacked on top of each other, pinning Zeppo against the wall. Harpo lay on the tiny bed, half-asleep. Groucho had his back against the door, guarding it. Chico shuffled about wherever there was space, often with roving, mischievous hands. He seemed to enjoy tickling Violet by slipping his hand under her skirt.

Once again, Groucho asked Ouida, "Are you sure you don't want a hotdog?"

"No, thank you. I'm not hungry," she replied, but considering she had too much to drink, maybe she should eat something.

Knock. Knock. "Who's there?" Groucho asked.

"Care to get your shoes shined?" a steward asked.

"I'd like to give you a shiner in South Caroliner if you think my patent-leather brogues aren't shiny enough. However, the tall, clean-cut guy in the corner always complains his shoes need a spit shine, and he's the one with the extra nickel in his pocket, so come on in." Groucho pulled the tubby guy, carrying a shoeshine kit, into the room, shoving the ladies onto the bed, who both rolled on top of Harpo.

Violet hopped off the bed, but Harpo, in his somnambulant state, wrapped his arms around Ouida like a child hugging a giant Teddy bear, but with extra groping as he squeezed her derrière. He honked his horn to celebrate his conquest.

Chico remarked, "He thinks you've got a nice piece of ass."

"Honk! Honk!"

"That means he agrees," said Chico.

"Ooooh!" Ouida turned red with fury. "You're making an ass of yourself!"

"Well, if I ain't a horse's ass," Groucho said. "But then again, I thought I was a monkey's uncle, and with all that honking, I bet you were ready to call my brother a silly goose. Well, anyway—"

Knock. Knock. "Who's there?" he asked.

"Singing telegram for Mr. Harpo Marx," a male voice said from the hallway.

"Come on in. It's so empty in here, I'd swear there must be a hole in my head." Groucho said, and he let him in.

Everyone shuffled around to accommodate the singing telegram messenger. He put a harmonica in his mouth to achieve the right pitch and sang from Wagner's, *Der Ring des Nibelungen*, quite loud, in German, which no one understood.

Knock. Knock. "Who's it now?" Groucho asked.

"You ordered hotdogs?" a voice asked.

"Corn dogs." Chico corrected him.

"Honk! Honk!"

"And chili dogs," Groucho said. "Maybe we ordered hedgehogs, but now I'm confused. Didn't someone also order Braunschweiger?"

Groucho let the server into the already cramped stateroom. Holding his tray above his head, he fell on top of Ouida and sandwiched her between him and Harpo.

"Let me go, you—" Ouida pounded on Harpo's chest. She was so infuriated; she didn't know what to call him. He honked his horn again. "You *Honk! Honk!*"

Groucho leaned over Ouida and almost poked her with his cigar. "Who's disputing that it isn't a dog-eat-dog world?"

"A dog's life, that's-a for sure," Chico remarked in his phony Italian accent.

Violet, silent the entire time, scooted around wherever possible.

"Let me out!" Zeppo shouted. "I'm getting seasick!"

Everyone reacted in horror, anticipating the worst.

* * *

Myrna and Powell went in separate directions. While he returned to the lounge, she clutched the counterfeit Asta and hurried over to the front desk to use their phone, insisting it was an emergency.

The concierge directed her to a bank of payphones. "We can't have passengers tie up our front desk lines, no matter how urgent."

Infuriated he wouldn't make an exception, Myrna grappled with the naughty dog. She squeezed into a phone booth and asked the operator for the Los Angeles Police Department, not realizing she should've called the Long Beach Precinct.

"Then transfer me," she demanded.

"Ma'am, you'll have to call them directly," the policeman replied.

Myrna blurted it out so fast he couldn't follow. "I don't have time. You must do this for me. A German woman is stealing dogs. She's selling them to the highest bidder. For some sort of revenge. That's what her name translates to in English. We're both at a party on the *Queen Mary*. She needs to be arrested, and the dogs need to be found."

The telephone operator interrupted. "Please deposit another twenty cents to continue your call for the next three minutes."

Myrna had no change left. "Please, I beg of you. Call the proper precinct. Report this—"

Before she finished, her dog broke loose. Myrna tried to chase after the little varmint, but she didn't realize her long gown got caught on the hinges of the phone booth's folding door. When she sprang toward Asta, she fell face-first on the carpet.

* * *

Zeppo Marx, dashing straight-man of the comedic foursome, slithered out of the impossible confines of the stateroom. He, who faked the entire episode of being nauseous in order to leave, took a deep breath before commencing a maniacal sprint through the lengthy corridors toward the bar. There, he grabbed Countess Velma's arm with such ferocity she lost her balance.

"You're needed now!" he said, panting.

"First, let me tell Errol." She pointed to another area of the lounge, where admirers surrounded him.

Zeppo didn't even give her a chance to ask where or why. He offered to sweep her up into his arms, but she declined. When he found an abandoned wheelchair in the hallway, he picked her up and plopped her down.

"Sit and stay!" he commanded, as if she were a dog.

Then he picked up speed by pushing her in the wheelchair, since she no longer had to run in heels. Zeppo came to a stop in front of the stateroom, where his brothers remained with Ouida, Violet, and the others. He assisted the confused countess out of the wheelchair and knocked on the door.

"Who's this now?" said a voice from the inside.

"Sounds like my brother, Groucho. We're here for the count," he replied. *His password.*

"I don't know. Last time I counted, it was getting pretty crowded in here and the people were not friendly. There was a book I wanted to read, but the lights went out after you left, so now it's pretty dark, too. Outside of a dog, a book is a man's best friend. Inside of a dog, it's too dark to read. Are you sure this is the right room?"

"Do you mind letting us in?" Zeppo turned to his ward and insisted they were in the right place. He showed her a note, as proof, with the correct room number.

"For God's sake, open the damned door!" shrieked a woman's voice from inside, who sounded like Ouida.

The countess cocked her head like a clueless German Shepherd. "He needs his head examined, and you're too polite. Try the doorknob. Maybe it's unlocked."

Zeppo tugged on the door. When it finally swung open, an avalanche of at least a dozen people tumbled out and fell on top of Zeppo and the countess, burying them on the bottom.

Part III

Babs needed to leave the lounge before Ouida returned. She sifted through the crowd to say one last word to Nigel.

"You look upset." He pointed out her furrowed brow with his index finger. "If you don't smooth out those wrinkles now, they'll come back to haunt you years later."

She ignored his warning. "I'm uncertain what your wife's been up to, but please do me a favor."

"Anything, dear. How can I be of help?"

"Maybe I should give Basil better credit for possessing the skills of a real-life Sherlock Holmes. He saw right through my disguise. Best to tell him what I'm doing, so he doesn't interfere with either of our plans—mine or your wife's detaining Ouida. Can you do this for me?"

"Don't doubt me for a minute, but one more thing. I don't know if this has any bearing on your plans, but recently, Basil and I encountered a disturbing situation."

Babs checked the time. "What happened?"

He whispered, "Quite by accident, we came across an underground dogfighting ring. Run by Nazi supporters."

"You can't be serious."

"Bloody hooligans. I didn't think people like that existed. Well, anyway, Basil and I found the situation horrendous, but weren't sure how to take proper action. I tried calling the police in my precinct because the ones downtown endorsed them. I must've bungled it and got nowhere. For Basil… Let's just say playing Sherlock Holmes on-screen worked against him. When he tried to make a few inquiries, no one took him seriously."

Just like when he tried to report his missing dog at the pound, Babs thought.

Nigel concluded, "Anyway, it wouldn't surprise me if they might have a connection with the dogs you seek. You are the real detectives, however, and I shouldn't be telling you how to do your job."

She thanked Nigel for the tip and readied for her next challenge. How was she going to cut across this gigantic ocean liner on her own without a map? Babs needed to find out if Wiggins ever reunited with Guy and Sir Henry, but first, she wanted to check on Ivan. He had waited by his limousine because he couldn't risk his employer seeing him. She also needed to know if Ivan had kept tabs on those who boarded or disembarked the ship.

Babs asked the bartender for a bottle of Coke and scooped finger food into a napkin. The least she could do for the poor guy, who was all by himself in a dark parking lot. Guy had instructed him to park next to Wiggins' truck, but when she located his pickup, she didn't see a limo parked anywhere nearby. Running short on time, she left his snacks for the seagulls before racing back up the gangplank.

* * *

Hammett and Hellman availed themselves of the open bar.

Lillian inspected the crowd from her comfortable perch. "Quite a full house tonight."

Dash inched closer and whispered, "You'd think with pretty much half the cast from *Oz*, their missing dog would materialize—courtesy of Glinda, the Good Witch from the East."

Lillian took out a tarnished brass clamshell case, containing her personal stash. "Gotta keep fumigating my brains," she joked.

He offered her a light. "Each coffin needs a few nails."

"What do you think of that sissy Sam Spade?" Lillian asked.

"Guy Brandt? Not so bad," Hammett said. "Tries too hard to be tough."

Lillian left a lipstick print on her cigarette. "Babs Norman... What do you think of her?"

"Drop-dead gorgeous, and yet she has a—how do I say it? A virginal quality. Yet I still can't believe we encountered an honest-to-goodness, real female flatfoot," he said.

"I'm not sure if I'm used to such a hard-edged woman who isn't either a criminal or a femme fatale, but this situation is as real as real can be. You're not doing the you-know-what with her on the side, are you?" Lillian asked.

He cleared his throat to make a point. "Seems like every healthy-minded male is being accused of hanky-panky with Babs Norman. When you see a broad like Babs, she breaks the mold, and I find that refreshing. Don't you?"

"Aren't you partial to promiscuous blondes or lanky brunettes with wicked jaws?" she asked.

"I'm partial to you." He gave her an unexpected nip behind her ear; she blushed.

"Lillian, give me your opinion of that snake in the grass who thinks he's God's gift to womankind."

"Assuming you're referring to Errol Flynn, let's say he looks about as inconspicuous as a tarantula on a slice of angel food."

"Be honest, honey. What do you think of Countess Velma?"

"Quoting Chandler once again, from thirty feet away, she looks like a lot of class. From ten feet away, she looks like something made up to be seen from thirty feet away."

Dash's tuberculosis gave him a kick in the chest. The moment he caught his breath, he asked, "Have you been reading Raymond Chandler behind my back?"

"What if I told you we were having an affair?"

"I'd say you're drunk, and you're lying.

Lillian swiveled her stool. The swift jerk caused her to slip, and the rest of her martini spilled on the counter. He helped her back onto her seat and pointed to the mural behind the bar.

"Called *The Royal Jubilee Week*," he said. "Depicting a circle of people. All holding hands, and dancing in celebration. See the woman on the left? She appears to have lost her footing, but the crowd carries her along. Reminds me a little of you and how sometimes I have to pick you up when you're down. There are other times you're there for me, so it works both ways. Enough of the shaggy-dog story. Is it already time to take you home?"

Lillian shook her head and examined her empty glass. Held up her hand to hail the bartender, but Dash gently pulled it down.

There was a slight slur to her words. "Do you think Powell was seeing double, or was he serious about placing that wager?"

"I think you're starting to see double. Perhaps you should slow down." He gave her a reassuring hug. "Powell didn't know which way was up, even more so after he rustled poor Myrna into it. I'm sure he heard an earful from either her, or he will hear from her husband tomorrow morning. However, he offered a handsome price."

Dash reminded her they still had a long night ahead. He grabbed a plate and filled it with hors d'oeuvres, and insisted she put something in her stomach.

Chapter Thirty-Six: All the Queen's Men and Women

Sir Henry had broken loose but found Babs, lost and looking for her partners. "To you, I must smell like my same old self, even if I look like Eileen Adlon."

He led her to Guy and Wiggins, who almost didn't recognize her after her glamorous transformation. Wiggins also joked about Guy's impersonation of a blind man with his guide dog and said he reminded him of an old sea captain with his fake beard made from castoff dog hair. Guy, relieved he didn't need the disguise any longer, pocketed his welder goggles.

Now, since she reunited with her friends, Babs couldn't get her questions out fast enough. "Have you located the rest of the dogs?" she asked. "I expect more than just Toto and Asta. I tried to check on Ivan. His car isn't there."

"Hold on," Guy said. "You're going in too many directions. Ivan will be back long before we need him."

Sir Henry took off again at a quick clip and stopped in front of an entrance to the engine room. He barked to signal they needed to enter. Guy went first. Wiggins second, but he retraced his steps when Babs hadn't followed.

"Whatcha waiting for?" he asked.

Babs took a hard swallow. It was even more of a labyrinth inside—and hot, dirty, and damp. If it wasn't from the filth, her sweat stains would ruin her borrowed couture.

Sir Henry's scruffy ears stood straight up. Must've sensed something the humans couldn't and took off again.

At a loss, Babs threw her hands up in the air. "Which way did he go?"

Wiggins reoriented their position on his map. "According to this, there are two engine rooms, two turbo generator rooms, five boiler rooms, which house twenty-seven boilers, and—"

"One crazy sniffer dog lost amid this maze," said Guy. "We're going to have to be on our guard."

Unable to find Sir Henry, Babs broke out into a sweat from the unbearable heat. "Feels like the soles of my shoes are melting."

Wiggins cupped his ear and swore he heard Sir Henry's barks. They came to a halt in the Aft Steering Room, where they discovered over two dozen snarling dogs penned in wire cages.

Stumped, Guy said, "These look nothing like the dogs we saw at the countess's."

He warned Babs to stay back and grabbed Sir Henry by the collar.

"I wouldn't want to keep any of these fellers around as my pet," Wiggins said. "They look like fightin' dogs. Ears chewed up. Raw sores. Broken teeth. The kind you'd throw into a pit for sport." He addressed Babs. "You're the boss. What next?"

She asked Guy for his handkerchief. With a loud, unladylike burst, she blew her nose like a bassoon. "Forgive me," she said.

"What for?" Wiggins asked.

Almost in tears, Babs stopped and panicked. "I think we just won the Academy Award for the world's worst detectives. Everyone gave us an impossible deadline. At times, I had to do everything on my own. We didn't have enough time to think this through. How are we going to get the dogs off the ship without getting caught? Plus, these aren't the dogs we want. I feel like someone spun me around in circles with a blindfold on, and now, while disoriented, I'm supposed to find my target."

Guy couldn't believe his ears. "Everyone makes mistakes. We'll figure this out."

Abel Wiggins reexamined his map and began whistling *My Bonnie Lies Over the Ocean*.

Babs lost her marbles. "How can you be so cheerful at a time like this?"

"Isn't there an old saying that you might as well belt out a ballad before you greet the hangman's noose?"

In an act of sheer madness, "Got to go," was all Babs said before she took off. Despite Guy pleading she couldn't quit on them now, and Wiggins shouting, "Have you gone bonkers?" she left startled faces in her wake.

* * *

Feeling something was wrong, Babs bolted out of the engine room and up to the top deck. She gritted her teeth—so nervous she could scream. Nigel Bruce had given her a tidbit of information that struck a chord. She didn't understand its ramifications at the time, but now it made sense. Not only that, but her gut feelings also told her one of two things: either Captain Irving knew nothing about the fighter dogs, or if he did, he was in on it. Those unanswered questions compelled her to abandon her friends and locate him. This was the complete opposite of what Sherlock Holmes would've done, but she also knew better than to ignore her intuition. She hoped her hiding place was safe, as she observed and overheard the goings-on inside the Captain's Bridge.

A group of firebrands, all armed, wearing leather boots, breeches, revolver belts, and swastika armbands, held Captain Irving and his crew at gunpoint. Ivan Alexandrescu, their chauffeur, stood among them. No wonder she couldn't find him earlier.

Their leader identified himself as Kommandant Walter Jäger. He spoke in German to his comrades, but communicated in clear, almost perfect English to the American crew. Weedy and angular, he reminded Babs of a watered-down version of Conrad Veidt from *The Cabinet of Dr. Caligari*, but shorter. His main stormtroopers: Otto Braun and Cig Angermann, the smoking man from the stateroom. All recent hires at the Hollywood Kennels. While Cig had his weapon drawn, Otto held onto a leash, restraining four vicious pit bulls.

Captain Irving stood his ground. "We know you use our ports to distribute significant sums of money, guns, and Nazi propaganda. We're also aware you dispatch these to places like your Aryan bookstore, meeting halls like *Alt Heidelberg* and *Deutsches Haus*, private supper clubs like *Wurst Haus* downtown, and other places beyond. I'm sure our Department of Justice already has undercover operatives who've infiltrated your Bund. Once they catch up to your German American League, Hitlerites, or whatever you call yourselves, they'll deport all of you."

"Don't be so sure," said Jäger. "Many of us have already infiltrated the National Guard and the Secret Service. Southern California has valuable, but vulnerable, aircraft production facilities and military installations."

The first officer tried to reach for a phone. Cig aimed his pistol and shot it out of his hand. Babs almost screamed from the sudden noise but was lucky she didn't.

"After your men finish the ship's retrofitting for combat, instead of sailing for Australia, you'll be heading into Japanese waters," said Jäger.

"They'll torpedo us!" the captain cried.

"On the contrary, they'll capture her and use her like a Trojan Horse," Jäger replied. "We'd have the German navy do it, but since Japan is closer and they're our allies, we've delegated that task to them.

"Our German Radio Hour broadcasts every Friday night on KRKD. When we play your pre-recorded Sherlock Holmes radio show, we'll transmit the ship's coordinates in an unbreakable code to the Japanese navy for intercepting this vessel."

"What do you plan with those dogs?" the first officer asked.

"The fighters are for sale to brother Bund organizations. One of our methods of raising money for our German cause is illegal betting. At the moment, they're caged in a secret location on one of your lower decks, separate from the others. They're dangerous and require special handling. Our transfer will occur nearby in San Pedro. Those Japanese fishing vessels along the coast are not as innocent as they look.

"When the *Queen Mary* arrives in Japan, we'll auction the celebrity-owned and movie dogs to the highest bidders," replied Jäger.

"Not only do you have my crew, but everyone attending the party downstairs."

"From this point on, consider them prisoners of war," said Jäger. "I'm sure the Japanese will get exorbitant ransoms for your Hollywood stars."

The captain continued his accusations. "You'll never get away with this. Your organizations are flawed. Just like those fighting dogs, you're often pitted against each other."

"Let me remind you which side of the gun you're on," Jäger said. "A New Germany will rise and destroy the pornographic and demoralizing films of Hollywood. The studios, producers, directors, and actors who make them will pay the ultimate price."

The first officer said, "You're all talk and no action."

Jäger gave an order in German to Cig. He fired at the rebellious first officer, to wound and teach a lesson, but not to kill. The bullet grazed his shoe, tearing off its leather. He fell and clutched his bleeding foot. Captain Irving ordered his staff captain to fetch supplies and administer first aid.

Jäger cautioned his hostages. "We are willing to die for our Fatherland. Are you?"

After a round of Nazi salutes and *Heil Hitlers*, Babs took off.

Chapter Thirty-Seven: Rogues' Gallery

Part I

B abs needed to warn the others. Crossing portside from bow to stern, she passed the sports deck and gymnasium and made a sudden stop in front of the ship's dog kennels.

Dog kennels? How come it never showed up on Wiggins' map? She did a double take and peeked inside, where someone had moved Asta, Toto, and many more celebrity dogs.

Babs took a quick mental inventory. Most had temporary tags dangling from their collars. If not, a handmade sign by their pen or cage. She bent over toward the German Shepherd. His tag said Rin-tin-tin, Jr. Another German Shepherd had a sign, Ace the Wonder Dog. Then she examined a Newfoundland named Cappy. "Oh, my! Humphrey Bogart is your owner."

More dogs: Owner: Shirley Temple Breed: Pekingese; Owner: Bette Davis, Breed: Scottish Terrier; Name: "Zero" or "Pard," Breed: Terrier-mix. Babs giggled when she saw two Dachshunds named Stinky and Poopshin, belonging to Joan Crawford. The list went on. Owner: Mae West, Breed: Borzois; two Cocker Spaniels, Owner: Elizabeth Taylor; an Irish Setter of Clark Gable's, named Lord Reily of Redwood, and a Standard Schnauzer named Arno, belonging the Errol Flynn.

"Imagine the surprise when they find out their missing dogs were right under their noses, or in actuality, the owners are right under the dogs' noses."

The animals went berserk the moment the ship's foghorn blared. Her ears rang, and her whole body vibrated with such severity, she didn't think she'd ever stop shaking. Afraid the commotion might alert the fifth columnists, she rushed toward the nearest exit.

* * *

Babs returned to her friends, perspiring and out of breath. Even though she'd forget half the names of the dogs and their affiliations, she unraveled what happened, but Sir Henry became anxious.

Guy attached a leash to his collar. "He's trying to tell us something."

"Maybe he smells their scents on me," said Babs.

Without warning, Sir Henry bolted, and the threesome engaged in the game of "Follow that Dog." This time, he dragged them into one of the ship's propellor rooms. Surrounded by railings, they noticed a dangerous drop into the water below. He circled the area and bayed like a hound, sparked by the sound of approaching footsteps. Guy tried to clamp his mouth shut, but to no avail.

A man with a slight Liverpool accent called out, "Ahoy! No one's supposed to be here."

Babs gave Wiggins the nod, figuring he'd look less out of place in his *Queen Mary* custodial uniform.

"Sir, these young'uns lost their pup, and I volunteered to help them. Can't figure out why he wanted to come here, but at least we found him."

The man introduced himself as Jack Stewart, chief engineer of the *RMS Queen Mary*. Guy continued to make an effort to muzzle Sir Henry with his bare hands. Jack and Wiggins talked shop, with their janitor bluffing through their conversation.

Babs intervened. "Sir, we need to level with you. Despite appearances, Wiggins is assisting my partner and me. I'm Babs Norman. He's Guy Brandt. We're private investigators. Metro-Goldwyn-Mayer hired us to return two of their most famous animal actors, Toto from the *Wizard of Oz* and Asta from the *Thin Man* series. We believed a group of people were hiding them on this ship, but just discovered they're a bunch of armed militiamen. A few minutes ago, I spied on one of their conversations. They're on your top deck and have taken your captain and crew hostage. If what they said is true, they plan on hijacking your ship, and holding the onboard celebrities for ransom."

Jack froze in place, speechless. He loosened his grip on his wrench, which dropped out of his hand and clanged on the floor.

She asked, "Did you or your men have anything to do with smuggling a bunch of dogs on board?"

"Of course—not," Jack stammered, his hands still shaking.

Babs disclosed she found two groups of dogs in opposite areas of the ship. "They must've had helpers. If none of your crew assisted them, who did?"

The engineer still appeared traumatized.

"If I can get Sir Henry to stop barking," Guy said, "he's got a talent for tracking scents, but it seems like we've reached a dead end."

Wiggins braced himself against the railing to check his map but dropped it into the water by accident. "Not sure if I could find my way to the top deck without it."

Jack regained his voice. "Don't worry. If anyone knows the ins and outs of this place, you're looking right at him."

Babs tried to figure where to go next. "When Wiggins and I found Asta and Toto holed up in one of your staterooms, two of their men almost discovered us. Wiggins hid in the closet. I crawled under the bed. Neither of us could see anyone's faces, but I heard the distinct voices of one German who had the upper hand, and one American, forced into cooperating with him. At one point, the American called him Cig.

"Later, I confirmed he was Siegfried Angermann, the trainer I met at Gale and Henry East's Hollywood Kennels, but I swore I'd heard the American's voice before. For the longest time, it drove me crazy, but I think he was Rennie Renfro.

"Guy, I know you thought I was going off on a tangent, but remember when I did all that research on Sherlock Holmes?"

"When you wasted our valuable time," he replied.

"Not if we use Arthur Conan Doyle's story, *The Adventure of Silver Blaze*, as an analogy."

"You were obsessed about the 'curious incident of the dog in the nighttime,'" said Guy.

"Correct. The stableboy abducted a stallion named Silver Blaze. Not a simple task. One would think the owner's watchdog would've barked and alerted everyone.

"That said, what if the dogs we're trying to recover didn't cause a stink because they knew their abductors, and that's how they smuggled them onto the *Queen Mary*? We need to find the animal trainers. They must be here."

Jack interjected. "Conan Doyle, you say? Interesting how life makes the strangest connections."

"What do you mean?" asked Babs.

"Not long ago, I befriended a neighbor after some speedster tried to mow him down. He also has an intimate bond with Sherlock Holmes—Basil Rathbone."

Guy and Babs gave each other guarded glances.

"Regardless," Jack replied, "your pup could never detect anyone's smell through all these tons of steel. The *Queen* is over one thousand feet long and high enough to rival a skyscraper."

"Let me ask you a question," said Babs. "Is there a holding area that might serve as a prison?"

Jack stroked his beard. "There's an Isolation Ward. A quarantine area for those with lice or contagious diseases, which the ship's medics don't want spread to other passengers. If someone's holding others hostage, it makes sense they would detain your people there."

Wiggins spoke up. "I say we go for it."

"It's off-limits to the public with few ways to access it," said Jack. "There's a staircase we can use off the First-Class Smoking Room. Should be empty tonight. None of your revelers would be interested since our captain confined the bar service to the Observation Lounge."

Everyone followed Jack through the covered promenade decks, up several levels, and down a narrow stairwell to the ship's Isolation Ward, where the lack of windows made the air smell stale and dank. Everyone's hunches played out. Gagged and secured to permanent fixtures by handcuffs, present and accounted for: Frank Weatherwax, the Easts, Rennie Renfro, and Alice and Carl Spitz. Neither detective had met the Spitzes before, but Babs recognized them from photos she'd seen in Strickling's office. They had trained Toto for *The Wizard of Oz*.

The detectives removed their gags. Jack instructed Wiggins where to find the nearest bolt cutter, and he cut off their handcuffs. After a round of questioning, no two opinions were alike. Babs summarized what occurred inside the captain's quarters and brought up the issue of Ivan.

"He came to our office and claimed the countess stole dogs from movie stars and planned to smuggle them overseas. According to his story, she forced him, along with others, to cooperate. He told us about her plans to ship the dogs to Australia and New Zealand, the *Queen Mary's* original route for troop transport. This differs from what I overheard about the ship being diverted to Japan. Between these two accounts, we have a lot of misinformation."

"A deliberate strategy to confuse you," Jack added.

Given Babs' disclosure, only some believed von Rache was the mastermind behind the dognappings and worked with the hostile Nazi sympathizers. Others didn't.

"Hold on a second," Babs said. She addressed the entire group but gave a special nod to her partner. He had always believed in the countess's innocence.

"Most of you admitted involuntary or blind participation with these— fiends, or whatever you want to call them. I also get the impression none of you knew about their affiliations with controversial politics. Don't think I'm taking sides, but I'm the one who overheard Jäger's plans. Not once did he mention von Rache's direct participation in their fascist coalition."

Guy expressed his concern about the dogs prepared for sport fighting.

"Were there pit bulls?" Renfro asked.

"Looked like it, why?" replied Guy.

"Thinkin' about Petey from the *Little Rascals*. He's a pit bull. Haven't worked with him since you saw me on the studio lot. Hope someone hasn't messed him up in this racket. He wouldn't survive ten minutes if thrown in the ring."

"Their network is far greater than we've imagined," said Weatherwax. "Whoever is behind this, they've kept us in the dark, on purpose."

Babs addressed Henry East. "Think back to when I visited your kennel. Remember when I got knocked down by a Rottweiler?"

"I haven't been able to figure out how those belligerent dogs got past my watch," he explained. "Somehow, they came and went, but never stuck around for long. Not sure why, but now, since this is out in the open, I think someone funneled them through us. Then on to someone affiliated with the countess."

Weatherwax added, "The German handlers you encountered have those answers."

"Are you also aware that von Rache hires a German household staff?" asked Renfro.

"Rennie, when we spoke at MGM," said Guy, "I'd like to know how you knew the countess wanted to acquire dogs?"

Renfro shrugged. "Word of mouth. Look, I'm innocent and on your side. Stumped like the rest of you."

The Rathbones had a provisional staff who was also German, thought Babs. They could've been behind Leo's abduction.

Jack asked her where she spotted the problematic dogs.

"Some sort of control room, but this ship seems to be full of them. Neither my partner nor I had ever seen them before. We sought the ones housed in the top deck kennels. If those trigger-happy fascists are still up there—"

"Too dangerous," said Jack, who began counting. "We've got eleven on our end. Babs, would you say that's an even match?"

"No idea. They might've stationed more of their men throughout the ship."

"Or they might bring in reinforcements," Jack said, "Because they can't sail this ship with the skeleton crew I hired for tonight's event. A smart move. This party is the perfect distraction, allowing them to work behind the scenes."

CHAPTER THIRTY-SEVEN: ROGUES' GALLERY

"Jack, you know this vessel better than anyone else," Guy said. "What do you suggest?"

He picked up the nearest in-house phone, but all those lines were dead. "I hope those Krauts didn't tamper with the outside ones."

* * *

Errol Flynn's roaming eyes would soon get him into hot water. Powell, who also lost all sense of propriety, egged on Flynn, starting with who could come up with the most poignant insults. With no sober bystanders as witnesses, no one was sure who threw the first punch. Rathbone accused Flynn of being a pompous ass and no longer cared whether his wife resurfaced and discovered his inappropriate behavior.

Quite plastered, Basil was in one of those wicked moods and wanted to match his machismo against a worthy opponent. He feasted his eyes on Captain Irving's collection of royal swords. "Tyrone, how fresh is your memory of that last scene we practiced for the *Mark of Zorro*?"

Power dodged a roundhouse punch, which almost grazed his cheek. "Fresh as Flynn's mouth, why?"

"We've kept tight lips on the highlights of our upcoming project, but there's always a chance he'd best me if I reprised scenes from either *Robin Hood* or *Captain Blood*."

Tyrone said, "Don't underestimate him. He's had recent practice filming *The Sea Hawk*."

"Ah... I forgot. Are you game for taking him on and teaching him a lesson? He wouldn't be familiar with our choreography from *Zorro*."

"Sounds like fun to me." Tyrone clicked his tongue with smug anticipation.

Basil plucked three of the captain's Spanish swords off the wall and tossed one over to Tyrone, who stretched and lunged to prepare for their big showdown. Then, the two of them marched over toward Errol Flynn's direction.

"Perhaps we should settle this like gentlemen," said Tyrone Power.

Basil recited his line from the *Zorro* script. "You wouldn't care to translate that feeling into action, would you?" He tossed the third weapon to Flynn, who licked his lips and grinned at the beckoning challenge.

Flynn tested the feel of his sword and warmed up while the crowd spread out.

Basil, also getting up to speed, slashed at a bouquet of roses and separated a few buds from their stems, witnessed by an awe-stricken audience.

Flynn gave him a shameless sneer. Always one to show off, he performed the technique of *sabrage* and opened a bottle of champagne with his sword. "This might not bode well for you, my friend. Did you forget I killed you in both *Robin Hood* and *Captain Blood*?"

Confident that Power was in his corner, Basil thrust his chin up and said, "Looks like we have a *ménage à trois de guerre*, and we outnumber you."

The theatrics began, although a threesome was not their normal way of practicing. Basil struggled to recall how a fight would play out if they were rehearsing a scene for *The Three Musketeers*. Dueling shadows projected as dancers on the lounge walls, adding to the ominous ambiance of impending doom.

Often, the fighting cavaliers got dangerously close to their onlookers. At one point, Tyrone Power missed a chance to skewer Flynn. Instead, he made a huge slash across Powell's suit and ruined it beyond repair.

Basil and Flynn closed in and locked hilts, head-to-head and eye-to-eye.

"It's curtains for you, Rathbone," Flynn called out, punctuating his sentence with an embarrassing hiccough.

Tensions escalated the moment Violet, Ouida, and the countess returned to the bar while their chaperones tried to outdo each other. Basil tried to take no notice, only to encounter more mayhem. An errant wire-haired Fox Terrier, on the run from Myrna and drawn by the scent of food, catapulted onto a wheeled serving cart and knocked it over. Ouida tried to rush in between the dueling trio but skidded on a fallen chocolate cream pie.

Flynn plowed into Clark Gable, causing him to tumble backward. Gable hit his head on the hard floor.

"He's dead!" The countess went into hysterics and called out for a doctor.

Basil overheard Flynn say to the countess, "Let's make a run for my car.

The gossip columnists love to get creative with their headlines and might give a whole new meaning to my film, *Captain Blood*, if I really killed him."

The brawlers barricaded Basil from chasing after Flynn as he dropped his sword and abandoned their battle of wits and wills. Flynn grabbed von Rache by the arm and used the chaos as camouflage as the two of them high-tailed it out of there. In the meantime, the lounge lizards and the barflies ignored Gable. They carried on with their name-calling while the slugfest continued, producing far better entertainment than the live musicians.

Hellman hopped off her barstool, informing Hammett she'd find the nearest payphone and call the police. She scorned Basil on the way out.

"How about some free advice?" she said. "From a familiar story, *The Thin Man*. 'The problem with putting two and two together is that sometimes you get four, and sometimes you get twenty-two.' Rathbone, there's a jail cell waiting—with your name on it."

Part II: Roundup

Babs let Jack Stewart take charge, given he knew the layout of the *Queen Mary* better than anyone else. She asked, "How can we smuggle the dogs off the boat without being noticed?"

"What about lowering them in the lifeboats?" Guy suggested. "Isn't that how people got off the *Titanic*?"

"Unlike the ill-prepared *Titanic*, the *Queen* should have twenty-five motor-driven steel lifeboats, most at thirty-six feet long," said Jack. "All unsinkable and with the capacity of carrying four busloads. Since Wiggins is a handyman, he and I will know the nuts and bolts of operating heavy machinery. I guess it'll be up to us to launch them, since we'll probably need to do it manually and not rely upon doing it from the Captain's Bridge."

Henry East said he felt confident enough to find the kennels on the top deck without their help and volunteered to lead the rest up there.

Guy tossed aside his blind man's cane.

Jack picked it up and claimed it as his own. "This might seem like a burden to you, but I'd never discard something I might need to beat off an angry mob—human, dog, or otherwise."

"I gave this lassie's ex-husband his just desserts by using my mop and pail," Wiggins said, referring to Babs. "You never know when an everyday object can come in handy."

Jack found a chalkboard and drew a rough diagram. "Here's the rundown. The dogs you want are in the kennels. Now, the bad news. They're near where those blackguards held the captain, and I'm sure they've left men on continuous watch. Therefore, we need to board the ones furthest away from trouble. Each lifeboat has a radio telephone, which I'll use to call for help. Give me a show of hands. Who knows how to operate a small motorboat?"

Jack frowned. "Not many. All I can say is once you rescue all the dogs, try to pair up the best you can."

"What about the portable cages?" Weatherwax asked. "That'll be the easiest way to transport the dogs in a hurry."

"Release them right before boarding," Jack said. "Choppy waters tonight. If anything happens and they go overboard, you don't want them trapped in a cage where they'll sink and drown. Find the flotation devices. Once we lower your lifeboat, put yours on first. The children's sizes should fit most of your medium to larger dogs. You might have to get inventive with the smallest ones. There will be quite a drop from the top deck to the water's surface, and they're liable to get excited."

"What do we do once we're on the water?" asked Babs.

"Wait for me," said Jack. "I know how to navigate these dark shores toward San Pedro, so you'll stay close and follow unless we run into snags."

"What about my truck?" Wiggins said. "I can't leave it here."

"He has a point. We need to coordinate what to do when we get to San Pedro," said East. "Babs, Guy, what were your original plans?"

"We had no idea the rescue would involve so many people," said Guy. "Even worse, now with one driver and vehicle—Wiggins' pickup truck. All of us can't fit."

"Ivan had volunteered to use the limo he borrowed from the countess," said Babs, "before we knew he'd turn traitor."

"What did you plan afterward?" asked Weatherwax.

"Put the dogs into both cars and take them straight to the pound until placed with their owners," said Babs.

"Except for Toto and Asta," Guy said. "We figured Sir Henry could babysit for them overnight at our office. Then we'd give them door-to-door service at MGM tomorrow."

East offered a better solution. "We'll make room for them at my place. Have you ever been to the city pound?"

"Just to file a report for the Rathbones. Why?" Babs asked.

"There is no actual shelter. Lots of talk about building one, but they'll just process the dogs and ship them out to the nearest humane society. Depending on space in those facilities, they might continue to break up the pack and disperse the dogs all over the county. Getting past all the red tape to return them to their rightful owners could get way too complicated. Boarding them at our kennels, even if temporary, will be a better choice."

"To be clear," Gale added, "We'll keep the celebrity dogs, not the fighters."

Everyone knew their orders. They synchronized their watches and aimed for success.

Jack wiped his brow and said, "Godspeed and God Save the *Queen*."

* * *

Everyone on the rescue team clambered to the top deck. In nothing short of a miracle, they retrieved the dogs without attracting attention. Jack and Wiggins shuttled the detectives and the trainers with their dogs into the lifeboats, with Carl Spitz being the last one to launch.

When Spitz was ready to board, trouble surfaced. Otto Angermann headed toward them, wrangling a group of bloodthirsty attack dogs. Giving them a command in German, he unfastened their leashes, and the dogs charged toward Jack, Wiggins, and Spitz.

"Forget about us. Get in the boat!" Jack demanded of Spitz.

Spitz shoved a small bag into Jack's hand. "Take these. They're dog treats. Throw them as far as you can in the opposite direction—to distract them."

Spitz scrambled into the lifeboat. Wiggins engaged its descent. When the attack dogs got within range, Jack pitched the kibble like trying to win the World Series. The dogs turned tail and went after the scattered treats, even harder to find in the dark. This bought valuable time for Wiggins to ready the final lifeboat for Jack, but his clumsy janitorial supplies kept getting in the way.

"Why do you insist on dragging those things around like they're prized possessions?" asked Jack. "You can always replace them."

Wiggins gave his reasons. "You saw value in Guy's cane."

Unable to use his dogs as weapons, Otto drew a pistol and charged forward. "Halt! How dare you steal our dogs!"

Wiggins swung his mop at Otto, but struck his shoulder, which caused its wooden shaft to snap. "I thought my mop would last me 'til Kingdom Come."

The German fired his last bullet, shooting a hole through Wiggins' pail, now useless.

This gave Jack the opportunity to put his fencing skills to use. Before Otto had time to reload, Jack lunged, and using Guy's cane, he knocked Otto's gun out of his hand. He pinned him against the railing by thrusting the cane into his chest. On that cue, Wiggins picked up his bucket and whacked Otto in the head, who passed out on the deck. Jack retrieved the gun and Otto's extra ammunition. Then he got back to his lifeboat, which Wiggins deployed.

* * *

Getting to safety proved to be another challenge, and one that would involve quick thinking. As soon as Jack's lifeboat reached the water's surface, the Germans mobilized at lightning speed. They launched their own lifeboats and followed. The pistol, which Jack lifted from Otto, was almost useless since it was a short-range weapon, and the fog made visibility difficult. The fascists also outnumbered them with both men and firepower.

Jack radioed for law enforcement while rough swells rocked his lifeboat. "Mayday! Mayday! Mayday! This is Chief Engineer Jack Stewart in a lifeboat launched off the *RMS Queen Mary*. Mayday! Armed men, holding the ship's captain hostage. Lifeboats deployed. Heading from Long Beach to San Pedro. We're being followed by Germans with weapons. Also in lifeboats."

All of the sudden, he realized he'd need to distinguish their boats from their enemies'. "Shooters wearing Nazi military uniforms. Our boats all contain dogs, except mine. I will signal using semaphore. Will also use signal flares and pneumatic air whistles for identification. Urgent! Need immediate assistance."

The Germans' boats drew closer, and much to Jack's surprise, they also contained dogs, but fighter dogs, so he had to radio once again to clarify. Even worse, as they headed toward safety in San Pedro, Jack noticed the Germans positioned their boats to trap the canine rescue team between them and their Japanese fishing boat connections.

He called again and asked to alert the Coast Guard. In turn, they must've received additional help from the fire department. When all the boats got close enough to shore, the local firemen turned on their high-pressure fire hoses to keep the German and Japanese boats at bay. This allowed valuable time to dock and for the rescue team to escape.

The doggy gang came ashore and met up with Wiggins waiting by his truck, accompanied by the police. After they settled a few of their immediate concerns, Babs scooted into the front seat of the pickup with Wiggins. Guy and Sir Henry sat in his cargo bed with Renfro and two German Shepherds. Since Ivan's limo was no longer at their disposal, the cops offered to pile the rest of them into the backseats of their squad cars. A motorcade of black and whites prepared to escort everyone up to Hollywood, with their red and blue lights flashing. Jack Stewart stayed behind with the Coast Guard to deal with the crisis on the *Queen Mary*.

* * *

Once Babs and Wiggins hit the road, she became anxious. "Fill me in on what I missed."

"After I launched the last lifeboat containing the engineer," he explained, "I made a mad dash down several levels to the gangplank to retrieve my truck. That's when I spotted Errol Flynn and the countess making a quick getaway. Police cars swarmed the place, but they managed to take off.

"I waited a few minutes so as not to look suspicious, but overheard on police band radios that a bar fight broke out. The cops had orders to haul everyone, save the ship's employees, down to the station. Thank my lucky stars, I still had on my custodian's uniform and hadn't had time to change."

"What about William Powell, Myrna, poor Nigel Bruce, and his wife, Violet? They didn't deserve this." Realizing Ouida Rathbone would also spend the night behind bars, Babs kept the humor to herself. Of all people, she felt the woman had dished out enough punishment that she deserved it to boomerang back.

"They'll prove their innocence soon enough," Wiggins said. "You worry too much."

"Let's hope the police will distract everyone from discovering the dogs are missing," she said.

A few miles later, Wiggins complained about his steering. "We passed a lot of construction back there. I could've run over a nail, and we have a way to go."

"Don't you have a spare?" asked Babs.

"That tire was my spare. I tossed the bald one after I distracted the security guard on the night you snuck into the place in the Hollywood Hills."

By the time they chugged into the Easts' kennels, Wiggins was riding on one of his rims. San Pedro police had already radioed the local Hollywood precinct. They came out to examine the dogs, took statements from the trainers, and put in a request for a search warrant for the countess's residence. The detectives decided it was best to keep Toto and Asta under the Easts' care until they could make the proper arrangements for a personal delivery.

Part III: The Raid

The following morning, the police stormed the von Rache estate, along with immigration agents and the FBI. Zoo officials seized the countess's leopard, along with any other exotic animals. Handlers took the house cats and promised to keep close tabs on them. Authorities warned Babs to keep her distance, as the frenzied countess hurled marble and bronze statuettes at her captors.

"Why are they destroying my house and taking my babies?" she shrieked in a feverish pitch.

At least nobody had to fire a weapon before they wrangled the irrational woman into handcuffs. Making a clean sweep of the property, the police apprehended her, along with her entire household staff, including Ivan.

Their shocking revelation came when Carl Spitz supervised a team of trainers and their assistants and rounded up the remaining dogs for identification. He summoned the detectives, since they were the ones who had been to the compound before.

He pointed to a group of cages. "These don't look like the fancy purebreds you described."

Babs' mouth got dry. "They're...a bunch of plain old mutts."

Guy confirmed they weren't the animals they witnessed earlier.

Weatherwax added, "None are mine. They look like strays."

"Like Sir Henry," Babs murmured. "Without the talent."

Spitz mentioned the countess might've found them wandering the nearby hills and wanted to rescue them from predators like hawks, bobcats, and coyotes.

Babs signaled her team to stop and excused herself to speak to the officer in charge. "Sir, my trainers just called to my attention. These dogs aren't the ones we're after. Woman to woman," she said, "Do you mind if I have a word with the countess—alone?"

Hesitant at first, he granted her request and explained his prisoner would remain handcuffed. Babs could have relative privacy while still under their watchful eye. She pulled the countess aside, and they sat under a shade tree.

"What is happening? Why are you arresting me?" Von Rache was almost nonsensical and wheezed from overbreathing. "I had nothing to do with the fight on the *Queen Mary*. Flynn might be guilty. Everyone was drunk, but I was just his date for the evening. I never even threw a punch."

Babs forced herself to remain calm and focused.

The countess choked out her question. "Oh my God, Clark Gable! Did he die?"

How come no one informed me? Babs had to pretend this was already old news rather than a sudden eye-opener. She took a deep breath, swore to herself not to react, and redirected her inquiry. "This is about another matter. When you...invited my partner and me over for the first time...dogs swam in your pool, and you served balls to dogs like Golden and Labrador Retrievers on your tennis court. These looked like show-quality dogs. Where are they now?"

"From day to day, it's impossible to keep track of them. I never noticed which was which."

Babs didn't buy it. "Have you hidden them? Were you tipped off? I'd suggest being upfront if you expect to prove your innocence."

"New animals came and went all the time."

"Why?" Babs asked.

"Because of my deal with clearing the animal shelters. To me, this was just a dog paradise. Since I knew I'd be giving them away, I never became too attached or gave them names, except Baby, my leopard. My only exception."

Shelters? Babs bit her lip and tried to read into that.

The hysterical woman continued to babble. "When we spoke at the dog show, I told the truth about not owning a dog. I loved dogs so much that I rescued a bunch of these mutts and swore to find them happy homes."

Nonplused, all that came out of Babs' mouth was, "You're a pound raider?"

Teary-eyed, the countess nodded.

Well, doggone it... "What did Ivan... Were you in alliance with those self-righteous fascists?"

"Dahling, what are you talking about?" Von Rache's eyes were bloodshot. Her makeup streaked. "When I moved to America, I escaped the Nazis. Are you telling me they're hiding here in Los Angeles?"

The countess pleaded her case. "I planned on teaming up with Bette Davis. She's the president of the Tailwaggers Society of Southern California. Two summers ago, she threw a party to raise money for an animal hospital and training programs for guide dogs. We discussed ideas for a garden party, which I planned to host right here in the next few months.

"If you ask her, Bette will explain that they held a raffle as part of their fundraising efforts. She'll also brag about how Howard Hughes purchased almost all the raffle tickets for a chance to have a date with her, which, by the way, never happened. Wallace Ford had the lucky ticket and won the prize."

Babs was still stunned but had a gut feeling the woman was telling the truth.

"Your name alone threw me. Why *Rache*? Why revenge? Arthur Conan Doyle used it as a clue in one of his Sherlock Holmes stories, but I guess it wouldn't mean a thing if you've never read them. How did you get your unusual name?"

The countess tried to laugh through her tears. "You can thank my great-great-great-great-grandfather for that. He vowed for the destruction of his enemies over a territorial dispute. Nobility nonsense. Now, it follows me like a curse."

Babs needed to avoid self-incrimination. "Then tell me this. Someone...in your neighborhood recovered Basil Rathbone's Cocker Spaniel roaming on your property. His home is in Bel Air, which makes it doubtful he got to the Hollywood Hills on his own. The person who found him reported it to the police, and they returned him to his owners. Are you saying that you had nothing to do with his disappearance?"

"I don't recall any Cocker Spaniels around here. Ivan, or one of my house servants, must've been behind it." The countess was so panic-stricken, she started shaking. "I'm sorry this happened."

Wait 'til I have a word with my partner, she thought. He was the one who had such a good feeling about trusting Ivan.

Babs gave the cops the go-ahead to take von Rache back into custody. She continued asking questions of the officer in charge.

"Looks like we've cornered the wrong person. I suspect Walter Jäger set her up as his decoy. She claims she has no notion of what was happening, and I'm inclined to believe her."

He went by the book. "That's for us and the Feds to find out."

"To be fair, I think she deserves some leniency. I'd bet that the gang coerced some of our trainers into stealing those animals and used her Bay of Wolves Canyon residence as a clearinghouse to re-distribute them elsewhere. Or the Nazis could have also done it behind their backs or used a combination of these methods. Who knows? She was so involved with her philanthropy, it appears their activities buzzed right past her."

Not everyone has the brains to match their bank account, Babs thought, but she kept those opinions to herself.

Before she left the premises, Babs wanted a word with Special Agent William Wright and Special Agent Sherman Lockwood, the FBI agents who gave her the third degree when she got arrested for trespassing. Compared to the Los Angeles police, they were less than cordial.

* * *

Babs returned to the Easts' by taxi. Since Wiggins left his broken-down pickup at the kennels, he wedged himself into Guy's sidecar, and they rode together on his motorcycle. City officials joined everyone at the kennels after their blitz at the countess's.

During a rare moment of calm, Babs contacted her studio rep at MGM.

"Operator, this is Babs Norman. I'd like to speak with Howard Strickling. Tell him it's a high-priority matter."

Three secretaries transferred her call before he picked up.

"Strickling here. Oh, Babs…the lady detective. Any luck?"

"Today's your deadline."

"I bet you felt like poor Dorothy, trapped in the witch's castle and watching the sand running out in the hourglass."

"We found both of your dogs and many more."

"I guess you're calling about the reward money."

Babs felt shy. "Well, that, and...my partner and I need to avoid publicity."

"This story is sensational! We have to post this in the *LA Times* and the trades."

"Sir, if you don't mind, please keep our names out of it. No photos, either. Just like you handled everything when we returned your stolen pairs of ruby slippers from *The Wizard of Oz*. As private investigators, it could undermine other cases in the future. We're the exception in this town. Everyone else wants to bask in the limelight."

"Gotcha. Where's everyone now?"

"For the time being, we've penned the dogs at the Hollywood Kennels. Long story—but the crooks behind the operation threatened many of the entertainment industry's top dog trainers into assisting them."

"You don't say? This calls for some kind of celebration. Let me arrange something for tomorrow."

"Too soon. We should honor our heroes after we return the missing pets. We also recovered the missing contestants from the Beverly Hills Dog Show. At any rate, we'll need to orchestrate a combined effort between pre-filed police reports, incidents filed at the city pound, and the ASPCA. Oh, yes...and the zoo."

"Why don't I ask my secretary to organize that? Producers from both *The Thin Man* and *The Wizard of Oz* should be able to lend some of their staff to help. It'll be great publicity for MGM to contribute back to the community. I'll invite the Mayor of Los Angeles, the Chief of Police, reporters, a few other muckety mucks, and all of those who reunited with their lost pets. This'll be the biggest blowout in town."

Chapter Thirty-Eight: Every Dog has its Day

After all involved returned the missing dogs, publicity hound Howard Strickling planned a gala event on the MGM studio lot, complete with the press. In his words, "Movies are magic, and this is where they're made." On the significant guest list, besides Guy, Babs and the Dog of the Day, Sir Henry, also hailed as a hero: Judy Garland to pose with Toto, Myrna Loy and William Powell to take photos with Asta, all the trainers, Basil and Ouida Rathbone, Nigel Bruce and Violet, Abel Wiggins along with his family, Jack Stewart, everyone's spouses, and the exonerated Countess Velma von Rache.

Also included: the producers and director from *The Thin Man*, as many as they could gather from the cast of *The Wizard of Oz* (including a few munchkins—good publicity), the Marx Brothers with the addition of Gummo, so all five brothers were present, and with a brief appearance of Gummo, the monkey, courtesy of Renfro who wanted to introduce him to his namesake. Guy kept a safe distance. He didn't want to lose another hat.

If it wasn't for Officer Jefferson Hope and Carlo from the LAPD Canine Training Center, Babs would've never had the chance to meet Sir Henry. Also in attendance were Dashiell Hammett and Lillian Hellman, Tyrone Power, and his wife, Annabella. Noticeably absent: Leo the Lion, MGM's mascot, because too many were afraid of him, and Errol Flynn, who spent the night in jail on a variety of violations, despite recovering his beloved dog, Arno.

Dog owners reveled with their reunited dogs. Even those who didn't own dogs wanted in on the action. According to a quote from the *Los Angeles Examiner*, "The dogs had the full run of the MGM lot. People tossed more balls than at a carnival arcade and threw enough sticks to thatch a roof."

Babs wanted to get down on her hands and knees in front of Countess Velma.

"From the beginning, all signs convinced me you were the guilty party. It's tough for me to admit I was wrong, but I'm so sorry."

"Dear child," the countess confessed, "I had no idea my butler helped coordinate a smuggling ring with members of my staff and others beyond. It's hard to believe I was too busy and perhaps too ignorant to notice. I'm the one who owes everyone an apology."

* * *

Rathbone had snuck up from behind and stood over Babs' shoulder. "Quick, open your purse. Make sure no one sees this."

She noticed a handful of crumpled bills. "Huh? What's this?"

"The best I could do on such short notice. It's my wife's fault the police got the reward when it should've gone to you. Ouida needs to thank you for retrieving our cocker. She was rude and now owes you an apology."

"Basil, please—"

"Once in a while, it wouldn't hurt her to eat a little humble pie," he whispered. "On another note, Nigel Bruce deserves some credit. Despite my animosities toward Errol Flynn, he suggested I throw down the gauntlet."

"Why he...I asked him to inform you what we were up to so your wife wouldn't spoil our plans. Not to provoke a free-for-all."

"Hold your horses. It was the perfect distraction. Kept my wife off your tail, so you could bring the real criminals to justice. You took them down, even if you went after the wrong target.

"In a roundabout way, he also clued me into those Friends...or whatever... of New Germany, and their plot to finance their organization from the seizure and sale of animals, along with assets from gambling from their dogfighting matches."

Babs didn't dare tell him those so-called "friends" also planned on holding him for ransom.

All of the sudden, a cocker ran toward Basil. He couldn't resist picking it up.

"That's not Leo," Babs said. "Whose dog is it?"

He enjoyed every bit of the dog's affection. "One of Elizabeth Taylor's, I believe."

"Better put him down. Your wife is making a beeline in our direction. All we need is another rampage."

Basil laughed it off and promised he'd return the pup to its owner. "One last thing. Who do you think won the contest?"

"What?" Babs' forehead turned into so many furrows, one could've mistaken it for a map of the Los Angeles freeways.

"For the better detectives—Sherlock Holmes and Watson, or Nick and Nora Charles."

"Since when did you have a competition?" she asked, but never received a satisfactory answer. Basil chased after the cocker, and Ouida approached her. Babs sensed her hesitance.

"I'm sorry for any inconveniences I made," she said in a soft tone and tried to keep it between the two of them.

"Please let me assure you nothing ever happened or will happen between your husband and me. As trite as this sounds, our association was in every respect professional," Babs explained.

Let's hope our peace treaty stands, Babs thought.

As corny as it sounded, in this doggone town, she needed more friends than enemies.

* * *

Guy knew his partner needed to tie up loose ends. While Babs tended to those matters, he enjoyed chaperoning Sir Henry, and others loved giving him a hero's welcome. Sir Henry took a fancy to his fellow canines, including a scruffy little mutt close to Toto's size whom Humphrey Bogart chased after.

"Hey Pard, come here, you cute little fella," Bogart said. The dog, always beyond an arm's reach, seemed more interested in Sir Henry than a human.

Rennie Renfro caught up with him. "His real name is Zero, and it was almost bon voyage for this poor little pup. Those Krauts had evil designs on him."

"Well, ya know...I kinda got used to calling him Pard after filming *High Sierra*," Bogie replied.

Guy put the leash back on Sir Henry's collar and joined their conversation. "He's in your next film?"

Bogart picked him up, and Zero licked him all over his face. "He steals the show. In the film, he's supposed to be my bad luck charm, but I guess I shouldn't give too much away. The studio won't do a widespread release of the film until the beginning of next year."

"Is he yours?" Guy asked.

"He's offered to buy him, but I don't know," said Renfro. "If every actor took one of their co-stars home, I'd have nobody left to train." He turned to Bogart and asked, "Come to think of it, don't you already own a few dogs?"

"My wife, Mayo, and I own a few. Those dognappers had their hands on my Newfie, Cappy. Thought he'd get too excited around all the people at this party, so I left him at home."

Guy handed Humphrey Bogart his business card.

Bogart's eyebrows arched as he did a double take. "You're a real son of a gun, shamus?"

"An actor, too, but it's doubtful any casting director would put me in that sort of tough guy role. I can talk the talk, but I'll never look the part."

"Everyone wants to typecast you as the patsy or the fall guy, am I right?" Bogart asked.

Guy nodded. "Once in a while, I'll get roles for a soda jerk or a filling station attendant. Even the dumb idiot. You'd be the dead ringer for an on-screen bird dog. Wouldn't you agree?"

"I dunno. A lot of folks have stereotyped me as a bad apple, if you know what I mean. Well, I'll keep your card in case another one of my dogs goes missing. Really appreciate you bringing Cappy back home. You've become somewhat famous among dog owner circles."

"This case was unusual. Our agency does more than pet retrieval."

"Just yanking your chain, bud." Bogart handed Zero back to his trainer and re-examined Guy's card before pocketing it. "Yeah, I guess you're right. There's always some nut job who wants to extort funds or threaten those with fame. You never know."

* * *

Despite rumors, Clark Gable was still alive. Henry East presented him with Bruno, the bulldog he'd been training, who ran off when Babs first came to visit his kennels. Bruno was one of the lucky ones whom the Germans hadn't dognapped.

"I don't know what to say," said Gable. "Didn't think I'd ever see the hind or hair of my Irish Setter, Lord Reily, and while filming *Strange Cargo,* someone gave me a Labrador Retriever. Add those in with the others, and I have my hands full right now."

Beside himself, East announced, "Anyone want a well-behaved bulldog?"

Babs nudged Wiggins' children to check him out. Between the kids and the dog, it was love at first sight. They convinced their pop to take him home.

Both Asta and Toto sensed the special scent of "hero" coming from Babs and wanted to show their appreciation. The moment she left the kids with Bruno, the two pups hugged her ankles and prevented her from taking another step.

She called out for help. "Am I being marked or cornered? Not sure if I understand this doggie language."

Carl Spitz, Toto's trainer, came to her rescue. "They just want to show you their gratitude."

"Do I have permission to pick one up?"

Spitz snapped his fingers to get Toto's attention. He gave her a funny whistle-like command, and she leapt all the way from the ground and into Babs' arms.

"You should've warned me," said Babs, shaking from the sudden surprise.

"I think she wants you to scratch her behind her ears," said Carl.

"Don't you think Asta might get jealous?"

Asta rolled over on his back with his paws in the air. He wanted a belly rub.

"I'll need an extra set of hands to play with both," Babs said.

Guy arrived just in time to bail her out.

* * *

Despite Babs' worries, Howard Strickling honored his word. He borrowed a bullhorn and stepped onto a small platform. "Stop your cameras!" he announced to the press. Then he invited the detectives to join him and handed a check to Babs.

He said, "Because of their persistence, ingenuity, and hard work, our movie star dogs are back in proper hands. Give these heroes a hearty round of applause."

Requests came from the audience to hear what they planned with their reward.

Cheered on by his partner, Guy went first. "My car bit the dust in the middle of our investigation. One of the first things I'll do is to shop around for a new one and trade in my motorcycle. Then maybe I'll fix up the office. I'd like to dedicate a special corner, complete with a soft bed and chew toys, for our valiant mascot, Sir Henry of the Baskervilles."

Upon hearing his name, Sir Henry woofed and sat up, begging for attention.

Babs waited for the applause to die down. "Given there's a *Wizard of Oz* theme today, and the film's last line is, 'There's no place like home,' all I can think of is that I need to move out of the residential hotel where I'm staying and settle into something more appropriate."

239

"Well, I might have the solution," William Powell shouted from the audience. He pushed through the crowd with his wife in tow and joined Babs onstage.

"The guy in Oz turned out to be a fraud, but this good old wizard might conjure some real magic."

He grabbed the bullhorn. "Some of you might know, I recently married this wonderful woman and fantastic actress, Diana Lewis. Before we were a couple, she made a handful of successful films. She purchased a modest house in the Hollywood Hills and paid off its mortgage. We've been so busy, we haven't even had time to take our honeymoon.

"Oh heavens, here I've done...how many? Maybe sixty movies or more by now, and I'm still a lousy actor and stumble over my own words." He turned to his wife. "Honey, why don't you explain?"

"In honor of bringing back Asta so William can continue making his *Thin Man* movies, I present to you, Babs Norman, the keys to this sweet little cottage," said Diana.

Babs almost lost her voice. "I...I don't know what to say except...thanks."

"Next week, we'll put the deed in your name," Diana explained. "As long as you can pay the property taxes and keep the electricity on, it's yours."

Once again, honoring the detectives' request not to have their pictures taken, Strickling rallied everyone else for a group photo, which included all dog owners who reunited with their pets. Babs took the break to walk over to Wiggins.

"Don't think I'm leaving you out, but I can't tear this check into pieces to divide it," she said. "Give me time to go to the bank. See me in the office on Monday, late afternoon. Have any plans with your share of the money?"

"When I realized the tow and new tires would cost more than I could afford, the Easts bailed me out," he said. "Need to pay them back. In the meantime, I also have to figure out where I can borrow stuff to clean your building. You were already in your lifeboat, but while I tried to ensure Jack's escape, I broke the shaft of my mop, and that no-good Hun, Otto Braun, shot a hole in my bucket."

Babs assured him they could've never rescued the dogs without him. He

240

gave her such a bear hug that her feet lifted off the ground.

* * *

Babs spotted Myrna and caught her attention. Up close, something looked out of place.

"Are you trying to hide a black eye with makeup?" Babs asked.

"Is it obvious? I thought it faded enough by now."

"Please don't tell me you got it in the bar fight," said Babs.

"Far more embarrassing. Happened when I ruined my dress, and it got caught in a phone booth. I hope the bruise doesn't show in any publicity photos," Myrna replied.

"Oh, about your loaner gown… Let's just say it met its demise in the engine room."

Myrna shook her head. "Don't worry. I can no longer squeeze into it."

"Anyway, I need to redeem myself," said Babs.

Myrna tried to focus through the haze of alcohol. "For what?"

"For your arrest and a night in jail. Please tell me. In your own words, what happened?"

Myrna threw back her head and laughed. "Police came and raided the joint. Anyone, including Asta's pup, who wasn't an employee on the *Queen Mary*, went into one of their paddy wagons. Our jailers fell in love with him."

"Myrna, I went into shock when you brought the fake dog into the lounge. I knew he was an imposter because I encountered the genuine Asta earlier in a locked stateroom. You must tell me where you found him."

"That morning, I went over to the Hollywood Kennels to pick up one of his identical puppies. Instead of finding the Easts, I encountered an ill-tempered guy, a thin man… Can't think of his name. He resembled that expressive German actor from *The Cabinet of Dr. Caligari*, but much shorter. Conrad Veidt, or maybe Max Schreck, but without his *Nosferatu* makeup. I always mix up the two."

Babs shuddered. *Kommandant Walter Jäger*.

"He gave me the toughest time, even when I insisted I'd give the dog back. I think he planned on selling the false dog, too. He'd pocket the money for his wretched organization and assume no one would know the difference."

"When the countess saw you bringing him into the lounge, I thought she would croak." *You don't even want to know my response.*

"Despite everything, Myrna, for the longest time, I imagined you were behind Asta's abduction. When you appeared with the look-alike at the Beverly Hills Dog Show, you convinced me you were up to no good. Well, I was wrong. Please set aside any hard feelings."

"Babs, think nothing of it. Contrary to what you'd think, William and I had a blast spending the night in jail. We recited lines from our films and entertained everyone. Even the drunks. We were more intoxicated than they were."

She couldn't understand Myrna's logic, but at last, Babs unloaded the burden she had kept inside.

* * *

"It wouldn't be right if I didn't acknowledge your involvement," Babs said to Nigel Bruce and his wife Violet, in private.

Violet gave Babs a hug. "Sweetheart, I had the time of my life."

Nigel chuckled like Old St. Nick. "Little lady, I have a confession to make."

Babs' eyes grew in size. "No, don't tell me—"

"Trust me. It's not what you think. I figured you needed a distraction. Can't vouch for Basil's display of bravado, but yours truly spilled his drink in Flynn's lap to help spark the fire."

Babs covered her mouth to avoid looking too unladylike in case she bellowed out loud.

"Getting me a role in the radio play was ingenious and far more fun than sneaking around as a cabin maid."

"My dear lady, your methods were unconventional and seemed far from logical," said Nigel. "In my book, you and your partner turned out to be smarter detectives than Holmes or Watson."

* * *

Now, since Babs and Guy wrapped this case, they needed to discuss their plans going forward. Should they share custody of Sir Henry, now, since Babs would be a new homeowner? Would she buy a car and relieve Guy of being her chauffeur? Two unlikely celebrants, however, cut short their conversation, FBI Special Agents Sherman Lockwood and William Wright. They congratulated the detectives for their return of the canine stars and for winning the reward.

"For a moment," Babs said, "the thought occurred to me that the Nazis might've wanted to collect the bounty for themselves—from the studios—for Asta and Toto."

"After we interrogated Jäger," said Wright, "He said the Japanese would pay far more at auction."

"Well, Ivan had everyone fooled," said Guy. "He and his cronies made everyone think von Rache was the guilty party."

"Speaking about Ivan," Babs said. "Is it true what Jäger said about the Nazis and the Japanese taking advantage of slackened security along the California coastline?"

The agents confirmed. The lack of protection allowed them the opportunity to exchange money, intelligence, and weapons. In their specific case, also for trading dogs.

"I guess now we know why Ivan always gave us the impression he had spent time by the water," Guy said. "He must've done his illicit business by the docks when he wasn't working for von Rache."

"My partner kept believing in the countess's innocence. I felt the opposite," said Babs. What I can't understand is how all their activity got past her."

"Her property has lots of acreage," said Lockwood. "One of our prisoners admitted he handed off dogs to whoever manned the guardhouse by her front gates. She would've never known what happened. That was one of many ways they pulled it off."

"If the Germans planned on turning over the Queen Mary to the Japanese, the dogs and the celebrities would be of value. What plans did they have in

243

store for the trainers?" asked Guy.

"They planned on confining the celebrities to their staterooms. Given the size of this ship, they could've kept the trainers in the Isolation Ward. That's, of course, before you released them. They planned on turning over the trainers to the Japanese as POWs to dispose of however they saw fit. I doubt if either the Germans or the Japanese could trust them to keep quiet," explained Wright.

Babs shuddered to think about a worst-case scenario.

"Their timing was uncanny," said Lockwood. "The Germans had prearranged to meet the Japanese fisherman to exchange their fighter dogs, but running into your group stealing back their celebrity dogs—that was never part of their plans."

"You were fortunate they launched their lifeboats closest to where they held the captain hostage, and you got a jump-start, using the ones on the far end, by the stern and under the cover of darkness," Wright said.

"We also had the ship's engineer on our side," said Guy. "How did they expect to hijack an ocean liner with limited personnel?"

Lockwood explained, "From what we've gathered, they had a trained crew ready to board the next day when everyone was sleeping off their hangovers. After all, the *Queen Mary* is a luxury hotel with plenty of staterooms. They had a backup plan to drug the guests to make sure they wouldn't be going anywhere."

Without warning, Guy flinched. Babs, embarrassed to mention it earlier, pointed out he had rubbed his arms throughout their entire conversation. Then she felt her skin prickle. The FBI agents also appeared to twitch and chafe with similar symptoms.

"Looks like our case has gone full circle," Guy said. He laughed, despite his obvious suffering. "We started out with a chance celebrity encounter at a veterinarian's office. Babs found a box of stray kittens in the alley behind our office building. She also rescued an adult, who she thought was their mother."

"I named her Miss Marple after Agatha Christie's character," Babs said, interrupting.

Guy tried to downplay the itching, but it only got worse. "Turned out the adult had fleas. Not much different from the Nazis spreading their insidious influence across Los Angeles."

Lockwood cracked a reluctant smile. "An interesting analogy."

Wright didn't get it and asked for an explanation.

"Think of it," Babs said. "They're great at hiding. Yet they make their host uncomfortable. When they infest the place, they're hard as the devil to get rid of."

"I'd say that's a close comparison," said Guy.

"Makes me never want to bring home a stray dog or cat," said Lockwood. "A good scare tactic to dissuade the kids."

"Guy, consider giving Sir Henry a flea bath after you return home," said Babs. "I think someone's pet brought along a few unwanted party crashers."

Wright concluded, "Despite our initial arrest of the wrong person, on behalf of the FBI, we'd like to acknowledge the two of you for your bravery and for helping solve this complicated but vital case for our national security. If J. Edgar Hoover was here, he'd thank you personally."

* * *

After the special agents departed, Babs realized neither she nor her partner received praise from the Los Angeles police. An ongoing problem ever since they started their agency. Guy gave her a kiss on the cheek for a job well done and headed in a separate direction.

When Babs went over to speak with William Powell and his wife, she didn't realize she'd have company. Nor did she expect to bear witness to an argument. Dashiell Hammett and Lillian Hellman also desired a word. Hammett gave Powell one of those *no excuses* looks. Powell scratched his head. His mouth opened, but nothing came out. His wife, Diana, held tight onto his arm.

"Aren't you forgetting something?" Hammett stopped to light his cigarette. Each passing second ramped up the tension. "Didn't you propose a wager the other night at the Observation Bar?"

"If you knew how much I had to drink, you'd consider it a slip of the tongue and call it a day," said Powell.

Hammett stood there with his hands in his pockets and stared at him in silence.

"What valuable contribution did you offer in recovering those stolen dogs?" asked Powell. "Every time I turned around, the two of you were at the bar with drinks in your hands and holding your own private party."

"You don't consider starting a fight to distract people from discovering the rescue operation a valuable contribution?" Hammett asked.

"You did that on purpose? So, are you taking credit for throwing the first punch?"

Lillian smirked. "No, I am."

Powell's eyes grew wide. In slow motion, the corners of his mouth turned into a disbelieving smile.

Myrna broke the stalemate. She surprised everyone by appearing to switch sides. "I like broads when they prove they're tough, but wasn't part of the wager about coming up with the best detective story?"

"Game's over," said Powell. "The countess is no longer the guilty party."

Myrna was in her cups. "I don't care. Show me your stuff. I'm in the mood to be entertained."

A flush bloomed all over Hammett's cheeks. Even his ears turned red. "Well, my lady and I didn't write any…"

"Too much of the free hooch gave you writer's block?" asked Powell. "That was some shindig on that fancy ship. All bets are off."

"'Tomorrow I'll buy you a whole lot of detective stories, but don't worry your pretty little head over mysteries tonight.' Well…this afternoon rather than tonight, if you want to be exact." Hammett quoted himself from *The Thin Man* with a slight hiccough.

"If there's any prize to be given, our real detectives deserve it—Babs Norman and Guy Brandt," said Powell.

Hammett took a drag and blew his cigarette smoke out in Powell's direction. "If you have another one of those houses you're giving away, I'll take that as a substitute."

"If I was more sober, I'd consider that a threat. Maybe I should hold you accountable for replacing my suit after a swarthy young swashbuckler sliced it like ham and fed it to the dogs."

"Oh poo," said Powell's wife, "There are enough suits in your closet for you to open your own haberdashery."

Hellman and Hammett aggravated Powell and backed him against the trunk of a spikey palm tree.

"Here's an idea," Hammett said. "How about a future installment of the *Thin Man* series? I'll give it to you right here, and right now."

"I'm all ears," Myrna said. "Go right ahead."

Hammett gulped down his drink and cleared his throat. "Provisional title: *Beware of the Thin Man*."

"*Oooh...*" Myrna kicked up her heels. "Tell me more."

He rubbed his hands together, eager to move forward. "All right, Nick and Nora attempt to lead normal lives. As parents of Nicky, Jr., they soon realize a so-called idyllic life of Boy Scouts and kids' softball games could still welcome danger at their doorsteps.

"One day, at a school picnic, Nick and Nora notice others paying too much attention to their son. Distracted by the music, the food, and let's not forget the drinks, someone kidnaps little Nicky, Jr., and..." He stopped and patted down his forehead with his handkerchief. "Sorry, I'm making this up on the fly."

To prove a point, Lillian let her head flop to the side and pretended to snore. "Dull as dishwater, Dash. You just won the grand prize for hackneyed prose."

Babs tried to suppress her giggles amid the standoff.

"Let me take over," Lillian said, "And to quote my boyfriend, 'If you have a story that seems worth telling, and you think you can tell it worthily, then the thing for you to do is tell it, regardless of whether it has to do with sex, sailors, or mounted policeman.'"

Powell bit his lip. She had recited another one of Nick Charles' lines from *The Thin Man*.

She snuffed her cigarette on the thick tree bark. "Picking up where Dash left off, their son's abductors served jail time. Incriminating evidence tied to the mob—an old case of Nick's. One of them kidnaps their son and demands a ransom, because Nora's rich, and she can afford it, and that's his way of getting revenge.

"In the end, Nick and Nora give credit to Asta. He leads them to their boy. By the scent of one of his toys, and you know what?" She looked at the gang. "If you gave me some time behind my typewriter, I could polish this up a lot better. Being sober would also be preferable."

Hammett clapped his hands in mock applause. "You think that was any better?"

Powell tossed the last of his drink on the grass. "Maybe I'm not the best judge. Dashiell's ideas have paid for my country club memberships and fancy automobiles, and all of us just went through this ordeal recovering Asta. Babs, you have no vested interest in who wins and who doesn't. Why don't you decide?"

He's trying to pass the buck. "They're a couple. What's the point? Aren't they going to split the winnings?" She flashed one last look at Powell and expected him to have the last word.

He decided, "Let's say we toss on it."

"A coin toss?" Hammett howled; his cigarette fell out of his mouth. "I haven't laughed so much over anything since hogs ate my kid brother."

Only Babs caught the joke. His line from his 1929 novel *Red Harvest* went over everyone else's heads.

Powell reached into his wallet, but all he found was paper currency. "Babs, got any spare change?"

She searched inside her billfold and held up a fifty-cent piece.

Lillian laughed. "I can't believe it's come down to this."

Babs figured a lot of clams were at stake, and this duo looked like a couple of bookies trying to rein in an overdue debt.

Powell asked Hammett, "What's your pick?"

"Heads. Guess you got dog tails," he said to Lillian.

Babs flipped the coin high into the air. With impeccable timing, Asta ran across the lawn, followed by Sir Henry and Toto. He jumped into the air, caught the coin between his teeth, and scurried off to dig a hole and bury it beside a tree.

"Just like when he hid Cary Grant's dinosaur bone in *Bringing Up Baby*," Babs said, although no one was listening.

All concerned chased after Asta to retrieve the coin, but Sir Henry and Toto stood guard and growled at anyone who dared to get too close.

Lillian laughed so hard she swallowed her ice cube whole. Clearing her throat, she said, "Guess we'll never know who won the coin toss now."

Relieved the ordeal was over, Powell looked daggers at Hammett and Hellman and took Myrna by one arm and Babs by another, who clutched Diana by the crook of hers.

"Come, let's rejoin the rest of the party. There's a martini waiting with my name already on it."

Historical Note and Disclaimer

This novel is a work of fiction. Although the author attempted to depict historical references as best as possible, she altered some dates and details in 1940 for artistic license. Winston Churchill credited the *Queen Mary* for shortening the war in her role of transporting Allied troops. The threat of a growing fascist movement on American soil was real, especially in Los Angeles.

Stay tuned for Book Two in the Babs Norman mystery series: *Bye, Bye Blackbird* featuring Humphrey Bogart and the cast from *The Maltese Falcon*.

Book Club Questions for Hounds of the Hollywood Baskervilles

1. What was your favorite part of the book?
2. What was your least favorite?
3. Which scene stuck with you the most?
4. Did you feel the book was educational? Did you learn something new from the book that you hadn't expected?
5. What surprised you the most about the book?
6. Does this book remind you of any other books or films?
7. Would you ever consider re-reading the book? Why or why not?
8. If this book were adapted to film, who would you like to see in the cast?
9. What characters did you like the best? Which did you like the least?
10. How did the setting impact the story? Would you want to read more books set in 1940s Hollywood?
11. Which twist surprised you the most?
12. Did you guess the ending? If so, at what point?
13. Would you definitely recommend this author and read other books that will come up in this series?
14. Are you curious about the other books this author has written, even if they are in a different genre?

Acknowledgments

My agent Elizabeth K. Kracht, Verena Rose, Grace Bradley, Pamela Beason, Kate Hirons, Kathy Bennett, Teel James Glenn, Jim Freund, Martin Page, Jonathan Goodwin, David Kaye, Andrew Solberg and members of the Stranger's Room, Kenny Lane, Bernd Willend, Dorothy Dobbins, and Paul D. Marks, a great mentor and lover of classic films. I miss him so much. Also a special thanks to the Mystery Writers of America – New York Chapter for the Leo B. Burstein Scholarship I received to help finish this project.

About the Author

Elizabeth Crowens is bi-coastal between Los Angeles and New York. For over thirty years, she has worn many hats in the entertainment industry, contributed stories to *Black Belt, Black Gate, Sherlock Holmes Mystery Magazines, Hell's Heart,* and the Bram Stoker-nominated *A New York State of Fright,* and has a popular Caption Contest on Facebook.

Awards include: Leo B. Burstein Scholarship from the MWA-NY Chapter, NYFA grant to publish *New York: Give Me Your Best or Your Worst,* Eric Hoffer Award, Glimmer Train Awards Honorable Mention, Killer Nashville Claymore Award Finalist, two Grand prize, five First prize, and multiple Finalist Chanticleer Awards. Crowens writes multi-genre alternate history and historical Hollywood mysteries.

Hounds of the Hollywood Baskervilles, First Prize winner in the Chanticleer Review's Mark Twain Award for Humor and Satire. Finalist in Chanticleer Review's Mystery and Mayhem Awards. Finalist in Killer Nashville's Claymore Awards for Comedy.

SOCIAL MEDIA HANDLES:

Facebook.com/thereel.elizabeth.crowens

X.com/ECrowens

Instagram.com/ElizabethCrowens

LinkedIn https://www.linkedin.com/in/elizabeth-crowens-5227804/

Goodreads https://www.goodreads.com/author/show/15173793.Elizabeth_Crowens

AUTHOR WEBSITE:

www.elizbethcrowens.com

Also by Elizabeth Crowens

New York: Give Me Your Best or Your Worst (photo-illustrated anthology), Grand Prize winner of the Chanticleer Review Shorts/Anthologies Award

Three novels in the Time Traveler Professor series (alternate history):

Silent Meridian, First Prize winner of the Chanticleer Review Goethe Award

A Pocketful of Lodestones, First Prize winner of the Chanticleer Review Paranormal Award

A War in Too Many Worlds, Grand Prize winner of the Chanticleer Review Cygnus Award

Printed in the USA
CPSIA information can be obtained
at www.ICGtesting.com
LVHW042137040324
773565LV00034B/280